Toxic

BY

RACHEL VAN DYKEN

Toxic
by Rachel Van Dyken

TOXIC

ISBN 13: 978-0991127399
ISBN: 0991127390
Cover Art designed by P.S. Cover Design

Prologue

The end of Spring Semester

I would have followed her anywhere.

It's funny isn't it? People claim to know what love is – yet the minute they're given the opportunity to prove it – they bail.

I wish I could have bailed. I wish I could have walked away four years ago. Then maybe I'd have the strength to walk away now. To look her in the eyes and say, "Sorry, but I can't do this again."

People rarely mean what they say. To me, *sorry* was just another word in the English language that people misused – like *love*.

I love ice cream, I love pancakes, I love the color blue – bullshit. Because when I said *love* – I meant I bled for you. When the word *love* actually leaves my lips – I'm speaking it into existence. I'm empowering my soul – I'm joining with yours.

I'd always heard about crossroads, how people are given choices in their lives, choices that either make or break them. I never realized that I'd be given that second chance; I never realized I'd fail to take it.

Her eyes pleaded with mine. My heart shattered in my chest, my lips moved to speak — to say anything to get her to understand the depth of what I was feeling, but I knew the minute I told her how I felt — it would be all over.

My heart, my soul, it couldn't survive anything happening to her. If she wasn't in my world, my heart would stop. I knew it was killing her — because it was destroying me.

But going back to that life.

Even for her.

Was out of the question.

Falling in love, jumping out, even knowing full well that she'd catch me. It wasn't an option. Because everyone knows, when it comes to love, it's not the fall that hurts… it's the landing. And I knew it was only matter of time before she gave up on me too and allowed me to break.

Because in the end… that's all I was — broken. A shell of a human.

"I don't understand!" She beat against my chest with her fists. "You promised me! You promised you'd never leave!" Tears streamed down her face, the face I used to love. I closed my eyes then looked behind me as Saylor clenched the keys in her hand, waiting for my decision.

I was at a crossroads all right. One path led to my future — the other to my past and utter self destruction.

I couldn't look at her. I ignored every thread of feeling — and relished the pain of my heart breaking into a million pieces as I held out my hand in front of me. "You're right, I promised."

"Gabe!" Saylor yelled from behind me. "It doesn't have to be like this."

"Don't you see?" I said quietly without turning around. "It's always been like this, it will always be like this. I warned you."

"But—"

"Enough!" I yelled, tears threatening to stream down my face. "I said enough. You should go."

Behind me, the door slammed.

"It's okay!" she said, cupping my face. "It will finally be okay!"

"Alright, Princess." I choked on the word. "Alright." I tightened the pink scarf around her neck and put my arm around her.

"Thanks." She sighed happily. "You always promised you'd take care of me. You can't leave, you can't—"

"I won't." I vowed, because it was my fault. Just like everything else.

"Can we go play now, Gabe?"

"Yeah, sweetheart, we can." I folded the blanket around her legs and pushed her wheelchair out of the room, knowing full well that I was choosing the wrong path — with every step I took.

Chapter One

Sad moment officially gone, just please, for the love of God, get a room —Gabe H

Gabe

Middle of Spring Semester

"Focus, Kiersten." I snapped my fingers in front of her face. "Stages of mitosis. Go."

We'd been sitting at the local Starbucks all morning. The smell of ground coffee was beginning to make me sick — I had nobody to blame but myself. Apparently ground coffee is what a new leaf smelled like. And I'd officially turned one over.

Kierten's eyes darted to the textbook. I scooted it away and waited patiently, folding my hands on the table.

Her mouth dropped open to answer, a blank stare followed and then a groan. "G-a-a-a-a-be." She smiled. "Can't we take a coffee break? Please?"

"Don't stick out your lower lip."

She stuck it out anyway.

"Kiersten..." I warned.

"Please!" She gripped my hands in hers and pouted some more.

I gave in with a heavy sigh — you know, to show that I wasn't happy about giving in to her demands even though that's how it always was with our friendship. She said *jump* and I said *where, how high, how long, and how fast can I do your bidding*? "Fine, we'll take a coffee break."

"Yes!" She slammed the book shut. "My turn to treat." Her ridiculously cute smile made me laugh. Hell, she always made me laugh, and I so needed to laugh at this point in my life. Besides, if I didn't laugh I was pretty sure I'd break down sobbing and the last thing the world needed was for me to suddenly make sure everyone was aware that I had feelings.

Damn, I didn't even want to be aware.

"Nope." I waved her off then had to physically restrain her from hopping off toward the counter. "I got it. Plus, Wes would kill me if he knew I made you pay for your own coffee."

"You guys spoil me too much." She sat back against her chair and crossed her arms. "You're going to have to let me go soon, Gabe. Both you and Wolf," she said, using Wes's nickname. "I can't live in your protective bubble forever." She yawned and accidently hit her hand on the wall beside her.

"Aw, little Lamb," I teased, using Wes's nickname for her. "Get a boo-boo?"

"Shut it."

"I'll just go get your coffee."

Her eyes narrowed. "You do that, Turtle."

If she was a dude, I would have flipped her off. Instead, I laughed and walked away.

I'd been making fun of her and Wes's nicknames for each other — Lamb and Wolf — and in return had been gifted with one of my own, on account of my idiot cousin, Lisa, deciding to tell them the story about how I'd had a pet turtle when I was little and had cried when it died.

But come on! That turtle was bad ass! I had a freaking funeral for the little guy — I full on wept.

Not a proud moment.

"The usual?" I called back.

She folded her hands in front of her like she was praying and shouted, "Please!"

With a smile I turned around and went to stand in line — trying to look casual, easy-going, normal. Ha! Funny how I used to actually practice being normal.

I'd looked in the mirror and had to tell myself to visibly relax my lips, shoulders, muscles. I had to own the look because things had been crazy for so long — and apparently I had a certain way of walking that made people recognize me. Who knew, right? At any rate, I was a bad ass ninja master of disguise, and it wasn't just my life that depended on it, but *hers* as well.

Maybe it was my graduation — but ever since the start of this last semester I'd felt edgy — irritated, as if I was some sorry ass sitting outside waiting for a storm cloud. I had no reason to feel that way — I just did, and honestly? It freaked me out a bit. I hoped it was just a side effect of not sleeping around with every single girl on campus. Maybe that was what not having sex did to guys… made them paranoid and jumpy as hell.

"What can I get you?" The barista asked, her demeanor cool, aloof.

I leaned forward and smiled brightly. "That depends, what are you offering?"

"Damn." She snapped her fingers. "You confused? The sex shop is just down the street." With a wink, she leaned forward and whispered, "We serve coffee here."

"How…" I licked my lips slowly, falling easily back into old habits. "…embarrassing." My heart started to race as I greedily scanned her tight little body, just barely hidden by the green apron. It was my game — the only thing I had going for me. The only thing that numbed me to my past — to everything. Don't feel sorry for me. I loved every damn minute of it — because it was one more minute I wasn't thinking about the past.

The past, the past, the past. Ah, there it was, the reason I kept it in my pants now. My promise to Wes, and worse — my promise to myself. She wouldn't want me to be this way — I was torn between feeling guilty about how I acted and also feeling relieved that at least there was still something that choked the sadness away from my existence.

"It happens," she replied breathlessly, her eyes widening as she took in my body. I was used to it. I lived for it. I survived on it.

And then, she flipped her hair.

A whiff of perfume hit me square in the face, shaking off any sort of lust I had going for me.

Shit. It was the same perfume.

Shaking, I jerked back forcing a weak laugh. "Anyways, um, can we just have two large caramel lattes? Triple shot and put extra whipped cream on one of them."

"Oh." The girl's face went completely red as she typed in the order and shook her head. "Is that all?"

Her voice was pitifully hopeful.

But I'd already made up my mind.

Or maybe it was my body that was made up first, then my mind. Either way, I felt like puking, like running outside and not stopping until I was either in the music room or on my Harley.

"Yup." I handed her my credit card, my fingers tensing around the sharp edges of the plastic. "That's all."

She swiped, handed it back, muttered *asshole* under her breath, and I walked around to wait for the cups and make sure she didn't spit in anything before our coffee made it into my hands.

Within minutes I had our coffee and was already sitting back at the table.

"So…" Kiersten took a slow sip. "How's life?"

I rolled my eyes. "Can we not do this?"

"Do what?" She shrugged innocently.

"The whole you ask me how I'm doing over and over again and just pray I'll crack or worse yet, start crying and spouting out all my dirty—" I leaned in. "Little." I leaned in a bit more "Secrets."

"Your sex eyes don't work on me," Kiersten said, her voice sounding bored as hell.

I shrugged helplessly and took a long sip of coffee. "Worth a shot."

"Worth *getting* shot?" Kiersten corrected. "Because that's what would happen. Wes would shoot you."

"Wes hates violence," I defended.

"No, he doesn't *hate* it." Kiersten laughed and looked to the door. "Oh my gosh… is that her?"

"Her who?" Kiersten knew I didn't do names — I rarely recognized the girls I slept with unless they walked up to me with their shirts lifted over their heads. Okay fine, so it wasn't that bad, but pretty damn close. I swear it was easier to tell people apart that way.

"Raylynn." Kiersten lowered her voice. "That's her!"

"Don't call her over," I mumbled under my breath. That bitch was psycho. I slept with her once. One time! And she all but stalked me for three months! Kiersten had really liked her and thought she was pretty; therefore, my opinion didn't matter. And nothing would make Kiersten happier than to see me settle down and stop whoring around, or so she told me every few days when she felt the urge to mama-bear me. Little did she know it had been months, which felt like years, decades… Oh, hell. Who was I kidding? It felt like death.

"Oh look, she sees me!" Kiersten said happily.

"I wonder if it's because you're waving."

"Stretching."

"Waving."

"Raylynn!" Kiersten said in a cheerful voice that sounded like she was a cheerleader in another life. "How have you been?"

"Good."

All eyes turned to me.

I stared into my coffee. Kiersten kicked me under the table. With a curse I looked up and said, "Yo."

"Yo?" Kiersten mouthed across the table.

"Er, hi." Raylynn blushed.

Damn it.

Her pale complexion and bright blonde hair did nothing to hide the fact that she was embarrassed.

I tried again. "How have you been?"

"Busy." She cleared her throat, her eyes darting between me and my coffee as if waiting for me to ask her to sit down or worse yet, ask her on another date.

And dead silence. Again. I suddenly experienced the exact definition of a pregnant pause.

"Well..." Kiersten cleared her throat loudly then kicked me under the table. "It was great seeing you!"

"You too." Raylynn looked at me one last time then, shoulders slumping, walked off.

"You ass!" Kiersten kicked my shin again. "And yo? Did you say *yo*? No one as white as you should ever say that word. Ever. I don't care if you get kidnapped and the only way to be free is to either say yo or gnaw your own arm off. Gnaw the arm, Gabe. Don't say...*yo*."

"Who said yo?" a male voice interrupted.

"Ah, Wolf." I teased, happy that I wasn't alone anymore with Kiersten's peering eyes and difficult questions.

"Turtle," he fired back.

"Gabe said yo."

"Out loud?" Wes all but shouted. "Is he trying to get

jumped?"

I groaned into my hands and waited for them to stop talking about me like I wasn't there.

It was a regular occurrence with them. Kiersten would say something like *I'm worried about Gabe,* then Wes would say, *Is he not eating*? and I'd raise my hand and say, *He's just fine, he ate a burrito a half hour ago.*

"Guys!" I snapped, and dropped my hands to the table. "I'm fine, everything is fine. I said yo, I'm gangster, deal with it."

They both stared at me as if I'd just announced I was going to be a monk.

"I heard something this morning." Wes reached for Kiersten's coffee and took a long sip then leaned back against the chair. If I wasn't his best friend I'd effing hate him. He was the ideal All American Football Star. Quarterback, dark blond hair, blue eyes, buff, easy going. Yup, I'd freaking hate him.

"Oh yeah?" My eyes narrowed. "Tell me, Gossip Girl, what did you hear?" I took a long sip of coffee.

"Dry spell."

I spit out the coffee onto the table and all but choked to death. Damn Lisa, damn family, damn *cousin*. "I have no idea what you're referring to."

"Right." Wes licked his lips but dropped it. He leaned over and kissed Kiersten on the top of her head, then pulled her silky scarf tighter around her body.

That simple motion — almost made me lose it.

The tightening of a scarf — made me want to end my own life. If people only knew — if only I could trust people enough to tell, to explain, how wrecked I was on the inside.

But no. I was playing a part. I was Gabe. I would never be *him* again, I would never be my past again.

Kiersten laughed and kissed Wes's nose.

It was too much. Everything was suddenly too much, and in that moment I knew. It was too much four years ago — my time was up. The storm cloud was coming. "Look guys, I gotta run."

"Alright." Kiersten barely took her eyes off Wes. "See you for Taco Tuesday?"

"Yup." I didn't turn around. I didn't wave. I grabbed my shit, and I ran out that door like the fires of hell were licking at my heels.

Because for the first time in four years — the time bomb was about to go off and I wasn't so sure how I was going to handle everything.

My phone went off with a text.

Puget Sound N: *She needs you. Can you call and sing? Or maybe send her a picture text?*

Oh look, the bomb… it was ticking.

Me: *Yeah. I'll call in a few.*

Chapter Two

People will go through their entire lives justifying every damn decision…they'll fight for all the wrong things, until finally the right thing stares at them square in the face. That's when the choices start to matter. Because in the end, you're a creature of habit. So you may want to choose right, but choose wrong in the end — because you're so damn used to it. It's tragic, then again, life's tragic, don't you think? —Wes M.

Gabe

"The dry spell's really getting to you, isn't it?" Lisa felt my forehead.

I smacked her hand away and rolled my eyes.

"You can't call it a dry spell when it's by choice," I grumbled. "And by the way, thanks for telling Wes." I'd run out of the Starbucks and headed directly to Lisa's dorm room in hopes of talking to her about everything. Instead, she'd answered the door, her sweet smile conveying without words that she would always be there for me and she'd always understand.

Except this time — I had refused to burden her.

I looked at her now, several days after making that decision, and realized that had been our entire relationship. I give you my pain, you give me yours. And I was sick of it. I hated that she was part of it, and I hated that for the first time in four years I'd finally decided to grow a pair of balls and leave her the hell out of it — she didn't deserve the darkness.

I, however, did.

"And cranky." She plopped down onto the couch and messed up my hair with her hands. "You need to get out more."

"Question." I put the TV on mute and pushed her away. "Weren't you telling me a few weeks ago that I was going either going to die alone or from too many STDs?"

Lisa's blue eyes twinkled in amusement as she snatched the remote and turned the volume back up "Don't be dramatic. I said you were going to die alone *with STD's*." She flipped her dark wavy hair over her shoulder and laughed.

"Right. Big difference, awesome encouragement. Cousin of the year." I groaned and leaned back against the couch. I was just getting comfortable when a pillow hit me in the face.

Swearing a blue streak, I jumped to my feet.

Wes held out the pillow and tilted his head. "Rough morning? Where'd you go anyways?"

"Dude." I croaked and just shook my head. Not him, not again. I was cracking.

The door to the dorm opened, revealing a tuckered out Kiersten. She was sweating like crazy, so I could only assume Wes made her workout with him after our morning study session. Swear, they did everything together, practically lived together since they'd gotten engaged. I didn't mind — correction I didn't mind that much, but the PDA was getting a little tiring. Case in point — today at the coffee shop I probably escaped right before he swallowed her whole.

"You look like someone just died," Kiersten joked coming

up alongside Wes and leaning against him.

Damn. Perfect-looking couple. They'd have beautiful kids. Wow, I've completely lost my shit. Was I really thinking about them procreating? And getting emotional about it? Oh look, there's something in my eye. A freaking tear. Hell, I needed to get out.

"Hah." My eyes narrowed. "Still too soon."

"Damn, no death jokes?" Wes laughed and pulled a sweaty Kiersten into his arms, attacking her mouth with such force that I, Gabe Hyde, slut of the year, felt like blushing.

"Guys, not here by the food." I pointed to the fruit on the table. "It's weird."

"Making out next to bananas?" Wes pulled away from Kiersten. "Really, man? Coming from you? Seriously, what's wrong with you?"

The room fell silent. Great. Perfect. I shrugged and forced a smile. "Oh, you know, my demented cousin claims it's a dry spell."

"Right." Wes snapped his fingers. "I almost forgot about that fun little piece of information."

"For the last time!" I all but yelled. "It's not a dry spell if it's by choice!" I rarely yelled. Everyone stared at me like I'd just lost my shit. I was a lover not a fighter. The slutty flirt that slept with anything it could. The guy who could charm the pants off a federal judge. Yelling? Anger? Yeah… I bit my lower lip and scowled at the floor. *Tick-tock, tick-tock.* I really was losing it.

"Right." Wes's eyes narrowed. "Hey, uh, Gabe, I need help with something. Can you come with me to my room real quick?"

"Sure," I said slowly, my eyes darting between him and Kiersten. She pretended to be totally oblivious to the tension between me and Wes.

"See ya, at dinner, Wes." She kissed his cheek and skipped into her room slamming the door behind her.

"Use protection." Lisa called after Wes and me once we reached the door.

"Hilarious!" I yelled above her laughter.

We walked in silence to Wes's room. Why did I suddenly feel like I was about to get a dad lecture? I was sweating. What the hell!

The elevator was silent as it made its way to the sixth floor. You could hear a pin drop. I followed Wes down the hall and finally into his room.

Even though he'd gone through cancer treatments at the beginning of last year, they still allowed him to stay as Freshman RA, so at least I knew we wouldn't have roommates barging in on us while he laid into me about raising my voice around girls.

Once we were inside, he shut the door, locked it, and threw one of his footballs at my face.

"Why?" I ducked. He threw another one. I barely caught it before it smashed into my nose. "What the hell, Wes!"

"Finally!" He all but shouted. "A reaction. You're like a freaking zombie. What gives? And don't lie. Kiersten said you were acting weird this morning too."

I yawned, attempting to look bored, even though my palms were sweating something fierce. "Nothing, man, just school stuff."

"School stuff?" Wes repeated. "You really wanna go with that excuse?"

"Drugs?" I offered.

He snorted. "Yeah, right."

"Jackass."

"Whore."

"Wes—"

"What?" He took a seat by his desk and crossed his arms. "What's going on?"

I didn't spill my guts. I knew I owed him everything — hell, I felt like he practically saved my life when he almost died, he made me feel like living again. His strength was like gravity, pulling everyone within a fifty-mile radius into its center. You couldn't help but want to be better when you were around him, and that was the problem.

"I'm aging man, and we both know cancer can come back at any time."

"Seriously!" I threw the football back at his face. "This is what I'm talking about!"

"What?" He caught the football and twirled it in the air. "Speak up, I can't hear you."

I groaned into my hands, "You're so damn perfect. It really is irritating as hell."

"Thanks." He flashed a smile.

"I'm serious."

"I know."

I groaned again.

"Gabe—"

I reached into my pocket — the locket was cold against my fingertips. "Have you ever messed up so bad that—"

"That what?"

I averted my gaze. "I just… you're my best friend, don't get me wrong, but I feel like you never do anything terrible. You're smarter than most therapists, you have tons of money, you're like a freaking god around this place… Oh right, and a walking miracle. Check all those off the list. I know life hasn't been easy for you, but you don't mess up, you roll with the punches and move on. I just wish I knew how to do that."

Wes laughed out loud. "Wow, a little freaked out that your opinion of me is that high. Do I really need to make a list of all the times I've screwed up in life?"

"It would help," I grumbled, crossing my arms.

A few seconds of utter and complete silence went by. I didn't mind though. Wes and I were like that. We didn't always have to be talking or arguing or laughing. Sometimes silence was what I needed most and he knew that about me.

He knew more than anyone — even Lisa. And I had a sneaking suspicion he knew every damn part I played was an act.

"What's really going on?"

"The weight." I cursed. "It's wrapped around my legs, pulling me deeper into the darkest depths of the ocean and for once, I want to let it."

"Why?"

My head snapped up. Wes's eyes didn't hold judgment, just concern. "Because I deserve to sink."

"Doesn't everyone?"

"No, you don't get it." I got up and started pacing. "You know how you always felt like nobody understood? Remember when you said you'd drink shitty coffee the rest of your life if you could just live? Remember all those talks about people just walking through life without a damn clue about your pain? Your journey?"

Wes nodded.

I started to sweat. I gripped the locket harder until it had to be making an imprint onto my fingertips. "How does a person deserve life?"

"Trick question," Wes answered softly. "We don't."

My phone simultaneously buzzed and sounded in my pocket, interrupting our talk. It was my mom's ringtone — she'd called at least five times in the last hour. I knew I should probably talk to her, but it just brought up too many bad memories. And, I was officially late for class.

I stabbed at the ignore button and grimaced at Wes. "Listen, I gotta go. Can we talk later?"

Wes waved me off. "Of course, just don't go jumping off any buildings or sleeping with the entire swim team again and we'll be good."

I rolled my eyes. "Later."

"And don't forget Taco Tuesday!" he yelled as the door slammed shut behind me.

Chapter Three

My reflection was foreign… I didn't even remember myself — the guy I was. I'd been living with that damn mask for so long that I'd completely lost it — all of it. Thank God. —Gabe H.

Gabe

I made my way to class. It was a bit of a trek — UW was a huge school and on any other day I probably would have ridden my Harley, but I needed the walk. I could only hope it would clear my head.

As I crossed the street, a prickling awareness wrapped itself around me. I stopped walking toward the business building and looked behind me. Nothing. Just people walking back and forth, talking, smoking, laughing — all of them in their own little worlds. I liked it that way. Really. I'd only had a few close calls over the course of the last few years, and now that I was graduating in a few months, I was almost home free.

I'd wanted to go to school — I'd needed normal more than I'd needed money, excitement, all of it. My parents hadn't understood. Then again, they didn't understand anything that didn't have to do with what they wanted for my life. How could they not get that the reason I almost died and ruined my life was because they wanted me to be something I wasn't? I laughed out loud and stuffed my hands into my jeans pockets to caress the cool metal locket. Each year I'd gone back to LA with a different tattoo. The next more offensive than the last. When I pierced my nose I think my mom about had a heart attack. Dad all but disowned me.

Pity. I would have liked to be disowned.

Lisa always warned me not to push them too far — she was afraid I might be tattled on. All it would take would be for my dad to announce my secrets to the media and I'd be done for. The secrets? My past? Front page news. The life I'd built? Changed forever.

I swallowed the fear and continued walking toward the building. Two months until school ended, and then I could start my own life, away from my family, away from the painful memories, and away from the man I used to be.

I felt better once I stepped into the old building. Homework was something I could focus on… I might look like I was part of some punk rock band, but I had straight A's for a reason. I needed to be successful in order to get the hell out from underneath my family's grasp. I could almost feel their hands wrapping around my neck, choking the life out of me just like before.

I jumped when my phone buzzed in my pocket. I quickly answered it and leaned against the wall, closing my eyes as my heart clattered against my chest.

I needed to get it together — fast.

"Hey!" Lisa said from the other line. "What'cha doin?"

"Going to class like a good boy. Why? Are you in trouble?"

Lisa rarely called me during the day unless she needed a ride… or food… or… Okay fine, so she called me all the time. It just felt lame that she was one of my only friends.

"Nah." She cleared her throat. "I, um, I just thought you should hear it from me."

"Hear it?" I repeated. "Hear what?"

"My mom called." She paused.

"Lisa, what the hell? Just spit it out," I growled, trying to sound annoyed, when really I was terrified of the news Lisa was going to tell me. I hated fear. It made me feel weak. And weakness was a close second on the list of things I never wanted to feel again.

"Your father... he's..." She took a deep breath then finished in a rush. "He's gotten into some financial trouble... nothing huge. I mean, he can't touch your trust found, but well, my mom talked to your mom, and she's worried he's going to sell your story to the media for money."

My heartbeat roared in my ears, adrenaline surged through my body as I looked wildly around me — for him, for cameras, for reporters. Shit, I was going to be sick. My hand started trembling so bad that the phone clamored against my ear. My entire body went cold. Shaking, I scanned the area again and stepped into the shadow of the building. "Sorry, Lisa. Thanks for letting me know, but I gotta go, I gotta—" I hung up and started running. I wasn't even sure in what direction I was going. I could have hit a tree for all I cared. My legs pumped harder and harder as the cold air hit my face. I could still feel them chasing me. I could taste the blood in my mouth from biting my tongue.

"Was it an accident?" the reporter asked. "You're over eighteen. Do you think you'll be held responsible?" She lifted the microphone in my face and waited.

I looked around for help.

No one.

Who was I kidding? Nobody was going to help me. She was gone.

"Um, no, no comment," I stuttered.

"Is that your answer for everything?" a male reporter fired out.

I stared into his cold black eyes and nodded. "For now it is."

"Shit! Shit! Shit!" I ran my hands through my hair and slowed down as I made my way back toward the dorms. What the hell could I give him to keep him from going to press? I had money but couldn't access all of it until I was twenty-two, which wasn't for another four months. I got a monthly stipend of five grand a month. I could take my money out of all my investments but would that solve anything? Would he ever stop? I could give him everything I had, which was roughly ten mill, and he'd probably still find a way to spend it all and come after me. It wasn't the money. I wasn't stupid. I was his cash cow. He was still pissed I'd walked away.

Funny. Dad hadn't been upset that my squeaky clean image had been wrecked by drug usage, drinking, and the horror that followed. He was pissed that I'd run, that I'd given up what was, in his estimation, a gold mine.

I jogged past my dorm.

And jumped onto my old Harley. I needed out — an escape. Drugs were out of the question — which left only one thing.

I rode as hard as I could toward the music building. My bike almost fell over as I parked it and ran up the stairs to one of the private rooms. Once inside I locked the door behind me, pulled the blinds down, and sat at the piano.

My heart pounded in my chest as the ivory keys stared back at me — called to me.

My addiction.

Four years.

I'd stayed away from the piano for four damn years.

Not anymore.

The bomb went off, the timer dinged, my hands caressed the piano. I groaned aloud and slumped onto the wooden bench, my body taking its natural position over the instrument.

I wasn't even sure I knew how to play anymore — how

to sing – how to communicate what was eating up my soul – slowly poisoning me.

But I had to try.

The minute I pressed the keys, need poured out until my shaking hands were hovering over the piano, and before I could stop myself, I started playing. I played the songs of my teen years, and then finally – as if my hands couldn't keep themselves from playing the melody – I played her song.

A strange sort of madness washed over me as I pounded harder and harder. Maybe if I played hard enough she'd come back, maybe I'd get a re-do and the last four years would be nothing more than a horrible nightmare.

I fought tears and then banged my hands across the piano as hard as I could. Cursing the past that was finally catching up to me.

Tick-Tock, Tick-Tock, with each slam of my fingers the cadence in my chest quickened.

I was so done.

Part of me had known I couldn't last this long.

Hell, it was a miracle I'd been able to put on such a show to begin with – then again I was an incredible actor. I should have won an Oscar.

My life was one big epic joke.

Finally, like a piece of steel getting manipulated and bent – I broke. A tear rolled down my face and dripped onto the piano.

My pointer finger slid over the tear as I wiped it from the ivory keys. Tears had never helped me. But sex? Hell, yeah. I was a freaking god with the right girl – most of the time with the wrong ones. And every conquest made me feel more godlike, impenetrable, stronger, able to withstand everything. Except it had really only been building a fortress around me. But in the moment, I could be everything I ever promised those girls – her – that I'd never really be. I could put away the fractured pieces of my heart and pretend like the past didn't matter, only the moment. So I took each moment with each girl for what it was, an opportunity to turn into what years ago would have been my worst nightmare.

For a time. It worked.

Because for a second I could believe I'd never been him to begin with. I was Gabe.

The only problem?

It wasn't even my real name.

Chapter Four

Pretty sure using drumsticks to play the piano was frowned upon. — Saylor

Saylor

It was my last practice session before my schedule change. I hated that stupid Freshman Seminar class. Right now it was the bane of my existence! The only way I could keep my scholarship was to have a high grade point average, and that was the one class I'd been slacking in, but only because they didn't take attendance, which meant I usually skipped in order to gain more practice time.

Unfortunately, it also meant I had no idea what was going on and usually flew by the seat of my pants. Let's just say the professor was less than impressed with my inability to get my butt into a chair, even when I told him it was because I was working hard in my core classes.

Ugh. I meandered down the hall and paused. The practice room that I usually used was occupied. It wasn't a big deal, but there was kind of an unspoken rule among music majors, if you were there every day for a year, and practiced at the same time — it was usually your slot. Anyone else was a dirty little poacher.

Okay, so my feathers were ruffled but only a bit. I mean, whoever was playing had some serious issues if the loudness was any indication. Hopefully, they wouldn't break the piano in the process of self discovery. Though, I probably wouldn't have chosen Ashton Hyde music to do said discovering. Eight years ago maybe, but not so much right now.

Geez, that music brought back way too many awkward dates, skate nights, and high school parties. All things I'd rather forget, considering I'd been the music nerd.

I sighed and went to the room opposite from where the music was coming, when all of a sudden the notes took a drastic turn.

A haunting melody floated into the air followed by cursing and then pounding on the keys of the piano. I took a few steps toward the room. The blinds were pulled. The pounding continued and then more cursing. Seriously, the dude needed anger management. I wasn't sure if I should go down and talk to the head of the department about how someone was literally beating the crap out of one of their expensive pianos, or if I should just mind my own business.

My problem was solved when the door flew open. I was so shocked that I fell backward directly onto my butt.

Great.

Now angry piano pounder was going to have something to hold over me — not only was I eavesdropping but I had fallen on my guilty ass.

"S-sorry," I said in a quiet voice, trying to scramble to my feet.

"For?" the guy asked. His voice was deep and smooth.

I looked up.

He was smiling at me. At me? Why was he smiling? Oh. He was probably trying not to laugh. I pushed down the embarrassment as much as I could and gave him a weak smile back. "I didn't mean to, um…" I pointed at the door and shrugged. I was still sitting on the floor, like a kindergartner at magic carpet time or something.

"Spy?" His eyes narrowed but his smile stayed. He was beautiful. With dark brown hair that fell just below his ears. His white t-shirt was stretched across a broad, muscled chest. Tattoos covered every square inch of skin on both arms.

"Yeah," I croaked, nearly choking on that one word as I felt a burning blush spread across my body. I tugged at the corners of my sweatshirt and cursed the fact that I'd thought wearing boots was a good idea. I was officially sweltering…

"No problem." He held out his hand. Confused as to why he was being so nice when about five seconds ago his playing made it sound like he was getting ready to commit some sort of crime, I examined his hand before taking it. Tattoos and some weird inscription covered a few of his fingers. With a frustrated sigh, I grabbed his hand and let him pull me to my feet.

His blue eyes were so bright and lined by really dark eyelashes. I swear it almost looked like he was wearing eyeliner, but I knew he wasn't. His eyes were just that beautiful. I'd never seen someone so good-looking up close before. The longer I stared at him the less sense it made. At first glance, all I saw were tattoos covering his arms. Now? I wish I had looked away, because in that moment, I couldn't. His eyes pierced through me, nailing my body to the wall, holding me captive until I felt like I couldn't breathe. They were the type of eyes that made you want to either confess your sins, or give in to them. I blinked a few times, hoping to break the connection that was slowly stealing every ounce of self-preservation I had, and finally was able to look away.

"Thanks for helping me up, and again, I'm sorry for all of that…" I waved into the air and walked to the other side of the hall to my own practice room and away from the dangerously sexy tattooed guy with the bright blue eyes.

"You play?" he asked as my hand grazed the door to the other room.

"Piano." I refused to turn around and get caught in his gaze again. As it was, my hand was shaking over the knob. Give me five more minutes and my knees would be knocking together too. Holy crap! I needed to get out more.

"You good?" His voice was smooth, clear. My musical side immediately surged with curiosity. Did he sing other genres? Opera? Classically trained? Was he a new teacher or something? His voice was extremely smooth. He'd said less than ten words to me and I was still thinking about the tone of his voice. The way it seemed to warm me up from the inside out — yeah, I needed to get more sleep, because in that moment I was ready to swoon because of his eyes and voice.

My fingers tapped against the doorknob as I thought about my answer.

"Cat got your tongue?"

"Yeah," I snapped a bit harshly and turned around, trying to give him my best glare when really the effect he still had on me was downright irritating. "I am."

He laughed, throwing his head back as the sound echoed down the empty hall. "So you do have a personality. Good to know."

My eyes narrowed. I opened my mouth to speak but he interrupted me.

"Don't ruin my fun by actually defending yourself. You a band geek?"

"Band geek," I repeated. Where did he come up with that? Did a time machine just transport me back to high school or something? Who even said that anymore?

He nodded toward my sweatshirt.

I looked down. Sure enough it was an old high school band sweatshirt. Really, Saylor? I was wearing the ugliest grey sweatshirt I owned. And, kill me now.

"Sure." I croaked. "I mean, I used to be, but—"

"Thought so." He nodded. "Want to know how I can tell?"

"I need to practice." I changed the subject and pointed back to my room. I was about ten seconds away from screaming at the top of my lungs. Though I wasn't sure if it was out of terror or something else — something that made my heart beat just a little bit faster and my palms start to sweat.

He stalked — not walked — toward me until he was inches from my face. "You scream innocence. Twenty bucks says you practice at least six hours a day, go to bed at nine p.m., and really think you can make it in the big bad world by majoring in piano performance." His lips curled into a mocking grin. "Daddy bought you everything you could have ever wanted, including the pink pony you probably still have in your room. Trophies line your walls, and the last time you even wore a color as scandalous as red was when you were alone in your room trying to see what it would look like on your tan skin. You think guys like me are trouble and by the looks of it — as much as you want to push me away — you want more…" He lowered his voice to a seductive pitch and I found myself leaning toward him so I could hear. "…you crave more."

Speechless, I didn't know whether to laugh, cry, or slap him across his gorgeous face. Was he serious? Where did he get off saying that to me? A complete stranger? Clearly something was stuck up his ass, and I was about ready to tell him where he could stick that something, but I was too late.

Had I known that any contact from this beautiful stranger would forever change me — would mark me for the rest of my life, wreck me from the inside out, completely break me down until I was nothing but a memory of who I used to be — I would still have made the same choice.

Funny, how people always say they want second

chances, yet had I been given one. I would have traveled down the same road. Every. Single. Time.

His mouth crashed against mine in a blur – hot lips pressed, sealed themselves into my memory until all I could think about was the hot slick wetness of his mouth and how every inch of my skin felt like it was on fire from his touch.

He pushed me against the wall, bracing himself with his hands on either side of my head. I'd kissed guys before – none of them had ever kissed me like the gorgeous stranger was kissing me. I didn't know where to put my hands. I pressed against his chest, which just seemed to encourage him more as his tongue dipped into my mouth.

I pushed harder against him. His hands plunged into my hair.

I squeaked when his hands moved my shoulders – his palms burning a hole through not only my defenses, but my excuses for pushing him away.

His mouth was hot as it pressed harder, his tongue doing things I didn't know tongues could do. All I could feel was him – I was on fire as his chest met mine. A loud bang clamored in my ears.

The beautiful stranger pulled back his eyes a blaze of fury. If I was scared before – I was petrified now. He looked like he wanted to kill me – and I didn't mean that in a joking sense. I was actually scared. Well, I was both scared and extremely shocked – let's just say it was a tie.

In an instant his dark look disappeared as if he'd just put on a Halloween mask and a smile returned to his gorgeous face. With a chuckle he spoke quietly, mockingly, "You're welcome."

Pretty sure I looked like I was about to stab him with something sharp because he laughed harder and backed up to his side of the hall. "Whoa, you're more feisty than I give you credit for – and the proper response is 'thank you'." He gave a little bow. Holy crap, I was going to murder him with my bare hands.

"For assaulting me?" I squeaked. "You want me to thank you for assaulting me?"

He winked. "Not assault if you beg me for it."

"Beg?" I repeated. "I begged to get sexually harassed?" I marched over to him and pushed against his chest. "Tell me, was it the band geek assumption that got you hot or the fact that you know just by looking at me that I have a pink pony hiding in my room." I rolled my eyes and stepped back. "You were wrong you know."

"About what?" he whispered, his bright eyes slipping back into darkness.

"The pony." I looked back and lifted my chin. "It was purple and it's not in my room back home."

"Oh?" His eyebrows lifted.

"Yeah." I narrowed my eyes and imagined tripping him down the stairs. "It's in my dorm, you ass."

With one final look that gave me shivers down to my toes, he gave me a nod and walked down the hall, "See you later, Pony."

"Bye, asshat." I called. "And thank you."

He froze.

I should have stopped talking. Normally I *would* have stopped talking. Crap! I never spoke out of turn or talked back. But something about him brought out the worst in me I guess.

"I always wanted to know what it would be like to kiss a tattooed bad ass with a chip on his shoulder. Officially crossed that one off my bucket list."

His shoulders shook. He turned, a look of complete amusement washed over his features. "Careful."

"Or what? You gonna pull a knife on me or something?"

"We both know I wouldn't need to use violence to get you to respond, sweetheart." His smile was crooked as he wiped his mouth with the back of his hand. "And you, little girl, better be careful. You're dangerously close to getting me to fall for you, and I don't do relationships, I do girls. Call me if you're ever lonely. I'm sure I can even make that purple pony blush crimson given the chance."

"Y-you're disgusting!" I called as he walked away. *Wow. Great, Saylor, way'ta add a stutter to really show him how much he affects you.*

"You're welcome!" he fired back, waving his hand in the air and making his way slowly down the stairs.

Shaking, I quickly opened the door to the practice room and then slammed it behind me. With a sigh, I touched my lips with my fingertips and leaned against the wall, then slowly sank to the ground. What. Just. Happened?

Chapter Five

What the hell had possessed me to accost a perfectly innocent girl in the hallway? Oh right, my squeaky clean past had come up to haunt me — it was annoying as hell. —Gabe H.

Gabe

My lips stung like hell.

I was losing my damn mind.

Embarrassment wasn't really an emotion I was used to feeling, but there it was, bright as a freaking rainbow raining on my damn parade. Right. Because rain came during rainbows. I winced at my inability to even get a metaphor right in my mind. Music had a way of sucking everything out of me, all my anger, hurt, frustration, sadness, helplessness. And there she had been, standing there just listening!

And her eyes.

Hell, those eyes.

I knew those eyes — those were the true eyes of a musician. She'd been impressed, stunned, and a bit worried about me. I could see it all, could calculate just what was going on in that innocent little brain of hers. She was curious about me, curious about the music, and, thank God, hadn't recognized me.

But the worst part?

Her face reminded me of the seas of faces. The ones I let down, the ones I left. The people who'd depended on me, who'd looked up to me, who — without knowing they were setting me up for failure — put me on the highest damn pedestal they could find.

My phone buzzed in my pocket. Ignoring it, I continued the brisk pace toward my bike.

Kim had looked at me like that, with those eyes.

"Why now?" I said aloud. "Why the hell is this happening now?" Of all times. Why. Now. It seriously felt like God had abandoned me. I was alone, stuck in a pit of nothing, defenseless, a sitting duck, wallowing in emptiness.

My brain chose that moment to remind me of the perfume I smelled earlier that morning on the barista. I picked up my pace.

My stomach clenched. Either I was going to be sick, or I needed to go for a long ride somewhere to clear not only my head but the perfume. It was as if the scent had a life of its own, swirling around my mind, consuming every part of me until it wasn't separate, but part of my soul. Its tentacles wrapped around my heart, and like any man with regrets, I felt them squeezing me so tight that my first response was to lash out and then retreat.

The perfume this morning, the phone call from Lisa, the girl in the piano room… shit. Worse of all, she'd heard the song. The one I'd written.

Worst timing in the world — because that immediately set me off. How dared she listen in on something so freaking private?

I hadn't planned on kissing her, but I was pissed, and thought if I just scared her off, she'd freak out or just slap me away, at least then I'd feel something, right?

Wrong.

She'd kissed me back.

Wrong move, considering the whole dry spell and all, her little body had fit exactly in the outline of mine.

I couldn't blame her — she had no way of knowing that the last girl that felt that perfect in my arms… was no longer present. So really it wasn't her I was angry at. Maybe it was myself.

"Come on, Kim!" I grabbed her hand and kissed each finger, dipping them in my mouth as my tongue swirled around her hot skin. Damn, she was hot. With a giggle she pulled away and teetered on her feet. I grabbed her to keep from falling.

"Babe!" She giggled again. Clearly she wasn't used to handling pot and alcohol at the same time. "It's freezing outside!"

"But you'll be with me, come on." I pulled her into my arms. "One quick run then we can go to the wrap party later."

Kim squinted and laughed again. "Right, but you're forgetting, we're a bit drunk and I'm not so sure it's safe."

"Again," I sighed and pointed outside the window. The snowy landscape was untouched by anything. "You'll be with me, and we won't go down a hard run, I promise. Come on!" I kissed her forehead. "It's not like anything's going to happen! There isn't even anyone out there! Look…" I stalked over to the window and pulled the curtains back as far as they would go. "It's incredible. You don't get this type of powder in California — only Whistler. Come on."

"Fine!" Kim shook her head and walked toward the bedroom. "Let me just get my stuff real quick okay? I don't care what you say, it's freezing outside."

Five minutes turned into thirty by the time Kim was ready. I grabbed the key to our hotel room and ran down the hall with her in tow. At sixteen it seemed kind of forbidden that we would be able to stay in the same suite, but my agent had said it was great publicity. We were basically the next teen heart throb couple and everyone wanted to see us together.

Which really wasn't a problem, considering I was freaking obsessed with the girl. Her life, her smile. Hell. I would marry her at sixteen and she knew it.

"Ready?" I asked once we were outside. There weren't any clouds in the sky, just stars. I winked at Kim. She shook her head and laughed, looking away as if embarrassed. Damn, I was lucky.

"Ready."

"One, two—"

"Wait!" Kim touched her head. "I forgot my helmet."

"One run." I tried not to sound irritated. We were already going to be late to the party. "It won't kill you. I swear."

Kim looked uncertain. Didn't she trust me to protect her?

"Well, okay." She aimed her skis down the hill.

"One, two—"

"Three!" She squealed and went flying down the run, leaving me in the powder. Laughing, I went after her. I could hear every swipe of her skis, and then all of a sudden I heard a scream.

Then nothing.

"Kim?" I screamed, "You okay?"

I wasn't going to make it.

I ran over to my bike and puked on the other side, wiping my face with the back of my hand. No matter what my dad did, no matter who found out about my true identity, one thing would always remain. It was my fault, my cross to bear, and there weren't enough prayers that could save my soul from burning in hell for what I'd done. For what I was still doing.

Once I'd puked my guts out — relieved myself of that bad ass Captain Crunch — I sat on my bike. Visions of the hot piano player ran through my head. I should have apologized instead of being an ass. Dry spell? Yeah, let's blame it on that.

How was it my fault anyway? That she'd been spying on me? Or that she was sexy as hell. Was she new? I shook my head. Probably not. The University of Washington was a huge school and it wasn't like I was a music major or anything — it was too close to my past, I had to stay far away from any hints of the guy I used to be, the guy I was running away from.

Cursing, I kicked the back wheel of my bike. The crisp spring air had a hint of moisture in it, causing an involuntary shiver to wreak havoc on my body. I pulled out my phone and dialed Wes's number. We needed to finish that conversation. Because if there was anyone that could help me, it was him. Wes and I were exact opposites. He represented everything I was running away from, yet he was different. A miracle. That's what he was. He'd conquered cancer this last year. He was also son to one of the richest men in the US – though you'd never know it from hanging out with him.

I'd met him this last year and promised, damn it, I'd promised I'd try harder to be a better person and I'd just screwed that promise. I hadn't slept around for weeks since his surgery. Clearing my head seemed like a good idea, and I couldn't do that while banging every girl within a twenty mile radius.

To be honest, I hadn't been tempted.

Not until this afternoon.

Gorgeous… forbidden. Those two words came to mind. Long chestnut hair with blonde streaks fell around her face in waves, her large blue eyes almost looked purple, and that tan skin.

I hated to admit it but she was like a hotter version of Miley Cyrus, you know, before she went all blonde and baller.

"Shit." I hit Wes's name and waited.

It rang and then I got his voicemail.

"I'm coming by." That's all I said. I hoped he was there and just not answering his phone. He was an RA at Lisa's dorm and usually hung around as much as possible, considering his *fiancée* and love of his life was my cousin's roommate. Lucky me, I was surrounded with all-American happy, and all I wanted to do was get high and prove I was nothing like them.

I started my bike and made my way across campus. By the time I pulled up, I'd made a list of hundreds of different things I'd rather be doing – proactive things like calling my out-of-this-world expensive lawyer and getting his ass on my dad so that nothing happened.

But, instead, of doing any of those things, I paused. I was doing that a lot lately, hesitating when I knew I should be taking action. I'd done it with Kiersten, Wes's girlfriend. I'd wanted so badly to be that guy for her. The one who brought flowers and wiped her tears, and when it came time to actually put any of that into action, my hesitation said it all. She was meant for something bigger, because in the end, I'd always let people down. I could be her friend. I could be Wes's friend. Hell, I could even been a good cousin to Lisa, but I'd never end up with anyone. My soul mate? I'd already met her.

And it didn't matter. Nothing did.

I turned off my bike as my phone rang in my hands.

"Hey, Martha." I bit down on my lip. I didn't need this, not now.

"Parker, I'm glad we could–"

"It's Gabe."

"Right," she said rapidly. "Sorry, it's just… she only calls you Parker so I tend to forget."

"Martha, I'm kind of busy, what's this about?" I shifted my weight to the other foot and waited.

"She's asking for you."

I laughed bitterly. "She always asks for me. They all do."

"Yes, I know, but, Parker – I mean *Gabe*…" I could hear the sadness in her voice. "It's bad this time. Could you stop by? Maybe bring your guitar or something? I know she loves that. Or color, she's been going through that weird coloring phase. The entire place has!" Her excitement should have rubbed off, but instead, all I wanted to do was get high. I wanted an escape.

But I didn't deserve one. Maybe that was the problem.

"Yeah." I wiped my face with my hands. "I can do that. Give me fifteen minutes."

"Thanks… Gabe."

"Anytime, Martha. Take care."

I hung up and stared at the dorm. Wes was a freaking miracle worker, no joke, like a walking male version of Mother Theresa.

Shit. I may as well be the devil.

Chapter Six

He tasted like cinnamon — too bad I was allergic to cinnamon. Good thing I didn't go into anaphylactic shock from the kiss. That would have been awkward. —Saylor

Saylor

I wasn't really sure how long I stared at the piano before I was able to function enough to play. Each time I tried to lift my hands, all I could picture were his. They'd had music notes on each knuckle.

Why I'd remember such a ridiculous detail, I had no idea. But it seemed weird that a guy who looked like that was capable of the music that had come from the practice room. What had come out of his mouth when the door was closed was completely the opposite of what he looked like and how he'd acted when I was eavesdropping.

Maybe it was my fault. After all, I'd been salivating over the music like a dog in heat. It was my weakness, my downfall. I hadn't heard those songs in a long time, they pulled at something deep within me, some untouched part that I longed to unleash but was too afraid to tap into. Funny, because it had nothing to do with the actual song, but the way it was played – with such passion and abandonment that I was immediately jealous.

It was why my music major wasn't performance, as the *asshat* had assumed. It was music theory. I wanted to be a professor. I wanted safe. Safe meant I'd have a job, that I'd be able to pay off my ridiculous student loans, and that I wouldn't fail.

Safe was all I had. Because when you took chances you got hurt and I was so done being hurt. Most people went to college hoping for an adventure – I'd be happy with a diploma and a mug with my alma mater on it. Nothing was more important to me than not having to worry.

Typical for someone who's been taking care of her family for the past few years. I was all my little brother and my mom had. They were counting on me to make something of myself so that I could, in turn, provide for them.

And it wasn't even like they were asking a lot. They just wanted me to graduate and find a job that brought in decent enough money so we wouldn't have to live paycheck to paycheck.

I shook my head. Practice. Mom. Eric. Those were my motivators, not some tattooed, spoiled bad boy who liked attacking innocent girls in music rooms.

Nice. I was a romance novel waiting to happen.

I closed my eyes and placed my hands on the smooth keys and so began my two hour practice session.

Chapter Seven

I kept a picture of us in my pillowcase like an absolute nutjob. She'd had it in her pocket the day of the accident. I wanted it as close to my face as possible when I slept every night. Because every night I went to bed hoping it was all a bad dream, and every morning I woke up to the terrifying reality that it was not. You'd think I would stop hoping…but I'd never stop. I'd never stop praying for God to take it away. —Gabe H.

Gabe

I pulled out onto 405 South and took the exit toward the other side of Seattle. How many times had I driven this same route over the years? Through rain, snow, sleet, hail. Shit, I was like a dog with a trail in his owner's back yard. Predictable to the extreme. I was either at school or at the Home. I increased the speed, hoping that it would decrease the sharp pain in my chest. I was messing everything up just by existing, it was too tempting. To end everything. End everyone's misery.

Almost as tempting as dropping the whole happy-go-lucky bullshit act and actually pouring my feelings out to anyone. Hell, I'd even pour them out to Lisa at this point, but she was too close to the situation. It would just make her cry, and I hated seeing that girl cry. Correction, I hated seeing any girl cry. The last time Kiersten cried I wanted to do a freaking heart transplant so she wouldn't hurt anymore. I would have gladly taken her pain. After all, what was one more broken heart when yours was in a constant state of being shattered?

The moist air bit into my leather jacket as I got closer to the water. I slowed down once I pulled up to the Pacific Northwest Group Home and put my bike in its usual spot.

The building had once been an old hospital but had been converted into a group home with an adjoining retirement home in the late fifties. Later it was remodeled to include a state of the art treatment center for people with brain injuries. Every time I parked in that spot, the same feelings washed over me. Dread, heartache, confusion, guilt.

Luckily, the building was a pristine white with exposed wood, making it look more like a set of cabins on the water than what it really was.

For some reason I was delaying the inevitable. My feet felt like lead as I approached the doors. It had been… different since Wes's surgery. Or maybe I was different? Whatever it was, I wasn't dealing with anything well.

I walked toward the main building — the treatment center — and braced myself for impact. The first steps into the entrance were always the hardest.

"Gabe!" Martha clutched a clipboard to her chest and let out a sigh of relief. "I know it's not your normal day but—"

"It's fine!" I flashed her a smile when I all I wanted to do was turn around and march back out to my bike and cry. I was here five days a week. You'd think it would be enough. But lately, even being there twenty-four seven wasn't doing the trick. She was failing. And it was my fault. Martha gave me a sympathetic pat on the hand.

Aw, pity. Lovely. I cleared my throat and forced a wider smile. "You look great. Have you lost weight?"

Good call, Gabe. Just hit on the elderly because that's been known to make everything better.

"Such a nice gentleman." She elbowed me in the ribs as I wrapped my left arm around her, pulling her in for a hug. "I still don't understand why you don't find a nice young girl and settle down."

My entire body tensed.

Did she still really not know? How in my heart that would be the final nail in the coffin? To settle down and finally — forget.

"Yeah, well." I laughed it off. "Most girls my age can't keep up. I'm into older women. You got any ideas of who I could seduce out of her scrubs?"

"Oh, you." She hit me with the clipboard. "I could be your grandmother and you know it."

"So you'll think about it?" I kissed her cheek in good fun.

"Oh, I never said I didn't." She winked. "Now, she's just in there. The nurses finally calmed her down a bit with a game of checkers."

"Let me guess, she's destroying everyone."

"It seems the only way to calm her down is competition." Martha shrugged and handed me the clipboard. "Just be sure to sign out when you leave."

I took the board. "No problem."

Nurses and staff shuffled by me, each of them hurrying off in different directions, getting things prepared for the day. Martha went back to the main desk while I made my way through the long hall toward the game room, passing the security team on the way. The two men nodded in my direction — as they should, considering I paid their asses — and opened the door to the room.

Laughter danced off the walls.

Her laughter.

I grinned despite my shitty attitude and the fact that I was sweating. When had I ever been hesitant to visit her? Or any of the patients? I shook it off as the large metal door closed behind me.

"Gabe!" Old man Henry wheeled himself over to me and held out his hand. "Didn't know you were gracing us with your presence today!"

"Count yourself lucky." I took his hand and reached into my pocket to pull out a piece of taffy. "Shh, don't tell Martha."

"That woman was a drill sergeant in another life." Henry shook his head, "Last time she caught me with pudding I was on bathroom duty! In my condition!" He pointed at his legs. They were strapped against the chair so he didn't lose balance and fall out. A farm accident had nearly killed him, but it didn't keep him from volunteering his time. Once his wife died he decided to move into the retirement home next door – unfortunately, Martha was head nurse for both buildings and had the ear of the cooks, meaning he never got sugar. Poor guy.

"Hey, Gabe!" Sarah practically tripped over Henry's chair to jump into my arms. She was my age but because of an accident had memory issues. For some reason, though, she remembered my name. Probably because I was the only constant thing in her life.

My heart ached a bit as I set her back on her feet and kissed her cheek. "Do a twirl for me, Sarah. Let's see this dress."

She laughed and did a twirl then went to go sit at the far table. Where I knew I was being patiently waited for.

"Henry." I saluted him and walked toward the table.

"Parker." A muffled voice rose from the table, nearly bringing me to my knees. I told myself to be strong, but it was so damned hard and getting harder. She reminded me of every mistake I'd made, every bad road I'd traveled.

She looked thinner than when I saw her last week. Her

blonde hair was pulled back in a pink scrunchie – her favorite color – and she was wearing her favorite Oregon Ducks sweatshirt.

Another really bad sign.

She only wore the sweatshirt on bad days.

She'd been having bad days for the past two weeks.

And every time I tried asking the doctors what was going on they'd just shake their heads and say the human condition was a mystery. Her health was failing and they had no freaking clue why. She'd already suffered through two bouts of pneumonia where she needed to be physically restrained so they could calm her down enough to put a tube down her throat to help her breathe.

The second time she'd screamed my name over and over again. I'd stayed overnight and prayed that God would just take her. Even though it would hurt like hell, I wanted Him to take her.

Watching her suffer was like going to bed and praying that when you wake up things would be better. I'd been told that all my life, just to sleep on things and they always look better in the morning.

It didn't work anymore.

Because now when I woke up, things always looked worse.

"Princess?" I knelt down next to her wheelchair and took her hand in mine. She was paralyzed from the neck down, so it was impossible for her to feel the warmth of my skin – but I still held her hand anyway.

One time I forgot to hold it and she thought I was mad at her. When I asked how she could feel my hand in the first place, she said she couldn't, but she did still have two eyes. I'd laughed and grabbed her hand, promising to never let go.

"You haven't been here, Park." Her lower lip jutted out as her mouth dropped open a bit. So she was pouting. Fantastic.

And this was what I was talking about. I'd done my daily duty by showing up for at least a half hour to an hour each day. But it still wasn't enough. She always forgot, meaning I'd had to start calling at night too. That had begun a month ago, and things still weren't getting better.

"I've had a really busy few months with classes." I lied, thinking it was easier to brush it off rather than explain to her that I had in fact been by her side like a freaking leach for the past four years and was slowly suffocating to death. She wouldn't understand. It would hurt her, and I'd already done that enough.

"Oh." Her empty blue eyes seemed to take the information as truth, "Well, since you're here, can we play a game?" The emptiness disappeared as excitement flashed across her face.

"Sure." I sat down next to her and looked at the table. "What are our choices?"

"Hmm..." Her smile was bright and eager. "How about Guess Who?"

"Awesome." I pulled out the game board just as my phone went off.

Not thinking, I went to answer it, momentarily forgetting how much Princess hated interruptions.

"No phones, Park! No PHONES!" She wailed shaking her head back and forth. "You promised, PARKER, you promised me! You promised!" Loud sobs escaped her mouth as a few nurses came running.

Well, shit.

"I'm so sorry, K, I forgot, I—"

"That's not my name!" She yelled. "My name's Princess!"

"You're right," I sighed, reaching for my guitar and motioning for the nurses to stop running. They'd do more damage than good. "How about I play you a song?"

She stopped yelling, but her lips quivered. "Play our song, Park. Please?"

"Of course, Princess. I'll play our song."

I was five seconds away from losing my shit. I strummed a few chords and started singing. Princess giggled and started singing with me.

She'd once had a beautiful voice. But her voice, just like everything else, had been taken from her. By the very person who promised he would never let anything happen to her.

My stomach clenched. I wasn't sure how much longer I'd be able to do it. But I had to try – for her I'd try, because I'd broken every other promise I'd ever made her. I had promised to protect her, to save her – sucks that the one person who promises you life – delivers death.

Chapter Eight

I couldn't get him out of my mind. Which was so stupid if you asked me. I dreamt of his stupid music note tattoos and that ridiculous kiss. I needed to get out more or something if I was dreaming of the devil and actually looking forward to falling asleep so I could dream of him again. —Saylor

Saylor

It had been two days since my run-in with Blue Eyes, aka Asshat. I was beginning to think he wasn't real. I mean, he played the piano like a dream but he wasn't in the music program — at all. Not that I shamelessly searched for any sign of him in all of my classes.

Or Facebook stalked him.

Or asked the dean of the department.

I was curious. That was it.

Besides, he was never in my building.

And I was in that building twenty-four seven.

Great, was I really practicing so hard that I'd started hallucinating?

I shook my head as I walked down the hall toward the practice room. So what if it was at the exact same time I'd been there a few days past? Was it wrong to feel hopeful that I'd hear that music again? It was my practice time —the only time I could manage to fit it in my schedule!

That man could be the devil himself — and probably was if his earlier behavior was any indication — and all it would take would be one song and I'd be putty. That's why musicians were dangerous, they made you forget yourself. The core of who you are can be so easily lost in music. They were our modern day sirens, wielding the power of persuasion with their gift. And the rest of the human population had no choice but to be caught in the trap. It was worse for a fellow musician because they could actually appreciate the raw talent and skill. It was beyond something sounding good — it was about life coming together for a few brief seconds while notes mixed. I shuddered.

I wondered if anyone had ever taken the time to tell him how amazing he was at the piano. How I'd kill to have that type of talent at my fingertips. My greedy little musician heart wanted to sit in the same practice room as him and just savor the moment.

"Geez, Saylor," I mumbled to myself. "Get a grip. Focus. Practice. Graduate." I reaffirmed my mantra with a nod as I repeated it to myself.

And then I heard singing.

The melody was familiar. I listened closer. The song spoke of messing up, being the reason for your own mistakes, and then walking away from someone you loved. My breath caught as he sang it perfectly. *Parachute* had always been one of my favorite bands.

My heart started slamming against my chest as I took a tentative step toward the practice room.

He was at the piano, his hands flying across the ivory keys like he was Mozart's long lost prodigy. His voice was like

— nothing I'd ever heard. So honest, so raw, so much pain came out of that mouth, that for some reason I felt like crying.

I gasped as he stopped playing and then with a yell hit the piano with his hands, over and over again like he wanted to hurt, like the song was pissing him off, along with everything else in the world.

Without thinking, I opened the door. "You probably shouldn't destroy school property like that." What was I? The piano police? Kill me now. The door slammed behind me and took all the oxygen with it.

His hands froze midair, with a curse he turned and stared right through me. His blue eyes were cold. Slowly, he stood and stalked toward me. "What are you going to do about it, little girl? Tattle?"

"Sure," I said in a confident voice. "If you want to pick a fight, at least choose something that can punch back." I was officially the worst trash talker on the face of the planet. Why hadn't I disappeared into the floor already?

"Maybe I like it when people don't fight back," he snapped.

"If you're that angry the last thing you need is to get into trouble. It will just make you more angry."

"Says Miss Perfect," he growled. "Tell me, is it curiosity, or are you really just stalking me? Taking me up on my first offer?"

"First offer?"

He leaned closer to me and offered a half grin. "To make your pony blush."

I felt my cheeks burn as I glanced down at the carpeted floor.

"Oh, so you *are* taking me up on my offer." He grinned and trapped me against the door. "Maybe it will help your music."

"I don't need help," I murmured, still not looking up.

"Passion." He ignored me, leaning in so I could almost

taste him. "Music and passion are one. And I've never seen anyone so lacking in my entire life."

I flinched as if he'd just slapped me across the face. With a grunt, I tried to push him away from me but he wouldn't move.

"I'm a great tutor."

"I don't doubt it. But I'm not interested in a one night stand."

"So you say." His hand moved down my arm. I shivered. "But your body says something else entirely." His lips grazed my ear and then my neck. I arched toward him, not realizing that I was pressed fully against him until it was too late. His warm chuckle should have infuriated me. Instead, it made me want to reach out, to touch him back.

See? He was a damn siren!

His mouth found mine, and I was lost. Fool me once, shame on you, fool me twice… well…

I'd never been one of those girls. The girl that kissed random strangers. I mean, seriously. I really did have a purple pony in my room.

His tongue found mine. I moaned as his hands tugged at my shirt. He smelled like fresh soap and spices. I wrapped my arms around his neck.

With a growl he pulled back, his eyes flashing. "We doing this here?"

"Wh-what?" My eyes darted round the room with confusion. What was he talking about? Palms sweaty, I wiped them on my jeans and took a hesitant step away from his muscled body.

His mocking chuckle vibrated off the walls of the room. "So, we doing it here? Or did you have someplace special you wanted to go for your first time? I mean, normally I don't do charity cases, but I could light a candle if you want."

I reared back, tears burning at the back of my throat. He caught my hand mid air.

"Tsk–tsk... and I'm the one who needs anger management." He winked. "Nice playing with you, Freshman, but if you don't wanna play then you're just wasting my time, and I'm really..." His eyes darkened. "...*really* careful how I spend my time."

"I think I may hate you," I breathed.

"Hate's a good emotion." He finally released me. "Fill your heart with hate, then maybe it won't hurt as much. That's what I always say." His smile was sad as he calmly stepped away. "Use it."

"Wh-what?" My head was still spinning.

"The hate. Use it while you play."

I opened my mouth to respond, but he was already halfway down the hallway by the time I could think of anything smart in response.

Once he reached the end of the hall he called back, "Interrupt my private session again, and I'll take that as an invitation. Believe me, you don't want to experience that, especially since you hate me."

As he disappeared around the corner, I let out the breath I'd been holding. Clearly, I'd completely lost my mind. My lips buzzed from our kiss. I should have run away. I should have slapped him! Instead I let him maul me... again.

Stressed. That was it. I was stressed and overworked and it didn't help that when I'd pleaded for the second time this week to get out of the stupid Freshman Seminar project, my professor had threatened me. Again.

I was going to have to start practicing late at night if I had any hope to impress the professors at the end-of-the-year recital. My scholarship depended on my ability to play.

My ability to make the professors believe I was worth the free ride they'd given me at this school.

Shaking thoughts of the dark stranger away from my head, I decided to stay in the same practice room he'd left. After all, I was already there and it wasn't like he was coming back.

Maybe some of his talent would rub off on me.

I didn't play like that.

I wasn't raw.

I was practiced.

To be out of control the way he was? To let the music decide what it was going to do and when — I didn't have that. I was lacking in the passion department.

My professors all said my music was perfect — but cold.

If I was cold — he was on fire.

Two hours. I had two hours to practice before I had to meet up with my class partner and go over plans for our project.

I set my notes and music on the piano and focused on the keys. My fingers tingled as I touched the ivory — they tingled when I thought of his hands.

For once in my life I wanted to know what it felt like to be free.

But something told me — the guy who had just left this room was anything but — he was trapped, and by the conviction in the song he sang — it was all his own doing.

Chapter Nine

Music is life — maybe that's why I'd abandoned it for so long. I didn't feel like I deserved life — not anymore. —Gabe H.

Gabe

I leaned against the wall as the music from the practice room filtered faintly into the hallway.

She was perfect.

Her timing.

The way the notes flowed together.

But I *felt* nothing.

The moment had finally come, the moment when music no longer made me feel. I wanted to hate her for barging in on me, for correcting me, for being so annoying and pretty at the same time.

For being one of those girls who actually fascinated me.

She'd tasted good. Kissing her had been a giant-assed mistake, because for some reason, I knew her lips were going to haunt me, the way her mouth felt against mine.

The last time I felt something while kissing someone was

four years ago and that hadn't ended well.

Her spunk reminded me of Kiersten.

Great, that's just what I needed... to lust after my best friends *fiancée*.

I stayed in the hallway for an hour. I listened as she changed from piece to piece, each one of them perfectly flawless but void of emotion.

For some reason, it made me sad.

Music wasn't really music unless your soul was exposed, unless your heart was either bursting or breaking.

And hers... was doing neither.

Then again, who was I to judge? I would have used the piano for kindling if she hadn't barged in on me.

With a sigh, I leaned back against the wall and closed my eyes. *What if.* Damn, I hated those two words.

"Are you lost?" A female voice asked.

I opened my eyes, a girl the size of a middle schooler was looking at me like I was the ghost of Christmas past. Her eyes went wide as she looked at my neck and then lower. Yeah, I really didn't fit the part of Musical Performance major.

"No," I said curtly, closing my eyes again.

"You look familiar."

My eyes opened, and then realization seemed to dawn in that smart little head of hers.

"Gotta run." I pushed away from the wall.

"Wait, has anyone ever told you, that you look a lot like—"

"Adam Levine?" I interrupted. "All the freaking time. See ya."

Close call, close call. I ran out of the building, pausing only to look at my reflection in the window.

Damn it.

My hair was beginning to lighten again. How had I not noticed that? I was starting to get careless — lazy.

And my entire existence depended on keeping my secret

from the world.

I made a mental note to stop off at the drug store and grab some more hair dye.

The guy with the sandy brown hair and smiling eyes was gone — and I'd replaced him with an imposter — a picture of what I felt like on the inside.

Dark.

An empty void.

Chapter Ten

Ashton freaking Hyde, how I loathe you! My roommate had found out about my obsession and littered my walls with his sexy face. I guess there were worse things to stare at. Damn his blue eyes. – Saylor

Saylor

By the time Tuesday rolled around, I was dragging my feet. All the late night practices were getting to me and I still couldn't get Sexy Stranger out of my mind. Yes, I'd officially resorted to calling him Sexy Stranger.

Ugh.

I walked back toward the dorms. I'd promised my study partner I'd stop by and go over our plans for our freshman project. I'd only met her once, but she seemed really nice. Added bonus, she seemed like the type of girl who didn't make the other person do all the work.

I kept my head down as people walked by me. Being a social butterfly was never high on my priority list. Plus, I never really knew what to do when people looked at me. Was

I supposed to smile? Wave? I always felt awkward and uncomfortable and then there was that whole long hallway scenario. Seriously. What are you supposed to do when you and one other person are on opposite ends of the hall walking by one another? Five minutes into walking and it's like, okay, let's just acknowledge that each of us are attempting to pay attention to everything but each other and then, boom, at the last minute, "Oh hey I didn't see you there, what's up?" Lame.

I reached for the door to the building and stumbled backward into something hard. "Whoa there," an amused voice said from behind me bracing my shoulders. "You okay?"

I nodded and turned to face whoever saved me from a concussion. Of course, as luck would have it, Football God, also known as the great Wes Michels, was my savior.

Naturally, because life was just that cruel. And I clearly hadn't had enough embarrassing moments in the past three days to last me a lifetime.

Unable to find my voice, I lifted my hands to my temples, faking the whole dizzy thing, buying me enough time to say in a voice that sounded like a three year old, "Thank you."

"No problem." He shrugged then opened the door for me. I walked past him, straight toward the elevator.

He followed.

I pressed *up*.

He stepped in with me.

I moved to the farthest corner of the tiny box and waited for the floor to ding. The minute the doors open, I nearly collided with another person getting in, but was able to sidestep the harried genderless student who was hidden behind an armload of textbooks and make my way down to Room 226.

Balancing my bag in one arm, I lifted my hand to knock when that same voice said from behind me.

"You a friend of Gabe's?"

"Who?" I whipped around. "Is that who lives here?"

With shaking hands I gripped the piece of paper with Lisa's contact information. "I was actually looking for Lisa. We're in the same business seminar class and we're doing a project together, but I can be super forgetful, so I'll just text her and see if I wrote down the wrong number and—"

"Whoa." Weston held up his hands. "Totally wasn't meaning to scare you shitless… Lisa lives here, and she probably won't hear you knock on account that on Taco Tuesday she turns up Mexican music so loud the rest of the building complains."

"Taco Tuesday?" I repeated.

"You'll see." He sighed and reached behind me, pushing the door open. "Lisa!"

He yelled like a football player. I winced as my ears started ringing.

"What!" Lisa yelled from somewhere in the apartment.

And he was right, the music was crazy loud. I couldn't even hear myself think, thanks to both the mariachi notes and the fact that Weston had just yelled in my right ear.

"Someone's here to see you!" he yelled back just as a girl walked out of one of the bedrooms. I recognized her immediately — Kiersten, Football God's *fiancée*. You'd have to be living on a different planet not to know their story.

He fights cancer, she fights for him, they fight together, he proposes during football game and what do ya know? He's miraculously healed! They were a living, walking, breathing Hallmark Movie.

"Oooo, are you a friend of Gabe's?" Kiersten's eyes widened with amusement as she stepped into Weston's arms. He kissed her on the head, and started toying with a piece of her dark red hair.

"Who's Gabe?" I said for a second time.

"Stupid dry spell!" Lisa yelled again from somewhere in the kitchen. At this point I still hadn't seen her.

"Am I missing something?" I said as loud as my voice

was capable of going, which wasn't very loud.

"It's a damn choice!" An even louder male voice said behind me. I could have sworn the hair on my arms stood on end as I slowly turned to face the owner of the voice, hoping, praying that I was wrong.

"You!" We shouted in unison. I dropped my bag to the floor and held my hands in the air like I'd just gotten mugged and was about to drop his ass, when really every meeting with him had gone far, far differently.

Gabe grabbed my wrists and grinned. "Back for more."

The darkness was gone.

Who was this imposter? He seemed… happy. But every time I'd seen him he may as well be wearing a sign that read: *Chip on shoulder, beware.*

Confused, I shook my head. His smile grew as his fingers tapped playfully across my wrists.

"Gabe!" Lisa yelled. "Release my partner or I'll put Pepto in your tacos!"

"What would that even do?" asked Weston from behind me.

The music was turned down and then Lisa was prying me away from Gabe.

"So…" Lisa's grin grew to epic proportions, as her eyes seemed to calculate our acquaintance. "I take it you know each other."

I yelled, "He assaulted me!"

At the same time, Gabe winked and countered with, "She's a damn spy!"

"Forget the movie," Wes said in an amused voice. "Gabe drama? Way better." He took a seat on an arm of the couch and smirked.

My eyes narrowed into slits as my hands twitched at my side. The guy needed to be punched. This time Lisa put a calming hand on my arm, while Gabe threw his head back and laughed.

Again with the laughing? Did he have multiple personality disorder? Were they aware he was mentally unstable? And if they weren't, wasn't it my duty to say something? So he didn't knife them in their sleep when he decided to take the train from happy land back into hell?

"Classic," he said, his stupidly long eyelashes mocking me with every damn blink. "You Lisa's new tutor too? Tell me, piano star, does the world ever tire of your Mother Theresa ways?"

Ah, there he is. To be honest, I had been getting slightly worried.

"That's it." Lisa grabbed Gabe by the ear and tugged.

"What the hell, Lisa!" Gabe whined as he stumbled toward her tiny body.

She released his ear and stomped her foot. "New leaf. You stopped being an ass remember?"

"He was never really an ass," Kiersten said coming to his defense.

I turned my head slowly to catch her expression. But she looked completely serious as if he wasn't a complete and total loser. He was talented and hot, but still a loser. Okay, so he had skills but… Wow, I needed to stop the arguing in my head before I got a headache.

Gabe formed his hands into a heart and pressed it against his chest. "Love you, Kiersten."

"Not your girl," Wes fired back.

"Is this getting filmed or something?" I threw my hands up in the air. "You guys are all crazy. You know that right? I'm here for Lisa, not Gabe. I barely even know him outside of the practice rooms.

"Oh my gosh! You're trying out for the spring musical?" Kiersten asked.

"Uh…" Gabe licked his lips.

"Wait, practice rooms," Lisa repeated. "Gabe, are you playing again?"

"Again?" Kiersten looked between the two of them. "What do you mean again?"

"Wow, thanks, band geek, seriously. Awesome. I guess I was right before. You are a tattletale. Oh, look at the time," he said, checking his watch. "Better hurry home so you can get in bed before seven and have your roomie braid your hair. Oh, and don't forget to brush your teeth and say those prayers."

"Don't you have an STD to spread?" I tilted my head with cool indifference.

He pushed away from the wall. "Why, you open for business?"

"Turtle!" Lisa shouted and stomped her foot.

The room fell silent.

I burst into a fit of laughter. "Turtle? Seriously?"

Gabe rolled his eyes and pinched the bridge of his nose as if every word out of my mouth was causing his head to pound.

"Sorry, Gabe," Lisa whispered and wiped her hands on her crazy looking Jalapeño apron. "I had a virgin margarita."

"Sugar makes you crazy," Gabe said, crossing his arms over his chest, "And yeah, it's my nickname. Why? You into nicknames and role play? Shit like that get your engine going?"

"Ew, Gabe." Kiersten walked over to us and put her hands up n the air. "I'm just going to stop you now before both feet end up in your mouth and you lose the ability to walk. Repeat after me, Hi…" She paused and looked at me. "What's your name?"

"Saylor."

"Hi, Saylor. Nice to meet you. I'm Gabe, and I promise I'm not as big of an asshole as you think I am. I promise to keep all parts in my pants, and I swear that if I attack you one more time, Kiersten has full permission to castrate me in my sleep."

Gabe glared and held out his hand. "Saylor, it's a

pleasure meeting you." His teeth were clenched so tight his jaw flexed. I'd never seen a guy with so many tattoos and piercings… never in my life would I ever imagine it would look so damn hot, but on him it did. And I wanted to hate him for it.

Because the opposite meant I liked it.

His face had just enough of a five o'clock shadow to be dangerous for any female with a pair of good working eyes. His dark as sin hair hung almost to his chin but had a slight curl to it, making him look like a damn pirate. A tattoo snaked around his neck, diving into the front of his shirt, and his arm muscles seemed to swell as I tentatively watched the swirl of tattoos almost move across his forearm. He was covered in what looked like lyrics on his right arm, and on his left, he had a few birds, more music notes, and a cross, everything was linked together. It should have looked stupid. But instead of looking stupid — like he was some sort of mismatched first grader — it looked sexy. Damn, damn, damn. I didn't swear often, but Gabe made me want to live up to my name. Swear like a sailor? Um yeah, it was happening.

"So…" Gabe eyed me up and down.

I backed up until my legs touched the couch.

"You gonna just stand there all day staring at me, or are you and Lisa actually going to do homework?"

"Homework." An arm looped within mine, and I looked up into Lisa's amused gaze. "But first, we eat!"

"Olé!" Wes clapped and smacked Kiersten on the rear, while Lisa kept her arm firmly tucked in mine.

Gabe continued to stare, as if it was some sort of weird stare off where if I backed off first, I'd be the loser and have to do something really embarrassing, like admit he had a physical effect on my body.

"Shh," Lisa said in a low voice. "No sudden movements. He'll take it as a challenge and start chasing."

"Me thinks she wants to be chased." Gabe licked his lips.

I rolled my eyes. "Yeah well *me* thinks the ink on your body has started seeping into that brain of yours… Tell me, do you enjoy harassing young women in order to get them into bed with you?"

Gabe tilted his head in thought, then raised an eyebrow as if the thought actually had merit.

"Come on." Lisa tugged my arm. "You can help me set the table. I hope you don't mind that we eat first. It's my turn to cook and if I punk out, Gabe throws a fit."

"Likes his food?" I asked, following her into the kitchen.

"No." Lisa pulled out some taco shells. "He's just really OCD about the dinner schedule."

"Odd," I admitted.

"Thank you." Gabe's breath was on my neck as he answered and then side-stepped me and started pulling salsa and sour cream out of the fridge, "Being called odd's almost as great as being called sexy."

"How do you figure?" I snorted, trying to ignore what his nearness was doing to my body at that moment. My breath hitched as another wave of desire hit me. Swear, it was like he was physically willing himself on me without even touching me.

Gabe's hand paused on the ketchup as he ducked out from behind the fridge door and sneered at me; his mouth curved silkily around his white teeth, sending an involuntary shudder through me. "Odd can mean any number of things." He closed the fridge.

There wasn't anything I could put between us, no counter, no ketchup, nothing.

"Odd means I stand out. It's an unintelligent way of saying I'm unique, different, special, one of a kind. Odd means in a lineup of twenty guys, your eyes would still find mine." He thumped the block of cheese onto the counter. "Every." Followed it with a jar of chopped tomatoes. "Damn." And then the salsa. "Time." Then he turned to face me, a smirk on his face so cocky that I wanted to launch myself at him. "So do I take it as a compliment that you call me odd? Hell yeah, I do. It means tonight when you close your eyes, you won't be thinking about all those cookie cutter all-American guys with clean skin and baby blue eyes. But you will be thinking of me." His grin turned predatory. "All me. And that—" He took two more steps toward me. I couldn't back up. It was impossible to move. "—makes me happier than you'll ever know."

My breathing was ragged. I was an idiot. Plain and simple. I was allowing the bad boy with no future to play with my feelings, but it was unintentional. Everything about my reaction to him was uncontrollable. I couldn't help but feel drawn, I couldn't help but feel irritated, and I couldn't help but want him to touch me one more time, even though it pissed me off as much as it turned me on.

"Move," he whispered.

"Huh?" I shook the cobwebs of lust from my head.

He tapped my shoulder and gently pushed me to the side. "I gotta set the table. I wasn't trying to be rude. Oh, and close your mouth. Gaping makes you look desperate."

I stepped out of the way, basically clattering my body against the oven hard enough to cause a permanent bruise on my hip.

"Don't mind him," Lisa said from behind me. "One day, he'll get his."

"Don't worry." Gabe poked his head around the corner and winked. "I already got mine." He disappeared then came back again just as I opened my mouth to speak. "Oh, and by the way, it was awesome."

"Pig," Lisa muttered.

"Aw, cousin." Gabe blew a kiss and this time disappeared for good.

I didn't realize I was holding my breath until Lisa tapped me on the shoulder, making me almost choke to death.

"Sorry about him. Sometimes I wonder how we're

related." Her blue eyes twinkled briefly before she shrugged and returned to the cupboard to pull out plates. "Grab the salsa and we can put the tacos on the table. Homework second, food first." For some reason I felt the need to it – maybe it was because of Gabe, or maybe it was because of me. Yeah, on second thought, it was me, because he made me feel out of control.

Chapter Eleven

Stupid Taco Tuesday and all it represented. I'd rather drive down to Mexico, buy some drugs, and risk the chance of getting caught on the Tijuana border by drug sniffing dogs than actually sit through an entire meal while everyone pretended life was perfect. —Gabe H.

Gabe

"You staying for dinner?" I took a swig of water and sat at the table. Wes sat opposite and chuckled, reaching for his own water and giving me that look that guys gave one another when they were enjoying the other's misery way too much.

"Thought I would." Wes's grin widened. "You know since things got so interesting."

"You should go."

"I think I'd rather stay and watch Taco Tuesday drama."

"I second that." Kiersten took a seat and slapped me on the back, "Olé?"

"Um, no, and please remove your hand." I glared.

She tilted her head. Ah, the pity look. Fantastic. Her hand

moved from my shoulder down to my arm as she squeezed. Great! Effing wonderful. I'd just been given the supportive friend squeeze on top of everything else. Fantastic.

I wasn't big on touch. I mean, I talked a big game, and sure I loved screwing around, but people actually touching me just to touch? Not a huge fan. It reminded me too much of them — the people at the home--of their touches, of their sad faces every damn day that week.

I freaking hated it when people felt sorry for me, or what was even worse, when I felt guilty for being thankful that I was actually in that position, thankful that the person they wanted most to live... was actually dying.

"Which one do you think she would like, Park?" Her mother touched my arm briefly before putting her hand back onto her lips as they trembled.

"Um," my voice croaked. I could barely keep my eyes open anymore. I'd cried so damn much that they stopped producing tears. Instead they burned like hell until I closed them.

The only problem with closing them?

I saw her.

I saw the damn scarf.

And I saw all the blood.

"That one," I whispered hoarsely. "She always liked pink."

Mrs. Unifelt smiled sadly. "Maybe we won't have to use it."

I didn't know what to say. I mean, what do you say to that? I hope your daughter doesn't make it? I hope she dies in surgery because I really can't live in world where I'm reminded of her every day but I never actually get to be with her again?

"Pink it is." The funeral director put a large check through the box on her sheet and gave me the same smile she'd been giving me for the past hour.

I wasn't sure whether I was too numb to react or just too pissed. A freaking check box? Was that all her life had been worth? A recycled piece of paper with tiny boxes to fill in?

The tears burned at the back of my throat.

"...of course she may make it through surgery. We always have hope. After all, the doctors are confident they can stop the hemorrhaging in her brain, though they're certain she won't ever be our little princess again."

I couldn't take it anymore. The dam broke and tears flooded my eyes and spilled over as I stared at the pink casket. What the hell kind of torture was this? Pick out your girlfriend's casket? The same way I go and pick out a tie for a movie premiere?

The entire business made me sick.

From the dim lighting in the funeral home—

—To the idea that they made thousands of dollars off of something that wasn't going to make me or anyone else feel better. She was going to die. And if she lived... Damn. If she lived, I'd wish she hadn't.

And that made me the worst type of human being.

Because anyone should want to live when faced with death. Any sane person would choose life. But me? If I was in her shoes? I would choose death. As far as I was concerned, the love of my life had already died, all I was waiting for was her physical body to follow suit. Her mind — everything that had made her who she was — was gone.

Mrs. Unifelt reached for my arm again, this time gripping it like a lifeline.

"And have you decided who will be doing the eulogy?"

All eyes turned to me. A weight descended on my shoulders as I hung my head and gave a slight nod. "I am."

"If it comes to that," Mrs. Unifelt added.

"Of course," the funeral director said quickly. "If it comes to that."

"Where'd you go, Gabe?" Kiersten snapped her fingers in front of me.

Everyone was seated at the table staring at me like I'd just grown a third eye and had demanded they call me Kanye.

"Uh..." I scratched the back of my head and let out a nervous chuckle. "Sorry, long night last night."

"Must have been," Wes muttered as his eyes flickered from Saylor back to me. "All things considering."

Choosing to ignore his slight to my inability to sleep with any female since his operation, I glared and started piling my plate high with tacos.

"So..." Kiersten stole the taco shell from my plate and began making her own.

Irritated, I shot her a narrow-eyed glare and pretended not to be interested in her girly talk.

"Tell me about this project you guys have to do?" She finished.

"Yes, tell us. We wait with bated breath," I said dryly, annoyed that I had to sit through dinner with a hot stranger who would rather see me choke to death than make it through the next ten minutes.

Someone kicked me under the table. I winced but otherwise said nothing.

"Well..." Saylor reached for a taco shell.

I swiped it away from her before she could grab it, pretending not to see her. So now I had like three naked taco shells on my plate all because I had the manners of a fifth grader and wanted to stick my tongue out at her — or maybe it was down her throat? I didn't say I wasn't confused about her.

"We have to do this Third Semester Seminar project about something that's important to us. Since Lisa didn't really know what to focus on—"

"—and since the most important thing to Lisa is the number of shoes she has in her closet," I sang.

"Thanks, Gabe."

I saluted her and piled some cheese onto my taco, hating that I was being put through the torture of watching Saylor nibble on a damn chip like a bunny who couldn't decide if it liked its food.

"Anyways..." Saylor stuffed the chip into her mouth.

Thank God. Then took another. Of course. "I decided that we could work on my idea together. The professor had already put a few teams together, and we were the last two left."

"Bummer, and I thought I was important," Lisa joked.

Saylor smiled, and I had to look away. If only she had lipstick on her teeth, or a damn tortilla chip stuck somewhere. Instead, it was blinding and way too happy for my taste. Playing the happy one was my job, but I didn't have to enjoy it. Happy just seemed easy for her, so basically, she reminded me of a female version of Wes. Great, now there were two of them in the world, and both in my life indefinitely. I could only handle Wes's wisdom in small doses; otherwise, I figured I'd strangle him or try to punch him in the face. Don't get me wrong. I loved him more than a brother, but when a person's so stuck in their own hole of darkness — it hurts like hell when someone shines a light on them. Your eyes have to adjust, and let's just say it isn't a pleasant experience; it's why people stay there. It's why a lot of us, and I do mean a lot of us, choose the façade rather than the reality of where we're living. Hell, I'd been living in my dark hole for so long, I'd set up camp, put up pictures, and ordered cable.

Light reminded me of *her* smile, of what I'd taken, of what I'd never deserve again. It reminded me of loss, and I hated being reminded of loss. At least in my darkness I was comfortable. I didn't have to think about the light because it was such a rarity I sometimes forgot what it even felt like.

"Stop smiling," I blurted.

All heads turned in my direction.

"What? Me?" Saylor, still smiling, pointed at herself.

"Yeah, you got a chip stuck in your teeth or something," I grumbled. "Didn't want you to be embarrassed in front of strangers." Holy Hell.

Her eyes narrowed.

"Chip free," Kiersten announced after a two second stare down at Saylor's mouth. "So what did you guys choose?"

Great, so everyone was back to ignoring me. I could handle that. I took a huge bite out of my taco and waited.

"One of the local group homes. The one down by the Sound."

I spit out my taco onto my plate and started choking.

Lisa's face went pale, and with shaking hands she reached for her water. "Oh, for some reason I thought you said retirement home this morning?"

"Oh, I did." Saylor grinned. "Only because I wasn't sure if they were going to let us into this other facility. For some reason the security is kind of crazy there. Anyways, my older brother did an internship there for a year before med school and said it was fantastic."

"Why the hell would you choose a group home?" I blurted, voice scratchy after nearly asphyxiating on a taco.

"Gabe!" Kiersten smacked me in the arm. "What's wrong with you tonight?"

I shrugged, not sure how long I could take the conversation.

"If you must know…" Saylor said in a tense voice. "My younger brother has Down syndrome. He had to go to a group home when he was really small because my parents had so much trouble with him. He wouldn't eat, would scream all the time… that is until we finally learned how to take care of him the way he needed. His ears were really sensitive…" Saylor's voice died off.

"And?" I prompted.

"And none of your business." There was that damn smile again.

"Great, so…" Lisa nodded awkwardly. "Guess we'll be going to the group home this weekend?"

"I'll have to call and—"

"—they have game night Friday nights. Better go Saturday afternoon." With that I pushed away from the table. My chair toppled to the ground as I made my way out of the dorm room and down the hall. I pressed the elevator button so hard I jammed my finger.

"You gonna tell her?" Wes's calm voice said from behind me.

"Shit!" I hit my hand against the elevator door, praying it would open soon so I could escape. "Tell her what?"

"About the fact that you basically visit that same group home at least four times a week?"

Leave it to Wes to stalk me.

"You have security detail on me or what, man?" I tried to laugh but the laugh got caught in my throat.

"Something like that," Wes's said softly. "You know you could have told me."

"Told you?" I croaked. "Just what do you know? I mean, what the hell Wes, what's left to tell? Seems like you know it all anyway."

The elevator dinged. I rushed in and pressed the lobby button.

"For what it's worth..." Wes swallowed and looked away. "I've known for months."

I swore and closed my eyes.

"Don't tell," I pleaded as the doors closed.

Chapter Twelve

Snap at my best friend? Lose my shit in front of everyone I love? Check and check. I was losing myself – again. And this time I wasn't sure I'd make it through. After all, being lost once is an accident... but if it happens twice, three times? A guy's gotta wonder if it's just in his destiny to never be found. —Gabe H.

Gabe

With a curse I kicked the door to the elevator, ready to break the damn thing in.

By the time I was in the lobby, I was ready to find an escape; anything would do at that point.

My phone rang. I reached into my pocket and cursed when I saw the number.

"Hello?"

"P—Gabe?"

"Yes?"

"She's having another one of those nights... we've tried calming her down, but she wants you to sing to her, think you could do that?"

"Sure." My throat constricted with tears. "Of course, just put me on speakerphone like usual."

The phone made a static noise and then I heard Princess cry, "Park, Parkerrr! Sing our song, sing it! They don't sing it right!"

"Aw, Princess that's because they aren't me."

I heard giggling on the other end. "Okay, Park, I'm in bed."

"Snug as a bug in a rug?"

"Snug!" she yelled in that high-pitched voice I'd grown used to. It had changed since the accident — it had become more childlike, more precious.

I looked around the lobby and went into one of the corners. Nobody was near me. so it's not like someone would record my little performance and put it on YouTube.

"I love my Princess, my favorite girl. Every time I hear her laugh, I want to save the world — cause she's my, my, my girl."

Princess started singing along with me.

"My girl, my girl, she'll always be my girl. And when the tears fall from her eyes, I'll swear to never let her cry… never alone, never without me, never without us together. My girl, her and I will rule forever. My girl. She'll forever be my girl."

"Thanks, Parker," she said in a happy voice.

Memories came flooding back.

"You're crazy!" Kimmy laughed as I twirled her around the small room. "Put me down!"

"Never!" I vowed and then kissed her hard on the mouth. "If I put you down, then I'll have to pick you up again, and that just seems silly since I want you in my arms forever."

"Laying it on thick, Parker." Her eyes twinkled.

"You love it."

She nodded and laughed again. "It's you. I love you."

"I love you too."

"Thanks for the song…" she said in a breathless voice. "I love

it."

"Every night." I vowed. "It should be your lullaby every night. So when you fall asleep, the last thing you think of is me, and when you wake up, I want you to think of us."

"I like that." She kissed my cheek.

I set her on her feet and cupped her face. "Kimmy, I'll always be there for you. You need to know that."

She nodded, her eyes welling with tears. "I'm afraid we don't have enough time — like something's going to happen."

"Stop…" I pulled her in for a kiss. "Regardless of what happens, it's you and me. Tell me you believe me. Abandoning you? It's never going to happen."

"Thanks, Park."

"Anything for you Princess, anything for you."

Rustling and static told me they were taking me off speaker phone. The airy echo sound was gone and the connection was solid again. "Thanks again, Gabe. You know how hard it is on her when she doesn't sleep."

"Anytime." My voice cracked. "After all, I made a promise." I'd vowed never to abandon her.

That was it.

I couldn't take it anymore.

There was a reason I lost myself in women — a reason I didn't do relationships, a reason I closed myself off from the world.

Because the minute you let someone in — they either die — or you kill them — literally. That was my truth. My life.

A girl stepped off the elevator dressed to kill. Her blonde hair was piled high on her head, her makeup so dark she looked like a prostitute.

"Hey…" I licked my lips as the girls head snapped up. "Where you off to?"

"Out."

I nodded and took a step toward her as the elevator doors opened into the lobby. "Out sounds good."

"'Kay." Her eyelashes lowered. "Gabe, right?"

"Right." I wasn't surprised. I had a certain reputation.

"So," she said, as a blush spread across her cheeks, "you can ride with me if you want."

My body trembled, I was ready to puke all over again. I wanted to run, I didn't even know where I wanted to run, but running never got me anywhere. Running still made it hurt.

I wanted to lose myself.

"How about…" I gripped her hand. "…we hang out for a bit and then we'll decide when the riding takes place?"

Her eyes briefly widened and then her mouth dropped open as a hiss of air escaped. "Sounds… good. Real good."

****

The club was filled with sweaty bodies grinding all up in each other's business. It may have appeared to be my scene, but I was more of a classic rock type of guy, so hearing TI play over the loud speaker made me wince, but I tried to appear into it.

A techno track came on, the green lights started to flash with the pounding music.

"Wanna drink?" Cee-Cee asked.

Hey, at least I'd learned her name.

Even if I did kiss her first and then ask.

Not that she'd minded. She already had her legs spread when I got into the car with her — I didn't take her up on that particular offer — at least not yet. I wasn't drunk enough yet, not high enough, not pissed enough.

"Shots." I licked my lips. "Let's order shots."

She shrugged and went over to the bartender while I just stood there and watched as people laughed and partied.

I used to party like that.

Hell, I used to laugh.

But after Wes's surgery — things had changed. I'd been

living a lie for half my life; how the hell did I somehow run out of strength to be the person I wanted people to see? It was like I was a burnt out actor, only it wasn't a movie. It was my reality.

"Cheers." Cee-Cee winked, her dark eyelashes fanning against her cheeks as we each did three shots without choking. She must be a regular. Most girls would be downing vodka sodas and asking about calorie content.

"Wanna dance?" She leaned in so close I could smell the vanilla perfume she wore. I fought the urge to push her away.

"Not really in the mood for dancing." Instead of pushing her, I pulled her against me, ready to lose myself.

"What's your story?" she asked above the noisy music.

"I don't do the whole deep emotional talking and spilling my guts out onto the floor. so if you're into that, screw off," I snapped.

"Good." She nodded in approval as she shoved her hands down the front of my jeans in front of everyone. "I don't either."

My body flared to life and I hated myself for it.

Without saying a word, I dragged her toward the back of the club.

"Wait." She winked and then pulled a joint out of her slim black purse, "You want?"

"Aw, honey, you think I'm into that shit? I go big or go home."

"I can tell." She looked me up and down, her eyes settling on my arousal before she reached into her purse and pulled out a plastic bag full of white powder and a mirror. "You like?"

"Very much," I lied and looked away. I knew how this scene would play out. I knew it like I knew the back of my hand.

I'd sneak her into the bathroom, she'd line up the coke for me to snort, we'd get high, we'd drink, I'd take advantage of her, she'd smell like cheap perfume. Her sweat would be all over me and I'd be caught up in the same damn trap I'd been caught up in years ago.

The only difference now?

Now, I was too numb, too indifferent to care.

You know you're in some deep shit when doing drugs doesn't make you feel – I felt nothing. I was empty. I lacked the energy to pretend.

I'd lost myself.

My identity had been music, and then her, and then I'd been happy just being Gabe, the happy little player with a heart of gold.

I was so damn tired of it all.

Cee-Cee's eyebrows rose. "So?" She held up the bag and tilted her head.

"I'm gonna pass, but you have fun getting screwed by complete strangers. I'm out."

"I thought you wanted to party," she said in a condescending voice as I started walking away.

With a snort I turned back and glared. "Honey, one of my best friends died from a heroin overdose, a family friend bought me drugs when I was thirteen, I lost my virginity to an A list actress twice my age. Believe me when I say, there is absolutely nothing you could do that would shock me, or make me feel anything but dead inside."

Her mouth snapped closed as her teeth ground together. With a jerk she walked off, her hips swaying as she made her way through the crowds.

I wanted to wake up drunk.

No, scratch that. I wanted to wake up and feel something – anything but the way I felt then – going through the motions, smiling and joking around as if I actually had something to live for.

My phone buzzed in my pocket.

I looked down at the text.

***Mom:** If he calls don't answer. He wants money. Love you. Mom.*

"Hello, final straw," I muttered under my breath as I shoved my phone back in my pocket and walked over to the bar.

"What can I get for you?" the bartender asked as he mechanically shoved drinks in people's faces and put tips in the jar in front of him.

"Whiskey." I sat down and drummed my fingertips against the countertop. "And keep 'em coming."

Ten. The number of times I got hit on while getting drunk off my ass.

Three. The number of times a woman brushed up against me and tried to cop a feel.

Two. The number of hours I spent torturing myself with memories of her laugh, her scent, the way she'd always seemed to make me feel like I could do anything in the world.

One. The number of minutes it would have taken for me to run back into the cabin and grab her helmet.

Amazing. How one minute can define the rest of your life.

Yeah, clearly I still wasn't drunk enough.

I lifted my hand but the bartender shook his head. "You've almost downed an entire fifth. I'm cutting you off."

"Asshole," I muttered under my breath.

He didn't even respond.

I stumbled to my feet and made my way outside. The crisp spring air didn't sober me up. If anything it made me feel nauseated.

Shit. I'd ridden with Cee-Cee. Cursing, I pulled out my phone and called Lisa.

Her shame was mine.

Our shame was the same.

Our pasts aligned in a way that both disgusted me and endeared us to one another.

She didn't answer.

I tried Lisa again.

And then desperation set in. I was cold, my buzz was starting to make me sway more on my feet, and a little voice inside me said that if I tried to walk back to campus I'd probably end up in the Sound face down with a belly full of water.

Shit, I was in a dark place.

I dialed Wes's number.

He answered on the first ring.

"Gabe?"

"I need a ride." I fought to keep the slur from my voice.

With a heavy sigh he answered, "Where you at?"

"Club by the school, uhh…" I started laughing hysterically. "Shit, I don't know, why don't you just ask NASA? You're the great Wes Michels right? Screw it, I don't need you."

I pressed end and stumbled toward the sidewalk and fell on my ass, leaning my head on my knees.

The images kept flashing. First the blood, next the cameras going off and the reporters. God, the reporters. I'd freaked. I'd lost it in front of them.

Minutes went by, maybe an hour, who knew… and then I heard a horn honking and headlights in my face.

I put my hand up to block the light but it didn't help.

Footsteps neared. I still couldn't see.

And then a fist came flying for my jaw. I hit the pavement so hard I could have sworn one of my teeth fell out of my mouth.

"Get up, asshole."

Wes? Did he just punch me in the face? And call me an asshole? I tried to laugh but my jaw hurt too damn bad.

"I said—" Wes grabbed me by my shirt and lifted my limp body off the ground. "Get. The. Hell. Up." Another punch came, and then thankfully I blacked out.

Maybe if I prayed hard enough – I'd stay there, in the darkness. Maybe then my sins would be atoned for.

Chapter Thirteen

The dude was hostile, as if he was pissed that I was even sitting at his table let alone breathing on his plate. What was his problem? I could only imagine that all the piercings had damaged his brain cells — that is, if he was still in full possession of any. —Saylor

Saylor

"So, he's..." I nodded then briefly looked away so I didn't appear to interested, or curious, or creepy "Abrasive?" Lisa and I had gone into her bedroom and were sorting out what the schedule would look like for the remainder of the weeks we had to work at the place of our choice for at least sixty hours in order to earn a passing grade.

"That's Gabe." She laughed. "I promise he's harmless."

"Harmless?" I repeated in a mocking voice. Right, because all those tattoos and piercings matched with those killer eyes really screamed harmless.

Lisa closed her notebook and shrugged. "I swear he's not as bad as he looks. He's just... different, that's all. Kind of had a rough life and all."

"Please." I snorted, hoping I didn't sound like I was fishing for more information.

Lisa's face fell as if I'd just slapped her.

"I'm sorry," I said quickly. "I don't mean to be judgmental but, it's just… life's hard, you know? It's what you make it."

Lisa's expression turned to something I'd seen my whole life. Pity. She reached for my arm and laid her hand on it. "I get what you're saying, but, promise me not to make such snap judgments when you don't even know what he's going through. He's protected me my whole life. I'd do anything for him and he'd do anything for me."

"It's fine." I pulled away from her touch. "It's not like you have to convince me to like him. I mean, for the most part we'll be doing our work at the Home." I licked my lips and started collecting my stuff and putting it in my shoulder bag. "And I'm sure you're right. I'm sorry I said that about him."

"It's fine," Lisa said with a much-too-quick smile and wave of her hand. "So, you'll take Fridays and I'll start this Saturday?"

"Sure." I walked into the living room and looked around for Wes and Kiersten. They'd been watching a movie but must have gone to bed or something.

"Bye, Saylor." Lisa called.

"Bye," I said without looking back and opened the door walking out into the hall. I probably shouldn't have opened my big fat mouth — another one of my bad habits. But where did she get off defending a guy like that? A guy who justified his actions by saying he'd had a rough life?

It pissed me off.

I hated it when people used excuses for their actions as if it was justification for being a complete and total loser.

It was the easy way out. The stupid way out. Which meant only one thing, I needed to stay the heck away from Gabe — he'd be toxic.

The elevator door opened and a guy stepped out. But it was what I saw behind him that made me choke on my breath.

Wes was holding up Gabe.

And Gabe was bleeding all over his shirt. His jaw was turning blue and the smell of whiskey filled the air.

How was it possible that over the last week I'd seen Gabe that much? Swear, he was haunting me, though right now everything about him made me recoil in disgust. He stumbled against Wes again, his words slurring all over the place.

Yeah, real winner there.

Poor me, my life's so sad and messed up I have to do drugs.

People like him disgusted me. They made me want to yell, scream, kick something.

What right did he have to mess up his life when most of us didn't even get a shot at a normal life? My throat started closing up as my thoughts went immediately to Eric. Normal was never going to be his reality. I'd kill for him to be able to do things that normal kids his age do, even though in his mind he had absolutely no limitations.

People like Gabe? Spat in the face of opportunity.

With a giant sigh, I got into the elevator and rode it up to the next floor. It was better to get on than have to wait for it to come back down.

"You have a good night?" Wes asked, breaking the silence as if his best friend wasn't bleeding all over him.

"Yeah, got in a few rumbles, did some drugs, lost my virginity." I nodded, "Top night. Total blast. I can't wait to ruin my life again tomorrow."

Wes grimaced. "It's not his fault it's—"

"You know what?" I interrupted. "I don't care. It's fine. I don't even know him. I don't know you. You guys are strangers to me, okay? Defend him all you want, it's none of my business anyways. I'm not even a friend. I'm just a person trying to graduate without losing my mind."

Wes looked like he wanted to say something. Instead, he

cursed and dragged Gabe out of the elevator. Just as the doors were closing, he whispered, "Just because his way of trying is different – doesn't make you any better than him."

Chapter Fourteen

I was dead. No. Seriously. I'd puked so much that my body was starting to shut down. I wanted the light damn it! Where the hell was the light in the tunnel? I could have sworn someone said death felt a hell of a lot better than this. —Gabe H.

Gabe

Moaning, I flipped over onto my stomach and reached around for my cell phone. My hand hit a lamp instead.

I tried opening my eyes, my cell fell to the floor, making a soft clunk against a red area rug I knew didn't belong to my room.

I rubbed my eyes. Colors blurred and ran together. Nothing floated into focus. I shut my eyes again and rubbed them for a few seconds. When I opened them a second time, I wished I had kept them closed.

Time machines. Someone really needed to get on top of that.

"How do you feel?" Wes asked, sounding calm as a cucumber. He was sitting directly in front of me. Arms crossed, and looking pissed as hell. How could he look both calm and pissed at the same time? Did he have some weird split personality that only manifested itself when someone pushed him over the edge? I'd never seen that look on his face. I hated it. I hated me.

"I really wish you would have just finished me off last night," I grumbled.

"Trust me." His jaw flexed. "I wanted to. Then I realized that's exactly what you wanted, so I chose not to beat your sorry ass and stayed up all night with you while you hallucinated about Bambi, told me stories about starting drugs at eight, and then finally — just when I thought you were going to pass out — you puked all over my bathroom — and me. Safe to say we no longer have any secrets after showering together, and if you ever, and I do mean *ever*, touch me there again I will end your life. Got it?"

I groaned and nodded, then winced because it hurt so much I thought I was going to puke again.

"Something you wanna tell me?"

"No offense, Wes, but I really don't want to talk right now."

"Funny, because I didn't really want to watch my best friend try to commit suicide last night, yet, here we are."

"You're pissed." I felt like crawling into a dark hole and staying there. Letting down Wes was like… true agony. He was the one person I admired. And I'd failed him.

"As hell," Wes said in a deadly voice. "How did we get here? A few months ago you wanted a new life — you weren't in a dark place anymore. What happened? I know the last thing you want to do is talk about your feelings — but, shit, man… you didn't just fall off the wagon. You made a purposeful jump and flipped off the world in the process."

I swallowed as tears threatened to pour down my face. The choking sensation returned, the same sensation I got when the guilt wrapped itself around me. It was like an old blanket, my comfort, every time I took it off, I was so freaked out it was going to come back that I just put it back on anyway.

"Nothing." I shrugged. "Old habits, I guess."

"You haven't done drugs in years."

"Things change." I didn't mention that I hadn't in fact done any drugs, though I had been tempted for a few brief seconds.

"You haven't drank in years. You've been sober."

"Right."

"Can I ask you something?"

"No. But you will anyways."

Wes sighed, his face turned a bit pale as he leaned forward on his knees and whispered, "Do you want to die?"

I couldn't answer. I could only nod.

"Why?"

"Because she didn't, and it's my fault. It's all my fault." I couldn't hold it in any longer. I burst into tears and then reached into my pocket and grabbed the locket, throwing it across the room, praying it would break.

Praying the hold she had on my heart would end.

It didn't.

I fell from the bed to my knees and rocked back and forth, the tears were dried up — they always were.

"Gabe…" Wes gripped my shoulders. "You need to talk to someone — you need help."

I shook my head. What I needed was music. What I needed was—

"Guitar," I said in a foreign voice. "Get my guitar."

Anyone else would have questioned me. Wes didn't.

Within minutes he was back in the room, guitar in hand.

I didn't say anything. I sat on the floor, put the guitar in my lap and started singing.

Seconds later I was focused — calm.

My therapy was music.

But I'd pushed music out of my life — because it was

another reminder of my sins, my regrets, so I felt guilty when I needed it, because what did she have? Nothing. Absolutely nothing. I didn't deserve comfort.

Two hours of playing music and my fingers hurt; they weren't as calloused as they used to be.

I set the guitar down and stared at the floor.

Wes sat down next to me. We both stared at the wall.

"Gabe."

"Yeah?"

"Tell me about Ashton Hyde."

I froze and then did something I never thought I'd ever do to my best friend. I lied and said, "I have no idea what you're talking about."

Chapter Fifteen

Watching my best friend wallow in the pit of hell? Not my favorite way to spend a Wednesday morning. The truth about hitting rock bottom? Sometimes you have to bang your head against the ground before you finally realize the way isn't down but up. —Wes M.

Saylor

"You'll have to sign in when you arrive and sign out when you leave." I glanced at her nametag — *Martha Hall.* I'd been told a Mrs. Hall would be the liaison between me and the school during my time served at the Pacific Northwest Group Home. She pointed to the two security guards at the door, "Every evening your bag will be checked for cameras, and you'll have to leave your phone at the front desk."

"My phone?" I asked. "Why?"

"Rules." Mrs. Hall's smile didn't quite reach her blue eyes. Her silver-streaked hair was pulled back so severely I wondered if she'd be more happy if she loosened it up a bit and let her face have a break. I shivered a bit, she reminded me of my first grade teacher – the one who wouldn't let me go out to recess. Great. "And our guests deserve their privacy, besides, you're here to work not text your boyfriend."

Uh. Okay. "Totally fine."

She sniffed. "Obviously this isn't a paid internship, so just do the best you can to make your hours each week. If you stay on track you'll be finished by the end of the semester." Mrs. Hall beamed. She had black owl-like glasses and a tight wide smile – though upon closer inspection a bit of lipstick had found its way onto her abnormally white teeth. So maybe she wouldn't be too bad if she just smiled more.

"Great." I swallowed and glanced around. The home reminded me a lot of the place where Eric had lived when he was small. It even smelled the same, like warm food, coffee, and people. At the time, I'd hated that Eric had to be there, but soon it had felt like our home too. People had been so friendly and he was happy. Maybe this place was the same.

"Now." Mrs. Hall cleared her throat and handed me a checklist. "If you'd just go through every name on the list here. These are the ones we signed up for your music class. Follow the hall all the way to the end, the two double doors will lead to the rec room where a piano is waiting. Enjoy yourself, honey."

With shaking hands I took the clipboard and quickly counted the names. Twenty people. Twenty had signed up for my class. It was supposed to be fun, you know, teach everyone a song, give them an instrument like a cow bell and then be on my way.

But twenty?

It was going to be a lot harder than I thought.

I followed the hall all the way to the end, opened the doors and took a soothing breath before walking into the room.

The smell of chocolate chip cookies filled the air, making me feel less afraid. Food always did that – there was a certain comfort that came along with it. Cookies made me think of home — homemade me think of my mom and Eric, and thinking of them made me feel safe, protected, and strong. I could be strong now, just like Mom had been strong for us.

Several of the patients were already sitting in chairs. A few were in wheelchairs. My heart broke.

"Um, hi," I said in a quiet voice. "I'm going to be your teacher for the music workshop."

"Speak up!" an elderly man called out. "Can't hear you back here!"

He was in the front row.

Clearing my throat, I spoke again. "My name's Saylor and — "

"Do you sail?" A girl in the front clapped her hands and then jumped to her feet and turned around to face the patients. "I love sailing! Who else loves sailing?"

Nobody said anything.

With a happy sigh, she sat back down and started talking to herself. "Sail, sail, sail. How I wish I could still sail. Nice to meet you, Saylor!"

She said my name so loudly that if the elderly man hadn't caught it that time, there really wasn't any hope for him — ever.

"As I said…" I offered a weak smile. "I'm Saylor and—"

I was losing them.

Already the eyes were glazing over. I knew some of the patients had memory issues, others struggled with mental handicaps, and I was boring them to tears.

Screw it. I raised my hand, "Who wants to make noise?"

"Me! Me! Me!" The girl from the front jumped into the air and started dancing while cheers erupted around her.

"Awesome." I smiled and started handing out the different instruments. I had recorders — you know, like the plastic looking flutes you get in fifth grade music class — a cow bell, a miniature piano, a harmonica, and three drums.

Yeah, we weren't going to be winning any Grammy's, but I had tried to pick out instruments I knew Eric would like, and although he hated loud noises, he was totally okay with being the one making them.

Last year Mom had bought him a drum set.

My ears had been recovering ever since.

"I want drums!" The old man got up from his seat, hobbled toward me, jerked the sticks right out of my hands, and brought the small drum back to his seat, smiling the whole time like I'd just given him a new hearing aid.

The girl who liked sailing picked out the recorder.

It took me fifteen minutes to get all the instruments out, mainly because every time I offered one, someone else piped up that they wanted it. I broke the groups up. The recorders sat in one section, the drums in another, and so forth.

"What about Princess?" a voice asked.

I turned around and scanned the room, squinting as I tried to identify the person who had spoken.

"Over here," she said smoothly, her voice was high-pitched but really pretty and clear, almost childlike.

I turned to my right and noticed a girl in a wheelchair sitting in the corner. She had really long blonde hair pulled back into a scrunchie and was wearing an Oregon Ducks sweatshirt.

Her smile reminded me of Eric, innocent and hopeful. Her hands were laid out in front of her, lifeless, and there was a bumper on either side of her head, keeping her facing forward.

"What would you like to play?" I took a few steps toward her. "I have drums left, but if you have any ideas I can get you something else."

"Guitar." Her mouth fell open a bit, as if she couldn't control it, and then her smile returned. "I want to play guitar like my Parker."

"Parker?" I repeated, my smile widening. "And who is

this Parker?"

"Oh." Her eyes were bright, but there were dark circles underneath them like she hadn't gotten much rest in the past decade. "He's my best friend."

"Best friends are nice," I said softly, the words clogging my throat as I watched her mouth fall open again and then close. Her eyes struggled to focus on me and then she blinked a few times, like she was clearing cobwebs.

"Guitar." She coughed softly. "I want to play Parker's guitar."

"Guitar it is." I looked down at her hands. They weren't moving; she had to be paralyzed. How the heck was I going to get her to play guitar if she couldn't move her hands?

"Ask Miss Janice, she'll bring it out."

"Miss Janice..." I stood to my full height, put my hands on my hips, and searched around the room, reading each nametag as I went.

"Red hat." The girl said. "It's a big red hat."

"Huh?"

My eyes fell on a red hat, then the nametag. Janice. "Be right back."

I jogged over. "Hey, I'm Saylor, a freshman at UW. I'm teaching the music workshop, and that girl over there said something about a guitar."

The woman's smile fell as her lips pressed into a thin line. "Yes, well, she can't play it. It's not hers."

"But she said something about a Parker. Would he mind, you think?"

Janice's eyes softened. "Honey, that girl is very special to Parker. It doesn't take much to set her off, and when she remembers she can't play guitar or even move her hands — she's going to lose it. It's near impossible to calm her down."

"But maybe if I just brought the guitar over—"

"I'm sorry. No." The woman offered a sad smile before walking away.

Well, crap.

Empty-handed I returned to the girl. "What's your name anyways?"

"Princess." She giggled and then coughed a bit, her face struggling to get the cough out. Like her body wasn't strong enough to actually use the muscles needed for such a strenuous action.

"Okay, Princess." I leaned down so we were face to face. "Martha's grouchy today."

She giggled more.

"So we have to do something illegal."

Her eyes grew wide as saucers. "What are we going to do?"

"We…" My voice fell to a whisper. "…Are going to steal a guitar."

"Oh yes!" Her neck strained as her head moved back and forth. "Yes! Can we, please? Parker would laugh so hard. He would laugh. I miss his laugh." Her smile fell, her face clouded.

"Hey." I touched her arm even though I knew she couldn't feel it. "Why don't I put you on look out? If anyone sees me steal the guitar, or if they're watching. I want you to yell, 'Ahoy Matey!'"

That did it.

Fits of laughter poured out of her. "You're really funny."

"Glad someone thinks so." I winked. Gosh, she reminded me so much of Eric it made my heart clench. I missed that kid.

"Okay," she whispered. "I yell *Ahoy Matey* if anyone looks, but you have to be fast."

"Deal." I tapped her arm again. "Now where do they keep the guitar?"

"Shh." Her lips squeezed together, her eyes darted back and forth and then with a small smile she said. "They keep it by the toys. It's in a box labeled *Parker*."

Yeah, I was so going to get into trouble. But the poor girl

deserved to be able to play something!

I gave her a salute and snuck over to the toy section. The guitar wasn't really hidden. It was in a really nice case labeled *Parker*. Easy.

I reached down and unlocked the case, letting out a gasp as my fingers fell on one of the most expensive guitars I'd ever seen in real life.

The Fender Stratt had beautiful carvings for an acoustic, almost like it had been made specifically for this Parker guy.

"Ahoy! Ahoy!" A loud voice jolted me out of my trance.

"Busted." Another voice followed. I knew that voice. With a muffled curse I turned around and slowly looked up.

Gabe.

Princess was right next to him in her chair giggling. "I did it! I warned you!"

"Forgot the *Matey* part." I winked, trying to lighten the mood.

"Oh, sorry." She cleared her throat. "Ahoy Matey!"

Gabe's eyes narrowed.

"It's uh…" I tucked my hair behind my ear. "Because I'm a Saylor."

"Caught that."

"So…" I stood, my knees cracking as I rose to my full height which still only met Gabe at his chest.

"Stealing?" He crossed his arms, muscles bulged beneath his long sleeve gray shirt.

"Sharing." I shrugged. "She wanted to play, and I didn't think it was fair that she'd be left out. Isn't that right, Princess?"

Princess ignored me completely. Instead, her eyes were for Gabe, and only Gabe.

"Besides," I said with fake confidence. "I don't see your name anywhere on that bad boy."

He smirked and pushed back his hair. It looked lighter than normal. Did he dye it? Why would he dye it darker? Was he into Goth or what?

"Princess," Gabe said, turning. "Did you want to play the guitar?"

"Oh yes, please. Just like you."

Crap. He played guitar, sang, and played piano. Great, so he was basically like sex on a platter for a girl like me. If he were ugly, I'd still be panting after him like a lost puppy.

Music people were weird.

Gabe's eyes didn't leave mine. "Not right now, Princess. I think your teacher's right, though I frown upon her methods." I rolled my eyes. "You should learn to play."

"Yay!" Her head moved back and forth a bit, and then some saliva fell from her lips.

Gabe gently leaned over and used part of her sweatshirt to wipe the wetness away. "Wearing my favorite sweatshirt, beautiful?"

"You noticed!" She beamed.

"I always notice what you wear," he whispered, then pressed a kiss to her forehead. She coughed, earning a concerned look from Gabe. "How about I grab the guitar and bring it over and you can join the rest of the group. You hum the song and I'll play it, sound good?"

"Like a team." Her mouth gaped as she stared at his eyes.

"We're always going to be a team, Princess." Gabe gently helped close her mouth and then wheeled her over to the rest of the group taking the guitar with him.

I was cemented to the ground. Was he stalking me now? Why was he here? And how did he know the girl?

"You coming, teach?" Gabe taunted, his eyes challenging. He turned around and said over his shoulder, a little quieter. "Or do we have to teach ourselves?"

"Right." I stumbled after them, losing a bit of confidence as I realized that if anyone should be teaching, it should be Gabe, not me.

Each group was already playing with their instruments.

Thumping mixed with a few people blowing into their recorders like they were going to war would give a normal person a headache. But it was music to my ears, even the misplaced cow bells. Because every single person was smiling.

Even Gabe.

Curse him for having such a captivating smile.

I hated that I was jealous. Because I had absolutely no right to be! I didn't even like him, but still… I wondered what it would be like to be that girl. The one who had held his smiles. Who deserved them.

Because he wasn't smiling at me — he was smiling at her. As if she was the only girl in the world.

Chapter Sixteen

I didn't know how much more my heart could take…each time she smiled, I lost a bit of myself because her smile wasn't the same, her eyes were lost to me, but I'd made a promise. I was stuck in purgatory…and anything looked good from where I was standing. Even Hell. —Gabe H.

Gabe

Saylor looked nervous as hell. She clapped her hands twice. Those who could do so followed her rhythm. Others, those who were paralyzed like Princess, were told to shout with the claps.

Pretty brilliant, because that way they didn't feel left out. And Princess had some pipes on her. I was probably going to be deaf by the time class ended.

Ten minutes.

Ten more minutes, then I'd take Princess on our Friday afternoon walk, read her a story, and kiss her forehead.

I'd say goodbye like I always did.

She'd make me promise to come back like she always

did.

And I'd puke in the bathroom before I left… like I always did.

"So that's it for today! Good job everyone!" Saylor clapped as everyone cheered and started handing their instruments in.

"Gabe." Martha tapped him on the shoulder. "Do you have a minute?"

"Sure." I looked at Princess. "Be right back. Be good, okay? No more stealing or talking to pirates." I sent a smirk in Saylor's direction. "Or sailors."

"Ahoy Matey."

Yeah, that was probably going to be her new favorite phrase for the next month. Thanks for that, Saylor.

I followed Martha to her office.

I knew the news was bad when she refused to make eye contact.

"What is it this time?"

Martha opened up her folder. "The good news is, we caught the lung infection in time, but she'll most likely need to go on oxygen."

"Shit." I hung my head in my hands. "She's too frail. Her body can't handle infection after infection." Pneumonia meant that whatever was caught in her lungs wouldn't be able to get out. Normal people hacked until the crap left their bodies. Princess would just choke on it until it killed her. Paralysis made pneumonia even more deadly than it already was.

"Gabe…" Martha licked her lips and leaned forward. "You're the only family that cares, really the only family she has. Maybe if you talk to her, she'll take the oxygen without us having to sedate her."

"Sedating her could kill her."

"Not if she's on oxygen."

The only sound I could hear was the clock on the wall ticking. Seconds went by, minutes.

I hated time. I hated that I was responsible for her and that I never felt like I knew what I was doing.

"Pneumonia is treatable, Gabe. She'll be fine." Martha closed the folder.

"Can I have a minute?"

"Sure." She scooted her chair away from the desk and left the office, the door clicking closed behind her.

Just me and the clock.

And more decisions.

Decisions I wasn't in the right mind to make.

"Don't!" Mrs. Unifelt screamed. "Don't let her die!"

I grabbed her arms and tried to pull her away from the hospital bed as the doctor rushed to Kimmy's side.

"Get her out of here!" He pointed at me. Mrs. Unifelt was strong, and at eighteen I still hadn't packed on enough muscle to pry her body away from her daughter. She was fierce that way, like a mother cub protecting her young.

"You have to do what you can!" Mrs. Unifelt yelled again. "Please!" Tears streamed down her face and landed on my arms. Her tears were warm as they slid down my skin, but I was cold, shivering, dying right along with Kimmy.

I knew it was for the best. Kimmy wouldn't want to live that way, trapped inside her own body, a vegetable. We'd never talked about it, but I couldn't imagine her wanting to live, yet never actually being free. To never run again, never have kids, never be normal again.

"We'll try," the doctor finally said. "But you have to leave."

Hours later, they let us see her.

I wasn't prepared for her to look so normal.

She looked like my Kimmy, though her face was still bruised, her jaw locked shut.

"Talk to her," the nurse said. "She can hear your voice."

"Kimmy?" I whispered. "It's Parker… I love you, Kimmy."

Her eyelids moved and then flickered open. She looked horror-stricken, like she'd been to hell and back.

Her blood pressure skyrocketed as the heart monitor beeped.

"No." she mouthed. "No, no!" Her head moved back and forth.

And then the seizure hit.

The next time she opened her eyes, they were empty.

The girl I loved was gone.

I slowly made my way back into the rec room. Most of the patients were watching a movie.

Not Princess.

She was positioned right next to the window, and it was open.

"Shit!" I ran across the room and pulled the window closed. "What the hell were you thinking?"

Saylor blinked innocently. "She said she missed the outside."

"Are you stupid?" I roared. "She can't go outside! If she goes outside she could die!"

"But—"

"Just go away. You've done enough."

"Gabe, I—"

"Go!" I yelled so loud my throat hurt.

Saylor took a step back, then two, then turned for the door and ran.

"You shouldn't yell, Parker," Princess said in a quiet voice.

"Yeah, well… she shouldn't make me yell."

Princess's face lit up. "The air feels nice."

"About that…" Here went nothing. "They're going to have to put some air inside you. You'd like that, right? Since you miss outside so much?"

Her face pinched. "Will it hurt?"

"Nah, it will feel like a kiss."

"I miss your kiss." Her voice sounded almost normal, like if I closed my eyes it would all be some crazy nightmare and she'd be whole again. In my arms, I'd kiss her lips, I'd tell her I loved her, we'd laugh, make love, and everything would be fine.

"Parker." The high pitched voice was back. "Open your eyes, silly. No sleeping."

"Right." My voice wavered. "No sleeping."

Truth? It had been four years since I'd slept peacefully. Four years since I could look at myself in the mirror and not feel hate.

Now? I didn't even bother looking. Not unless I had to. I knew what my reflection looked like. Pain. Sorrow. Guilt. But worst of all? Fake. My reflection was fake.

I wheeled Princess back to her room and dialed Wes's number.

"Yeah?"

"I'm ready."

"For?"

"The talk."

"Ah, man, can't someone else explain how babies are made?"

"Cute."

"You're smiling."

"Shut up."

He sighed. "So talk."

"Meet me at the campus Starbucks."

"Alone or with Kiersten?"

"Better bring her. I'm going to need both of you if I have any hope of staying alive... Kiersten would kill me, we both know this."

"See you in ten."

Chapter Seventeen

Everyone wears masks. They come in all different shapes and sizes. The only problem with trying one on — is that it fits. How easily we fall into the trap that we don't have to be who we really are. How easily we convince ourselves that we need to cover up what we were born to be. It's a tragedy — that fear keeps us from our destiny. It's hell — when the person you were created to be — is covered up by some cheap imposter —Wes M.

Gabe

I walked into the coffee shop like I was marching to my death. I knew Wes knew. I wondered what was worse. Him knowing and me not telling? Or me actually telling him the entire truth and having him look at me with that look. Epic disappointment in my character.

I hated that damn look. It's the same look her mom gave me that day in the hospital. The same look my dad gave me when I gave up my shit career and moved to Seattle.

Pity? I hated it. But someone judging my character? Someone finally discovering I wasn't even close to who I said I was. Well, hell. I wasn't sure I was ready for that convo with Wes. He was the closest thing to family I had and now I was throwing a giant-assed wrench in our friendship.

The bell to the door gave a little jingle as I opened it and stepped in. Wes was in the corner. Kiersten was sitting right next to him, snuggled to his side. They didn't see me, and maybe it was better that way.

It would have been nice.

To have a girlfriend. A normal life. To go to a coffee shop and wrap my arm around her shoulders when she got cold, to pull that scarf snug around her neck and kiss her cheek.

Kimmy had loved Seattle — was obsessed with it actually. She'd always had this weird fascination with rain. Swear, I kissed her in the rain so many times, I even started to like it. That's what movies to do chicks. They make them bat shit crazy, but I didn't care, because it was her. And I would do anything — anything for her.

I clenched my fist at my side and took a few shaky steps toward the corner table. Shit, I was borderline hyperventilating by the time I made it to my chair.

Tired. I was so damn tired of it all.

"Hey." Wes's voice was gentle, caring, understanding. Holy shit, I wanted to punch his perfect face. "Um, Kiersten, why don't you grab Gabe some coffee. I think he needs it."

"Sure." She gave me a sympathetic look then left.

"Don't tell Kiersten," Wes blurted, surprising the hell out of, well, probably both of us if the look of shock on his face was any indication.

"What?"

"Don't tell her." Wes leaned forward. "She was with me, otherwise, I wouldn't have had her come."

"But—" My mind was reeling. "She's your *fiancée*. You guys tell each other everything. It's fine, I need to get this out, it's—"

"—it's not about her knowing," Wes interrupted and

pulled his phone out. "It's about it affecting her safety. She's already bombarded with reporters and fans thirty times a day because of me. What do you think's going to happen when she knows about this? She's going to want to be there for you, by your side, I'll have to freaking pry her from your clutches — and your father..." Wes sighed, "Man, there are things you should know."

"Wait." I snorted without humor, hating that he knew more than I thought he did "Wasn't this my time to blurt my feelings and seek your wisdom?"

"Too late." His eyes darted away from the table then closed. "Look, I know you're pissed..."

"Pissed?" I laughed. "Try betrayed, but hey, it's cool as long as Kiersten's safe, right?"

"Gabe—"

"Don't call me that."

"Would you rather I call you Parker?" He glared. "Or how about Ashton? Is that what you want? Everyone to know? If Kimmy—"

"Don't you dare..." I lunged for his neck and grabbed his shirt, pulling him to his feet. "...utter her name!"

Wes's eyes narrowed. "Let me go."

"We're done."

"No," he said, too calm for my liking. "We're not. We're a team. I'm going to help you through this. We'll figure it out. All I'm asking is that you leave the girl we both love out of it."

Hands shaking, I released his shirt and plopped down into my seat, rubbing my face with my hands, my tattooed, poser hands.

"Whoa, you sure Gabe needs more coffee?" Kiersten joked setting a cup of black liquid in front of me. "Maybe you do need sex."

I groaned into my hands.

"Gabe." A warm hand touched mine. I peeked through my fingers to see Kiersten's warm smile. "Is everything okay?

You know you can talk to me, right? Is that why you wanted to meet?"

Damn it, Wes. Lies. More lies. How many more before my soul was black as hell? "Yeah," I croaked. "I um, wanted to talk to you guys about Lisa's birthday. It's coming up and I thought we could do something fun."

"Oh yay! I totally forgot!" Kiersten clapped her hands together and began talking wildly about surprise party ideas while Wes met my gaze next to her, and mouthed, *Thank you*.

I nodded.

An hour later, Kiersten finally left for class. I'd consumed at least three cups of coffee and was exhausted. On a good note, the Home hadn't called, so that meant Princess was alright — for now.

Wes leaned back in his chair and sighed. "Let's walk."

"I'd rather punch you in the face," I sang. "But sure, walking's a good alternative."

Wes smirked. "You're kind of an ass, you know that?"

"Part of my charm."

"Maybe that's it." He snorted. "Haven't been using much of that charm lately, hmm?"

"Shut it."

We walked out of the coffee shop and slowly made our way back toward the dorms.

"So, Saylor's cute."

If this was his idea of small talk he had another thing coming.

"So are cats. Doesn't mean I want to buy ten then die alone with my hand down my pants."

"Dude." Wes shook his head. "Worse visual ever."

"What?" I kicked a pinecone and shoved my hands in my pockets. "Besides, she's annoying as hell, and she's not even cute." Oh look, more lies. I should make a career out of it. Cool, so my future was that of a con artist, not a far mark from reality.

Wes dropped it, not saying anything while we made the trek all the way back to the girls' dorms. Then finally said, "Are you sure you don't think she's cute?"

Irritated, I raised my voice. "Wes, Saylor is the most annoying, irritating, undesirable girl I've come across in the past four years since being here at school — and that's saying a lot. Drop it, man. Besides, I thought we were going to talk."

Someone gasped next to me.

I turned and came face to face with Saylor. Her eyes blurred with a mixture of tears and hostility as she pushed between us toward the door to the lobby.

The door slammed behind her

Wes winced. "Think she heard?"

"What the hell is wrong with you?" I wanted to hit him, to hit something.

His eyes flashed. "Can I be honest?"

"I'd rather you just not talk for a while, but sure," I grumbled, fingers itching to rearrange his smug face.

He shrugged. "If you can't even be honest about who you're attracted to — with your best friend, then we have no business talking about your past. You're not ready. You want to tell me out of guilt. I want you to tell me because you want to. Because you want help — because you need it — not because it's time you told me. Hell, I know most of it anyway."

I scowled. "You're not making any sense."

"Tell me your story," Wes said smoothly. "Not when it's your last option — but when it's your first. Don't come to me when you've finally used up every ounce of strength you have to push me away and lie. Come to me when I'm your first choice. Because right now, you're not ready and I'm about five seconds away from knocking you on your sorry ass."

My breath came out in a gust as if he'd just punched me in the stomach. Where the hell did he come off saying those things to me? I wanted to yell, to scream, but when I opened my mouth only a croak escaped.

Wes slapped me on the shoulder and walked toward the door. With his hand hovering over the handle, he turned and said, "By the way, your dad's been looking for you."

"How—"

"I took care of it. I was at admin when he stopped by and made sure he was satisfied with the lie. But Gabe... your time's up. You need to start thinking about how you're going to handle this — if at all. Running isn't the answer, but neither is exposing that poor girl to that life again. Just... make a decision and know that when you do. I'll be ready to listen." With that, he walked off, making me feel like even more of an ass than when we started.

Shit.

I hated that he was right almost as much as I hated that I was wrong. Damn it! I kicked the brick wall with the toe of my boot over and over again until I thought my toe might have broken.

"Easy, killer," Lisa said, coming up behind me. "Walls don't fight back."

"Go away." My voice shook.

"Wes texted."

I groaned, what? It took him two seconds to text Lisa and tattle? Awesome.

"Wes needs to stay the hell out of my life."

"Ash—"

"Don't." I shook my head. "Just don't, Lisa. I can't. Not right now."

"We're family."

I laughed out loud at that and looked at her straight in the eyes when I said, "Funny... the first lie we told."

Chapter Eighteen

What had I ever done to him? Besides listened to him beat the crap out of a piano and open a stupid window? Nothing. Gabe was bad news — bad, bad, news. He was a thunderstorm and he'd caught me without an umbrella. —Saylor

Saylor

I took the stairs two at a time, fighting tears the entire way. I didn't want Lisa to see me this way. And I sure as heck didn't want to cry actual tears over an asshole like Gabe.

Sure. I knew I wasn't supermodel caliber, but did he have to say it that way? Did he have to be so harsh? Hot embarrassment washed over me all over again. His face — it was complete and utter revulsion. Like I smelled and carried some sort of incurable disease.

My chest hurt.

I hated that feeling. I'd spent way too long with that feeling when I was young. When Eric cried all the time, it made me cry because I was helpless. I couldn't help him. He was lost in his own mind, unable to differentiate between someone wanting to help and someone hurting him. At the time, we hadn't known it, but he'd been suffering with a sensory processing disorder on top of everything else.

It had been a while since I'd cried.

My tears even tasted bitter. Did it matter what Gabe thought of me? So he thought I was ugly. So he hated me. It meant nothing, right?

Except for some reason he was stalking me.

Well, not really stalking, but when I'd left the Home earlier that day I was told that Gabe had free reign over the entire property, and that if I had a problem I should just ask Gabe.

As if it was the easiest dang thing in the universe.

Just asking Gabe was akin to walking into the *It's A Small World* ride, and then not having the song stuck in your head for the next twelve hours.

Freaking impossible.

By the time I reached Lisa's floor, my tears had dried up. I could do this. I had a few weeks until school was over. All I had to do was pass this one class. What was the worst that could happen? So Gabe hated me. So he was a volunteer at the same place I depended on for that passing grade and my scholarships.

It was fine.

It would be totally, absolutely fine.

Chapter Nineteen

There was a sickness in my soul — it was starting to take hold. It seeped into every part of my existence. The name of my sickness? Well that's the fun part. I had three. Gabe, Ashton, and Parker. And they say people with multiple personalities have problems. I'd do anything to kill off all of mine — the only problem? That left me with nothing. And she wouldn't have wanted that. No, that desire was all mine. All. Mine. —Gabe H.

Gabe

A week had gone by without any contact with my father. I'd changed my phone number again just in case and called all my credit card companies to make sure he hadn't somehow used old power of attorney paperwork to get on anything that wasn't legally his.

I was safe.

Another fire was put out — for now. Hell, it was put out as long as he didn't find me — as long as he didn't connect the dots. Which he would. One day. One day the dots would maybe connect themselves. Shit, I was losing it.

Now all I had to deal with was Saylor working at the group home.

I'd already decided it would be pointless for me to stay behind on the days she worked at the home. If anything, it stressed me out more because she was that close to exposing everything about me. One slip and a quick search on the Internet and I was done.

Four years of hiding. Gone.

With a sigh of resignation, I walked up to the building and found Martha. "Hey, thanks for meeting with me."

"Sure." She smiled warmly. "You want some coffee, kid? You're not looking so good."

"Aw…" I pressed my hand to my heart and smiled. "You wound me. How do you think that makes me feel?"

"You'll survive," she said dryly, eyebrows arching as she set her own white foam cup down on the table and leaned forward. "So, what's going on, boss?"

"Ha!" I rolled my eyes. "Good one."

"If the shoe fits."

I cleared my throat and changed the subject. "I want to up the security on the place."

"I see." She tapped her nails against the counter. "Is there a reason?"

"Do you need one?" I snapped.

Her face fell. "Gabe, what's going on, honey?"

I stood abruptly. "Nothing to worry about."

"If you're sure…"

"I am," I said smoothly. "Just call the security company. I'm sure they can add two men to the front entrance. Make sure everything goes on lockdown during all hours, so we don't have anyone coming on or out who isn't approved. Oh, and I'm going to start helping with the volunteer program."

Martha coughed. "Are you firing me?"

"Not at all." I sighed in relief. "I need you, Martha, you know that. I just, I don't trust that Saylor girl. I mean, we don't really know much about her and she's too close to—"

"—Princess."

"Yeah," I croaked.

"Well..." Martha stood. "As I said, you're the boss so what you say goes. But Gabe...

I looked up into Martha's blue-grey eyes. I'd known her for a long time. She'd never asked anything of me, not when I made crazy changes or asked for things that sounded impossibly stupid. "Yeah?"

"You know I'm always here if you want to talk."

Ha, if only she knew how many offers I had on that front. Talking was not what I needed.

"Thanks." I licked my lips. "I'll remember."

With a sad nod, she walked out of the room.

Sighing, I ran my fingers through my hair and looked at the clock on the wall. It was ten till. Saylor would be arriving any minute.

I could do this. I had to.

Closing my eyes, I reminded myself why I was choosing to put myself in her life — when really I wanted to run in the other direction, because Wes had been totally right.

I was attracted to her... and that was a feeling I hadn't had in a really long time. The last time I'd acted on my feelings, things had gone horribly wrong.

Besides. It would never happen.

Because I still had Princess.

And that was the problem. I hated that I wanted something I couldn't have, and Saylor? I wanted her, very, very much.

Chapter Twenty

Watching someone you love go through difficult times is like being trapped in your own body but paralyzed. You want to yell at them, scream, help them, but your body won't move, and you know that no matter how hard you try, in the end, the path is theirs to choose. You can't choose for them. What a terrifying concept, especially considering we hardly see every option when we're stuck in our own self-defeat. Sometimes, I just want to yell, "Look up!" But it always seems the time I say that, is the time Gabe closes his eyes. —Wes M.

Saylor

I forced a smile as I greeted the security guards at the door and made my way to the sign-in desk.

Martha eyed me briefly before asking for my cell phone and sending me on my way.

I was planning on showing everyone a musical for my instruction today to get them excited about learning a few new songs, so at least I wouldn't have to stand in front of everyone and talk, not that I minded it. It was just kind of stressful, and ever since Gabe's outburst about me being ugly — well, let's just say I was feeling a bit self conscious.

I'd even thrown away that stupid sweatshirt.

At least I didn't look homeless anymore.

I pulled open the metal doors to the game room.

And almost turned and ran.

Gabe was fidgeting with the TV/DVD player, while a few of the residents sat around and waited.

My palms started sweating as I took a few cautious steps toward them. Okay, don't freak out, he's probably just helping set up the movie for me.

When I reached the front of the room, I forced myself to give him a friendly smile as I tapped on his shoulder.

"What?" He didn't turn around.

And politeness just ran out the window.

"What are you doing?" I snapped.

"Oh!" Gabe jerked his hands away from the DVD player and stood to his full height making me feel the need to back away. "Just setting up the movie for you."

My shoulders slumped in relief.

"Oh and also, I'm in charge of the program now, so we're going to partner up on the days you're here."

I swayed on my feet a bit. "You're kidding right?"

"Afraid not." His eyes narrowed. "You have a problem with that?"

"Am I doing a bad job?" My chest heaved. "Is that what this is about? Or do you just hate me that much?"

Gabe tilted his head to the side and crossed his arms. "If I hated you, I'd just fire you."

I sucked in a breath full of air in order to keep myself from yelling. I knew he couldn't technically fire me, but he could make my life hell and also tell my professor I was doing a crappy job, dropping my grade.

"We done?"

Words still wouldn't come.

"Good." He turned back around and flipped on the TV. I was still standing there in shock when the main menu for the DVD popped up onto the screen.

Gabe clapped his hands four times.

Those who could clap followed loudly after him.

"Listen up." His smile returned. "Saylor's going to show us a movie today so we can learn all about musicals."

A chorus of cheers went around the room at his announcement.

"Saylor?" His smile faded a bit when his eyes met mine. "Do you want to explain what they'll be watching?"

"Sure." My voice was hoarse with emotion. Why was I letting him make me feel that bad about myself? I tugged at my plain white t-shirt and forced myself to keep the tears in.

I'd never had anyone hate me so much.

Or humiliate me so many times.

And then charm the pants off of every single breathing thing on the planet, including small animals and children, right in front of me as if to show me that I really was that much of an outcast to him. An undesirable.

"So, today, we're going to watch…" My voice wavered as my mind went completely blank. All of the residents' faces were eager as they looked up at me, but I couldn't find my words. My throat was so thick with tears it physically hurt. I placed my hand over my chest and told myself to breathe — to focus on inhaling and exhaling, I was just making myself anxious.

Instead, my lower lip started to tremble. Tears welled in my eyes as I looked around the room and said, "Excuse me, I'm sorry."

I ran out of there and into the closest bathroom and slammed the door behind me falling into a fit of sobs over the porcelain sink.

The door clicked open.

Crap. I'd forgotten to lock it. I whirled around and came

face to face with the cause of my breakdown.

Gabe.

Tears blurred my vision as I backed up against the counter. I could only discern the outline of his face, nothing more. I promised myself I'd never be one of those girls that let a guy have that type of power over me. He couldn't see my tears — *I* didn't even want to see my tears. I didn't want to feel them. I wanted them gone, and it was his fault that I was even feeling this way!

"Are you okay?" he asked in a gentle voice.

"Do I look okay?" I snapped, wiping my eyes. "Just leave me alone. Please. It's embarrassing enough."

"Embarrassing?" He sounded absolutely clueless.

"Yes! Embarrassing, okay! Just being next to you is embarrassing. I'm so damn worried about doing something wrong that I can't even breathe, let alone teach a class! Whatever I did, I'm sorry, okay? I'm sorry I was spying on you but the music was..." I choked. "Beautiful. It was beautiful, and I'm sorry for opening the window. I didn't know! I just wanted her to smile more and—"

With shaking hands I covered my face and tried to level my breathing.

"Freaking hell," he said under his breath. "Are those tears because of me?"

Was he that dense? Seriously?

I didn't have the strength to lie — but saying yes just deepened the embarrassment.

"Saylor, I—" He cursed.

And then Gabe did something incredible.

He pulled me into his arms and hugged me.

And I cried into his chest.

I cried in the arms of my tormentor.

I cried like he was my savior.

When he was the cause of it all.

After a few minutes, he released me, and used his thumbs

to wipe the tears from underneath my eyes. "Take your time, I started the movie."

No apology.

No words of encouragement.

He just… left.

Leaving me more confused than before – but less broken.

Chapter Twenty-One

Did I mention I hate tears? Hold heart, insert arrow… blood, blood, lots of freaking blood. —Gabe H.

Gabe

And the asshole of the year award goes to… ding ding ding! We have a winner.

I was caught between wanting to comfort her and wanting to tell her to suck in her damn tears. There were bigger things in the world going on than her own insecurities.

But a part of me — you know the human part of my heart that was still beating, though just barely — clenched at the thought that I'd made her cry over my rash actions and words.

It wasn't that I didn't feel bad or that I didn't want to apologize.

But I was so sick of lying that the only option would be to tell her the truth, and telling her the truth — although it would take a hell of a lot off my chest — would just make things worse.

So I hugged her.

Only that had been an even worse idea, because my entire body had jolted at our touch.

The girl was gorgeous. Her honey brown hair had actually smelled like honey, and her bright blue eyes were even prettier when she was crying.

Hell.

I groaned into my hands.

"Gabe?" Princess tried whispering, but her whisper was like a freaking yell. "What's wrong?" They'd started her breathing treatments, so she had one of those oxygen things in her nose, so she could still talk, or in her case, yell like a lunatic.

With a heavy sigh, I lowered my hands and met her gaze. "Nothing, just… tired."

"Me too." She sighed. "I'm always tired."

"Really?" I went on full alert, using my eyes to examine her face or body for any hint of that her condition had worsened. She was still pale, she was still coughing, but the oxygen seemed to be helping. "Are you feeling okay, Princess?"

"Look!" Her eyes rolled away from me to the screen. "They're singing again!"

"Yeah." I continued holding her hand.

The metal doors behind me clicked shut, and just like that I knew Saylor was back in the room. I could smell her now. Her scent was on me, I knew it like the back of my hand.

I was in so much trouble.

A whiff of honey-filled air hit me as she took a seat beside me and folded her arms across her chest.

We sat that way.

In complete silence, while the movie played.

When it ended, she stood, walked to the front of the room and started talking like she hadn't just had a emotional breakdown. The good news? None of the residents would care. Half wouldn't even remember — hell, half forgot their own names, so she was safe.

"The three songs we're going to be learning from The Music Man are, Shipoopi—"

Next to me, Princess fell into a fit of giggles. I smiled at her obvious interest in the name of the song, and looked back to the front of the room.

Saylor's eyes met mine.

But she didn't shy away.

She stared right freaking through me.

My heart started hammering against my chest. I refused to look away; instead, I kept my smile in place and directed it at her.

Because she deserved more.

She was here for the same reason I was... to make Princess laugh, to bring about joy in a world full of hate and darkness.

And for that reason — I owed her my respect, even if it meant I had to be careful as hell around her.

Saylor's gaze finally fell away from mine as she named the next two songs and then dismissed everyone.

"Parker!" Princess shouted. Funny because she hadn't full named me in a really long time. Usually it was just *Park* or *that funny guy with the guitar.*

"Hmm?" My knees cracked as I leaned down to eye level.

"Parker?" Saylor's voice said behind me. "But I thought your name was Gabe—"

"No!" Princess started thrashing. "I hate that name! That's a stranger's name. His name's Parker! P-parker!" Tears fell down her face as her mouth dropped open. A shriek fell between her lips as she continued thrashing.

Muttering a curse, I ran to grab the guitar and quickly sat down next to her and started playing.

Once I strummed the first few chords of our song, Princess stopped yelling and closed her eyes.

"Beautiful girl," I sang, "My girl, beautiful girl. Don't let me be lonely without you in my world."

I strummed the last few chords.

Complete silence greeted me.

The residents were used to her outbursts and had the songs memorized just as well as I did, but it was my voice that did it. We even tried a recording once — didn't work.

"That makes me happy." Princess giggled. "Park, remember when we danced?"

"Yeah." Visions of her dancing in front of me on two legs that worked flooded my mind until I wanted to bang my head against the wall. "You were always so much better than me."

"Hmm." She sighed.

The doors to the room opened and Martha strolled in.

"Hey, Princess, why don't you and Martha go grab a snack while I talk to Saylor for a bit."

"Okay!" Princess yelled. "And Saylor, his name's Parker, not Gabe."

"Got it," Saylor said quickly. "Thanks for your help, Princess."

"It's okay," she said, surprising me. "You didn't know. But now you know, so you'll call him Park."

I didn't want her calling me Park.

It was too much.

Too close.

"Yup!" Saylor's voice had a cheerful edge. "I'll call him Park, though it sounds like he's a car."

Princess laughed as Martha wheeled her off.

When Princess was out of earshot I grabbed Saylor's arm and took her out the doors on the opposite end of the room — the ones that lead outside to the water. "Let's take a walk."

Chapter Twenty-Two

And we're back to my original hypothesis – multiple personalities, well at least he named them. That had to be a good sign, right? – Saylor

Saylor

I followed Gabe silently out the doors into the crisp afternoon air. The home was nestled right up against Puget Sound. It had to have cost a fortune. It was prime real estate. Everywhere you looked you saw the tall buildings of downtown Seattle.

I'd grown up in the area – but the view never ceased to take my breath away, or calm me down. There was just something about the ocean that made you feel small.

It made you realize life was bigger than just you.

And I was beginning to think I needed that reminder on a daily basis.

"So..." Gabe thrust his hands into his pockets and fell into step along side me. "Wow, amazing. I can't even come up with a lie that makes sense."

I shrugged. "So try the truth."

"Haven't made a habit of that." He stopped walking, and lifted his head. "That's the truth."

"Maybe you should." I swallowed and gave a half shrug. "Make a habit of it, I mean."

"Hmm." He put his arm around my shoulders and in silence led me closer to the water.

When we reached the edge, he bent over, picked up a rock, and threw it.

He picked up another rock and examined it in his hand. "I used to be like this."

"A rock?" I lifted my eyebrows. "As in you used to be really buff and let yourself go recently or…?"

Gabe threw his head back and laughed.

Holy. Heaven on earth. I loved his laugh. I mean, at the moment I kind of hated him, but his laugh was… something else. It made me want to fall prey to his charms — but I knew better. He didn't do nice. He just… did girls, which apparently worked well for him.

"Cute." He licked his lips, smile still in place. "No, but good to know my body ceases to impress you."

Oh, it impressed me. I just didn't want to give him any ammo to embarrass me again.

"I mean…" He bounced the rock in the palm of his hand. "I used to be solid like this. I was strong, unwavering, knew exactly what I wanted in life. But the thing is, I had no idea that I was in a bubble. I was on the shore where it was safe."

I took a step toward him. "What happened?"

"Life." He bounced the rock again, once, twice, a third time. "Circumstances out of my control, ones I thought I could control." He shrugged and then sent the rock flying into the water, "Can you count the ripples?"

"Ten?" I guessed. "Maybe more?"

"More." He nodded. "Because even when you no longer see the ripples, there's still a vibration. I think so many of us go through life not realizing that when we get tossed like that, it's no longer about us, but about everyone around us. The human condition is a type of infection. Selfishly, we're under the impression that our bodies are our own, our thoughts, our actions — everything is all about our own choices, our own rights, to do whatever the hell we want and damn the consequences."

He shrugged. "Until."

With a curse, he looked down.

I wasn't sure what the heck I was doing, or why I was offering the olive branch when I'd rather hit him over the head with it. But I grabbed his free hand and pressed my palm against his.

"Until," he continued, seeming to draw strength from my touch, "something so horrific happens to you, or to someone you love, and suddenly you see the ripple effect of every single action and choice you've ever made. Sure my body's mine to do with what I want, but the choices I make with it, still affect others. How I spend my time is my right — but in the end, it still affects those I don't leave time for. There's a yin and yang in life. But people seriously don't ever realize it until it's too late."

"And it's too late? For you?"

"Yeah." He sighed. "It is."

We held hands in silence.

I took a deep breath and blurted, "I don't know what you're going through or what's in your past. Clearly I don't even know what your name is."

He laughed again.

"But, I do know what it's like to have your choices affect others. My brother… growing up, he was confused. He had no idea how much we were all hurting for him, and it was… awful. And now, having the pressure put all on me to get an education, to graduate, to be perfect in every single area. I get the choices thing… I get what you're saying, because my life hasn't been my own for a very long time."

"Hmm," Gabe whispered and looked down at our hands. "The perfect fit."

I smiled. "Yeah, it appears so."

"She calls me Parker…" He averted his gaze to the ground and squeezed my hand tighter. I held my breath, my heart pounding like crazy. "…because after her accident, that was the only part of my name she remembered. It's still part of my full name, but not my first name."

"Because your first name is Gabe," I said. "Right?"

"Do you like fish?"

"Huh?"

Gabe released my hand and laughed. "Come on, either you like fish or you don't." His eyes were teasing as he bit down on his lip and crossed his arms. "I'm going to take you for fish."

"Uh, as in we're going fishing, or we're buying a goldfish?"

Gabe shrugged and flashed me the same smile I'd been craving for two weeks. "Neither. Now, let's go."

Chapter Twenty-Three

I think...I was letting her in. Is what that felt like? To talk to someone and have them actually get it? I mean I was as honest as I could be and she didn't freak out, call me crazy, try to kiss me, shout my name, though I wouldn't be against the shouting, she just...listened. I liked it. —Gabe H.

Gabe

"Where are we?" Saylor asked, getting out of the car. It was one of the rare days that I'd actually driven my car.

A car that even Wes hadn't sat in before.

I usually let Lisa drive it around when she needed it, but for some reason, it was one of those days and I'd decided to use it instead of my bike.

Saylor hadn't said much when I told her to get in.

Though I had to admit a bit of pride when her innocent eyes took in my BMW coupe.

"Anthony's," I answered. "My favorite restaurant. I said fish, didn't I?"

Saylor froze. "But, Gabe, my clothes. I'm not exactly

dressed for—"

"You look perfect." I shrugged. "Besides, who cares?"

Her gaze narrowed. "Do we really need to rehash that conversation?"

"I was pissed." I looked away, shame washing over me. "Let's just leave it at that."

"How do you get so many girls?" Saylor asked.

I stumbled a bit. "Sorry, what?"

"No." She smiled. "I'm dead serious. You are seriously the worst smooth talker I've ever heard in my entire life."

"False." I snickered. "I could charm the dress off a nun — I just choose not to when I'm around you."

Her face fell.

"Shit." I wiped my face with my hands. "Let's try that again, shall we?"

Yeah, or she was going to impale me on the sharp side of the swordfish decorating the wall.

"With you…" I said, sighing. "I can just be me."

"A non-smooth talking jackass with shifty eyes?" she asked dryly.

I winced. "Ouch. You beat all your dates beyond recognition, or is it just me?"

"Just you." Her smile was wide. God, I'd forgotten about that mouth of hers. And officially looking at anything but her mouth.

My eyes lowered to her chin. Perfect. There was nothing attractive about chins. Except they were attached to mouths and, well, hell, right back where I started.

"Can I help you?" The hostess asked.

"Two for dinner." I didn't take my eyes off Saylor. I should have. But I didn't want to, and it was a day of not wanting to do the things I'd been doing for four freaking years.

So I continued staring.

I was probably going to get slapped soon but whatever.

The hostess handed us menus and filled our water glasses.

Saylor took one look at her menu, slammed it closed, and paled. "Gabe, we don't need to eat here. The fish... it's like, really expensive and you're a college student and—"

"It's fine." I fought the urge to laugh out loud. I couldn't spend all my money even if I wanted to. "Trust me."

Her eyes narrowed. She crooked her finger for me to lean in.

"Do you sell drugs?"

"Holy shit!" I burst out laughing. "No! What the hell? Why would you think I sold drugs?"

She winced. "Mood swings, nice car, money, er, yeah, I'm just going to disappear under the table now."

"I would *love*—" I accentuated the word love. "—to see what trouble you could get into under the table."

"Ah-ha!" She pointed her fork at me.

I shoved it to the side.

"There you go again!"

"Go? I'm right here."

"No." She set the fork down and picked up her knife. To be safe I leaned back. "You do this all the time."

"And by *all the time* you mean like in the last few times you've met me?"

"Don't be an ass," she muttered.

"You say *ass* funny, like you're embarrassed you're saying it."

"Ass." This time it was loud, unapologetic, hot as hell. "Better?"

"Yeah," I croaked, felt it too.

"And don't try to get me off topic. You do that too."

"No idea what you're talking about." I lifted my napkin to my forehead and patted. I was officially sweating. It was like we were on *Law and Order* and I was on the bad side of the metal desk. Sitting in a metal chair. Balls to the metal. Wincing.

"One minute you're charming anything with a pulse, the next minute you look so angry you want to set me on fire, and then all of a sudden it's like you snap out of it."

I shrugged. "Maybe I'm mentally unstable."

Saylor pointed the knife towards me, an unapologetic look on her face.

"Hell, put the knife down, I was kidding."

Our waiter arrived. "Would you two like to hear the specials?"

"Fish." I watched Saylor's expression with interest. She had a facial expression for everything. It was…distracting. "What's the fish of the day?"

"We have a lovely salmon that's—"

"Good." I handed over the menus. "Two of those, and can you bring some bread and sparkling water?"

"Sure. Salads?"

"Caesar," Saylor and I said in unison

The waiter gave me a firm smile then, thankfully, left us in peace.

"He's so going to spit in our food," Saylor groaned.

"I've come to this restaurant for four years straight."

"Er…" Saylor nodded slowly. "Awesome. Good for you. Are you saying this is your booth? Or that you're on a first name basis with the staff?"

"Nobody. Not even Wes, orders a Caesar salad."

"So that was a test?" She squinted her cute little eyebrows together. Why did everything about her tempt me?

I laughed. "Um no, but after the Caesar salad you're going to be breathing fire for days. It's basically the only way to make sure you don't get kissed. Wes calls the salad the kiss of death."

"That's not funny," she grumbled.

"Thank you!" I slammed the table with my hand. "I say no to death jokes. Bastard."

At that she grinned. "Well, all death jokes aside, I'm not

worried about the kiss-of-death salad."

"Oh yeah?"

"Sure." She took a long sip of water and paused to answer, "Because I'm in no danger of getting kissed tonight."

Waving a flag in front of a bull. That was what she as doing, and she had no freaking idea that she'd just opened the gate. "Oh yeah? Says who?"

"Me." Saylor laughed. "You got the salad too, buddy. No way am I getting near that mouth of yours."

Her laugh was infectious. I joined with her, then clinked my water glass against hers. "To the kiss of death and fish."

She grinned. "To fish."

Chapter Twenty-Four

Getting comfortable with someone like Gabe was risky — especially considering our shaky start. But he was impossible to resist — especially when he was himself — something I noticed he hadn't been a lot lately. —Saylor

Saylor

"Tell me one scary thing," Gabe asked once we were in the car driving back toward campus. He'd called Wes to tell him that we'd gone out to dinner, and Lisa and Kiersten were more than happy to go pick up my car for me so he could take me home. I wasn't sure if that was the girls playing matchmaker or just being nice.

"Oooh, only one?" I teased.

We'd spent three hours at the restaurant — and he'd actually behaved. Had it been Christmas, it would have been a Christmas miracle, like something you'd actually watch on TV. We didn't fight, the insulting turned to teasing, and honestly it felt good.

Everything except the fact that the more Gabe showed me

of himself—

The more I liked him.

I was more comfortable hating him.

"Only one." He turned briefly toward me and flashed a gorgeous grin. A totally, mind-numbing, rock star grin. He reminded me of someone, but I couldn't quite put my finger on it. Maybe he just had one of those faces, or maybe he was just that gorgeous that my mind was playing tricks on me.

"Performance anxiety," I answered honestly. "I always mess up when I have to perform my pieces. My hands freeze up and I don't know. It never fails. I'll practice for hours on end and still nothing. I always end up messing it up. So I kind of hate large crowds or auditoriums and baby grand pianos."

"That was like five things." Gabe pointed out.

"Hey!"

He patted my leg. "I'm kidding, Saylor."

That hand may as well have burned a hole through my jeans. I could feel him all the way down to my toes.

As if noticing the effect he'd suddenly had on me, he jerked back and cleared his throat. "So, performance anxiety. I think I can help with that."

"I've pictured them naked. Doesn't help," I muttered lamely.

"Clearly you're not picturing the right naked people."

"Gabe, I could picture you naked and I'd still freak."

The easy smile froze on his face. Wrong thing to say. Why did I have to be such an idiot?

And then the mask fell again and he shrugged. "Honey, if you saw me naked it wouldn't be fear causing you to mess up the notes, trust me."

"Cocky."

"Absolutely," he said quickly. "Although according to some, I've let myself go."

"Let it go. Will I ever live that down now?"

"Probably not." He chuckled as we pulled into the

freshman dorms parking lot. "But seriously." He turned off the car. "Let me help."

I sighed. "Gabe, look... tonight was fun, right?"

"Yeah." His brows knit together as if confused. "Of course it was."

"And I really had fun with you." I chewed my lower lip. "But last time we were in a practice room together, things got ugly. You were—"

"—not myself," he inserted smoothly. "And I was pissed — not at you, just life. Wrong place, wrong time..."

"Twice in a row?"

He winced. "Afraid so."

Logic told me to say no. Let it end here. Draw a line in the sand, so that we both knew where we stood. We were barely friends, and I would already be seeing him on a weekly basis because of the whole volunteer thing.

"Saylor..." His eyes pleaded with me. "Let me make it up to you."

"I don't know."

"At least let me make up for five of them."

"Five?" I shook my head. "Five what?"

"Tears." He swallowed. His Adam's apple bobbed up and down as he leaned in and brushed his thumb across my lips. "Let me make up for five of them. I know there were a hell of a lot more. All I'm asking for is five."

"And then..."

"Give me the five tears... the five chances..." He sighed. Warmth radiated from him. "And then I'll leave you alone."

I looked at his lips then back at his eyes. "Okay. Five." I reached for the handle to get out of the car, but he grabbed my other hand holding me in my spot.

"And just in case it wasn't clear..." he whispered, his eyes taking on that dark hue I craved. "You really are."

"Are what?"

"Downright. Beautiful. And I'm sorry." He released my

hand. Slowly, I inched out of the car and walked in a daze back to my dorm room.

I was half-tempted to bang my head against the brick wall too. Was tonight a dream? It sure felt like it, because the impossible had just happened.

Gabe had flown down to the pits of hell, bargained for his soul back, won, and returned to make amends.

Huh. Apparently miracles did happen.

Chapter Twenty-Five

I was whistling. Dear God save us all from such a fate. When grown men whistle you know something's up. Yet, I couldn't find it in me to stop… whistling or smiling. And for the first time in years when I looked in the mirror, I didn't wince. I… smiled. —Gabe H.

Gabe

"Either you fell off the wagon or you got some." Wes's voice said behind me. I jumped and nearly face planted against the mirror in the bathroom. It had been a week since my dinner with Saylor and things felt... *normal*. For once in a really long time, I looked in the mirror and I wasn't met with a scowl, but a freaking smile.

"Do you knock?"

"No." He made himself comfortable against the wall and smirked. "Not since my best friend started acting like a total lunatic… I feel like a damn babysitter. Don't make me get you a bodyguard."

I rolled my eyes.

"Then again you know all about that headache." He

whistled and examined his nails.

"Wes..." I groaned and stared at him through the reflection in the mirror. "I'm not high, I didn't have sex. I'm just... feeling better."

His chest puffed up as a cocky grin appeared across his face, "Would this have anything to do with a certain individual whose name starts with an *S*?"

"Oh, look at the time. You need to go. I have to get dressed, and for the last time, no, you may not see me naked."

"Hurts, dude." He thumped his own chest. "Right here."

"Play fair." I narrowed my eyes.

"Sharp pain." He winced.

"Son of a bitch. You're a pain in my ass."

"So?" He grinned.

"What? Your heart feel all better now?"

"Oohhh." He bent over a bit.

"Yes. Okay? Happy?"

"Healed." He jumped to his feet. "Oh, and thanks for being honest with me after I begged you for five minutes."

"Three minutes."

"I'll give you four."

"Wes?"

"Yeah?"

"I'm not ready. Not now. To tell you everything, but... my dad, did he — did he say anything?"

Wes sighed heavily, all traces of amusement gone. "No, he was looking for you under your real name. The one on your license."

I felt cold all over. With a shudder I exhaled.

"Should I be worried about our safety?"

"No." I ground my teeth together. "He's just... desperate, but it will blow over. This isn't the first time he's come up here looking for me, and every single time he goes back home with his tail between his legs. I'm careful. I won't let him find me. Plus, he would hardly recognize me now."

Wes stared at me for a few seconds before saying, "Do you even recognize you?"

"No." My laugh was hollow. "Not really."

"Thought so."

"I'm meeting her, you know. In a bit."

"The girl you said was ugly who you actually find really pretty and then treated like shit in front of everyone? That girl?"

"Yeahhhh."

"Good luck with that." Wes smirked and made his way toward the door. I was beginning to regret the fact that I said he could come into my dorm any time he wanted, especially now, considering he was all up in my business. Then again, he was worried and I'd made him that way.

"Hey, Wes?"

"Hmm?" He paused in the doorway.

"Thanks."

"For?" He actually looked confused.

"Making sure I was okay."

His face relaxed. "Sure, Gabe. Anytime."

****

"You ready for this?" I cracked my neck, then my knuckles.

Saylor yawned. "Yeah, and that's really bad for you by the way."

"Thanks, Mom."

She glared.

"I may have multiple personalities but you're freakishly bossy."

"I knew this wouldn't work." She slumped a bit.

"Sorry," I grumbled and placed my hands on the keys of the piano. "Swear, we can do this. Music just makes me edgy."

"Why?" It was an innocent question. "I mean, you're

incredible. You can play guitar, the piano, sing — you're a triple threat. I can barely hum."

"But—" I patted the piano seat next to me. "—you can play. You just don't know how to breathe."

"Huh?" She inhaled then exhaled as if to show me she knew exactly how to keep living.

Good, at least I'd changed the subject.

"Watch." I started playing, confident that nobody would barge in on us because, well, the *barger* was in the room already, and I'd pulled all blinds and locked the doors. Good thing she actually trusted me… a little. Thank God for fish.

I started slowly, my hands moving effortlessly across the piano. It was perfect, but I wasn't into it. I couldn't care less about the song. I tried to focus on something boring like dirt.

Which was really saying something, considering I was already starting to respond to the scent of honey and the way her warmth enveloped me.

"Now," I said, picking up speed. "Note the difference."

Same song. Different type of playing. I let every note flow from my fingers all the way through my body like my soul and the music were one.

When I was done, I opened my eyes.

To see Saylor crying.

"Shit." Yeah, because saying shit immediately made girls stop crying. Brilliant move. "Are you okay?"

"That was beautiful." She sniffled, her blue eyes glowing with excitement. "I've never heard anything like it. I'm sorry for crying. Ugh." She wiped her cheeks with the back of her hand. "You must think I'm such an idiot! I've cried twice now."

I shrugged. Actually, she'd cried once and even then it wasn't some crazy sob-inducing spectacle, she cried with… restraint. It was almost weird. "At least this time I earned the tears."

Saylor smiled. "Yeah, you really did."

"Alright." I stood and slid my hands around her waist gently pushing her toward the middle of the bench. "Now, play one of your songs, any one of them, and I'm going to help you feel."

"Feel what? It's just music."

"Just music?" I repeated. "That's like saying you're just breathing, or I'm just existing. Not true. Music is a story. And you're the author." I placed her hands on the piano and put mine over them. "Each stroke of your fingers is a different word that describes the story. By itself it's meaningless, but—" I pushed down on a few fingers helping her play a few notes. "String them together and you have a melody. You have a story. So, Saylor, what story do you want to tell?"

Her entire body froze in front of mine. Her warmth against mine drove me insane. Saylor began to tremble as if the closeness was too much for her to handle. If I were being honest, it was taking every ounce of restraint I had not to touch her more. Being near her was the closest to living I'd experienced in a very long time. And damn, damn, damn, I really did want to live, didn't I?

For some reason I felt like we had stepped over some invisible boundary, but I wanted to help her. It was almost as if helping her find that passion was redeeming my own damnation.

Music made me feel alive.

And those who made beautiful music? Were like an addiction all by themselves.

"Yours." She said it so quietly I almost didn't catch it. "You won't use words to explain – part of me thinks you never have and never will. So, show me through the music, show me your story, Gabe."

The room was suddenly too small.

"Please," she whispered.

"Saylor, my story… It isn't a happy one." I pressed down on her fingertips anyway as I helped her play a melody.

"I don't need a happy story."

"And the ending." I continued helping her with the melody, my abdomen pressed against her back as I hovered over her. "It's one of those endings…"

"What kind?" she breathed.

"A sad one." My voice quivered.

Her fingers became strong underneath mine, her body stopped shaking. In an instant, her hands slipped out from beneath mine and moved to press over the top. "So change it."

Chapter Twenty-Six

Life has two stages. Birth and death. That's it. What you do in between the two? Well, that's up to you, isn't it? —Wes M.

Saylor

Behind me, Gabe ceased all motion. The only way I knew he was still there was from the heat that seeped into my back from where his body touched me. More warmth rolled off his hands where they seemed fused to mine. Any minute now, I expected him to pull away, to slip into mask number one or mask number two. Instead, he flipped my hands over, gripping them with his fingers and exhaled, long and slow. Seconds went by, but they may as well have been years. Each time he let out a breath, my heart skipped a beat of longing, needing more of his touch — more of something. My back tingled as the hard planes of his stomach pressed against me. I was in a Gabe cocoon.

And I loved it.

Until the music started.

With slight pressure, Gabe moved my hands to the piano,

slowly, effortlessly placing them on each key.

He was playing *through* me, using my body as an instrument to convey the story of his life. Each time he pressed down on one of my fingertips or guided me to another area of the piano, I felt the sadness of the song clench deeper. The notes became floating tendrils of pain, each one of them slowly invading my body and taking hold until it hurt to breathe.

He moved faster and faster, my hands couldn't keep up. I pulled back as he continued the song, in such a rush it was like he was yelling but doing it with music. Unable to convey it in any other way.

With a final burst of movement, he lifted his hands off the piano and smashed them against the keys, causing a chaos of notes to burst forth.

Gabe's breathing was uneven, ragged as he leaned heavily against me, his chin resting on my head, and he whispered brokenly, "I can't."

"You were doing so good."

"It's like getting into a car with suicidal tendencies. You keep going faster and faster, needing the adrenaline to keep you alive until suddenly you turn the wheel and everything goes black. The notes, they go higher and higher, and right when I feel like I can change the outcome — I panic. Some things..." He sighed and pulled away. "Some things are better left in chaos."

"Are you sure about that? Are you sure about perfection?" I folded my hands in my lap, but didn't turn around.

"Sure." He moved from behind me and sat on the bench. "If life was perfect, how in the hell would we ever learn to depend on someone other than ourselves? If anything, that's what life's taught me. The need to be perfect is stemmed in the very belief that it's actually something we can achieve. Self-actualization — doesn't exist."

I licked my lips and looked down at the keys. "Does that

mean we don't try then?"

"No." Gabe tickled a few of the ivory keys in front of him, the music note tattoos on his fingertips looking darker against the white of the piano. "It just means when you reach the end of your rope, you shouldn't regret a damn thing, but applaud yourself for trying to do the impossible."

I felt like he was using double meanings. The philosophical Gabe was a bit terrifying because he made me feel more insecure than the jackass Gabe. But the guy sitting next to me right now? I was beginning to understand, he wasn't just one person. He was every person, everything, whatever he needed to be, he was.

Like a chameleon.

And suddenly the ending to the story made sense.

Ten different notes all clamoring at once.

Chaos.

Gabe was Chaos.

"So." He sniffed and cleared his throat. "Now that I've totally ruined the moment by talking in my serious voice and scaring the shit out of you — why don't we work on one of your performance pieces?"

"Okay." I placed my hands on the piano again, careful to angle my wrists at the perfect degree and keep my eyes on the music ahead. Sometimes I wondered if my posture was better than my playing.

"What the hell are you doing?" he asked in calm voice.

I turned and gave him a resolute nod. "I'm getting ready."

"To go to battle?"

"What?" I relaxed my hands a bit. "No." I straightened. "This is the right posture, it's—"

"If you say perfect, I'm going to kill myself."

"Someone should have majored in drama."

He burst out laughing. "Oh, honey, you have no idea."

"So?" I lifted my wrists again and looked ahead.

"Fine." He smirked. "Play just like that."

"Okay." I started one of my harder pieces, Piano Sonata 14. It felt exactly the same. The movement wasn't as fast as some of the others, but the timing for it had to be perfect.

"Close your eyes," Gabe instructed.

"But—"

He swatted my wrists. "No arguing with your piano master."

"Fine."

"Say 'yes, master'."

I smiled tightly, my eyes focusing on the music in front of me. I started slowly playing. "Not in this lifetime."

"Bet I could make you say it." His voice had an arrogant lift to it, which made me all the more irritated. Master? Um, no.

"Eyes." He growled again.

With a resigned sigh, I closed my eyes. "Better?"

"Immensely," he said smoothly.

Darkness enveloped my world. All I had were the notes at my fingertips. All I had was the music — that and Gabe.

He wasn't saying anything.

Which killed me.

It also made me want to open my eyes, but I knew he'd probably just tell me to close them again, so I kept playing.

And then, with a teasing touch, his fingers grazed my chin, slowly tilting it down toward the piano while his other hand went to my upper back then slowly moved down until it was in the middle, with a gentle push, he urged my body closer to the keys.

Eyes closed, posture completely off, I leaned over the piano. Everything felt wrong as I continued playing.

"Slower," he said softly.

With a sigh, I started playing slower. His hands moved to my hips. And stayed there. Other than jumping a foot, I was still able to concentrate.

"The music," he whispered, "It's not just your story – it's your lover."

"Okay," I squeaked. Heat washed over me as the word *lover* bounced around in my brain. I knew it, but I'd never experienced it. How was I supposed to use something I didn't know how to use? And how embarrassing was it that I was stuck in that tiny room having never been... stuck in a tiny room with any guy? Lover. I'd take him. If I got a choice. It would be him. But people like Gabe, beautiful people who had music in their soul, who knew how to speak without words... they weren't for girls like me.

"Each stroke..." His hands pressed against my hips making me gasp. "You need to feel it not just on your fingertips – but everywhere."

Holy. Crap.

"Feel it here," he squeezed and then ran his hands lightly up my sides, then resting right underneath my breasts, he pressed again. "And here."

My breathing picked up speed, as did my music.

"Slow down," he commanded in that same irritating patient tone. "Where is this story taking me? Where are you taking your lover?"

"Huh?" I breathed.

"Use your hands to tell me the story – use your body to propel the story forward, what happens next... Tell the story, Saylor. Make me feel it without even touching you."

"But – that's impossible."

"You can feel a kiss without touching someone's lips."

"I'm confused."

"Concentrate." Gabe's voice was firm. "I want to kiss you."

"What?" He was lucky I didn't actually collapse against the piano this time.

"In the story." He chuckled. "I want to kiss you in this story, so kiss me."

"You want me to get up and kiss you?" Mind you, I was still trying to play a difficult piece as he was asking me this, which basically meant I must have had talent, because my body was on fire.

"Without our mouths meeting."

"Through the music." I clarified in a doubtful voice.

I could hear the smile in his tone as he answered. "Yes, through the music, show me what the kiss would feel like. I want to taste it."

"But how?"

He laughed softly. "I'm touching them."

"What?"

"My lips," he countered. "They're soft, open, wet..."

I squirmed on the piano bench, squeezing my eyes shut. "What else?"

"As I part my lips... I wonder what your tongue tastes like, what type of pressure you'd use as you pressed your velvety smooth mouth against mine. I imagine exploring your mouth not just because I want to — but because I can't help it. I'm lost. And your kiss is my salvation... so, Saylor, will you save me?"

My fingers glided effortlessly over the piano as I imagined his mouth — the way he smiled, the way he took his lower lip hostage when he was deep in thought. The dark look he got in his eyes when there was something he wanted. Our kiss would be epic.

The music picked up speed as I leaned over the piano, pounding each note with the rhythm of my footsteps as I approached him.

His hands would reach for my hips as he pulled me closer. My hands hovered over the keys making my hesitation known.

And then I pressed softly against the ivory, leaning forward as if I was leaning into Gabe with my body pressed against his. My breasts brushed the keys. I moved closer to the piano and then slowed the music.

His eyes would close.

His lips would part.

And we'd meet in the middle — because both of us wanted the same thing. Both of us wanted to taste, to explore, to feel.

I slowed my left hand as my right hand moved quicker across the keys, to show the anticipation.

And then, our mouths would touch.

I pounded the keys with my left hand, making it the loudest part of the piece which wasn't normally how it was done.

Our tongues would tangle.

I pounded the piano harder.

His fingers would dig into my arms as he lifted me into the air.

I pulled back from the piano, stopping the music, and then gently started the rhythmic cadence again.

Our kiss was the perfect joining of music.

He was the left hand, I was the right.

Separate they sounded like silly scales.

Together — they were beautiful.

When I stopped the piece, I was sweating.

"Open your eyes," Gabe whispered.

He was breathing so heavily it looked like he'd just run a marathon. With a smile he tucked my fallen hair behind my ear and tilted my chin toward him.

"That…" He leaned in. "…is how you perform. Like every kiss is both your first and last — like you're saying both hello and goodbye — like you've just been born… like you've just died."

Chapter Twenty-Seven

In all my years living — I'd never experienced such a powerful kiss. The force in which our mouths met, our bodies fused, was electrifying — and we hadn't even touched. How's that for insanity?
—Gabe H.

Gabe

I was going to kiss her.

I don't know what the hell I'd been thinking to give advice like that, especially considering I knew I was already attracted to her and we were locked in a small confined space. Bad enough that the music was adding to her intoxicating scent. Worse — that in order to live I kind of had to breathe.

So I greedily sucked in every inch of air — praying that it would be permeated with her — I wanted to taste her that bad.

But each greedy inhale — left me parched.

My gaze lowered to her lips — and stayed there.

The bench made a cracking nose as she moved forward. An inch closer and our mouths would be touching.

I hadn't kissed a girl out of pure savage need.

In four years.

A small sigh escaped her mouth as I moved my hands to the side of her face and pressed a tender kiss right on the corner where her lips met.

Another sigh.

Another kiss on the opposite corner.

She clenched my wrists with her hands.

Next, our mouths collided.

Notes fused together.

I flattened my hands against hers then interlocked our fingers, slowly pulling her up from the piano bench and walking her backward toward the wall.

Her soft tongue pushed against my lips. When I opened my mouth, everything about Saylor became my identity as her scent and warmth swallowed me whole.

She moved her hands to my shoulders and then gave my long hair a little tug.

Of course she'd have no idea that hair pulling was my Achilles heel — but it was almost worse than that.

Because it turned off my need to be safe with her.

And made me want to give her everything.

My phone started buzzing in my pocket.

Not now. Anytime but now.

Her body was pressed too tight against me, the kiss more urgent then before. My phone kept buzzing as if reminding me that my time wasn't my own — not anymore.

I broke off the kiss. "I'm sorry." I fumbled with my phone and glanced at her swollen lips. "Damn sorry." I shook my head and cursed all phones to hell. "But I have to take this."

Without offering any other explanation, I answered.

"Oh Gabe, good." Martha let out a shaky breath, "I was hoping you'd answer. Listen. There's been a situation. A man came by—"

"What did he look like?" And just like that, reality hit me smack in the face. I still couldn't have a normal life. An innocent girl like Saylor? Not my reality. No matter how bad I wanted it.

"He had really light brown hair and blue eyes." Martha cleared her throat. "He asked for you by your real name."

"Parker?" I asked.

She was silent and then said quietly, "No, your other name."

"Shit."

I heard Martha fumble with the phone a bit. "Not to worry. I set him to rights, but he wasn't just looking for you. He asked for her."

"By name?" God, I hoped… I prayed.

"Her full legal name."

Guilt assaulted me. While I was here playing passionate music lover with Saylor, someone could have taken my world from me while simultaneously exposing every last private detail to the media.

"Do you need me to come?"

"No." Martha let out the mother of all heavy sighs. "Just come on your normal day, and I'll let you know if we see him again. He may still be hanging around, so just—be careful. And, Gabe?"

"Yeah?" My voice was hollow.

"Do you know who he is?"

"My dad." I licked my lips. "And he's finally figured it out."

I ended the call and made my way toward the door. She'd heard me say something about my dad, but I knew I'd been far enough away that she didn't hear anything that Martha had said. My secrets remained safe. For now.

"Is everything okay?" Saylor asked.

I couldn't even look at her — didn't want to see the disappointment in her face when I rejected her.

"Sure, um, look I have to go take care of something. Why don't you keep practicing a bit longer and I'll see you later, okay?"

"Gabe..."

"Yeah?" I had the door halfway open. So close.

"Why won't you look at me?"

Steeling my resolve, I forced a happy go lucky smile and turned, giving her a sly wink. "Sorry, just lost in thoughts, you should probably practice another hour or so. No worries, everything's fine."

Her eyes scanned my face. "Is telling the truth so hard, Gabe?"

My smile fell. "You have no idea."

I pulled the door shut behind me and made my way down the hall. It was time to ask for Wes's help — because someone in my family had finally told my dad about Princess.

Meaning. My time — really was up.

I took time to memorize the way the building smelled — I'd miss it. The way the architecture of UW was old yet managed to still feel new and exciting.

The salty smell of the ocean.

The mist hanging in the air.

My past had caught up to me — and I had to run.

For both our sakes.

Chapter Twenty-Eight

I wondered if there would ever come a day when Gabe would finally be free enough to be himself — the person he was born to be, not mask number one or smile number two. I wondered if he even knew how lost he really was — or if he was happy making the maze his home, the mask his identity, his life a lie. —Saylor

Saylor

"So, how are things going for you at the Home?" Lisa asked, taking a large bite out of her pizza and smacking her lips together. We'd been working at the Home for well over three weeks. "I've been doing some really cool art projects with everyone, but other than that it's been pretty uneventful." Lisa sighed heavily and took another large bite out of her pizza.

Just with her mention of the Home — my body went hot all over, because I associated the Home with Gabe, and when I thought of Gabe, I thought of kissing.

It had been two days since my kiss with Gabe.

And yes, I was counting. Because that was also two days

during which I hadn't heard one word from him. It wasn't like I could go to the Home and see if he was there; that's something called *stalking* and it's illegal. I even thought about lying and saying I left my cell phone, but with my luck he'd see right through it and know just how pathetic I really was.

And how much I wanted him to kiss me again.

I wasn't sure if that's how it would always be with Gabe. Either we were arguing or kissing. Regardless, I recognized something. Being with Gabe was like going to a zoo and watching the lions stalk in front of the windows of their cage. Give them their freedom and they'll devour you, but as long as they keep themselves contained — keep everything in check — they're safe.

Gabe was only as safe as he allowed himself to be.

And that was both alarming and enticing all at once.

Then again, scary things always were. Scary and beautiful were always interchangeable in my mind. Maybe it was because of the music.

"Whoa, lost ya there for a minute," Lisa joked. "So, things at the Home? That boring? Or is it just my charming personality?"

"Sorry." I felt my face heat, and I picked up a piece of pizza. It tasted like sand in my mouth, but whatever. "It's been great. I mean, at first it was kind of uncomfortable, but now I love it."

Lisa smiled happily. I'd always wondered why she didn't have a boyfriend. She was one of those girls that, if you didn't know them really well, you would assume was stuck up and rude. But she was the exact opposite.

"Good, I'm having fun too. Then again, I'm reading them stories, not teaching them how to play music, but we can't all be that talented."

I laughed and set my pizza down. "Well, we only have what? Six more weeks to go?"

She groaned. "Don't remind me. Mr. Miller keeps hitting

on me. I finally took away his walker and said I'd only kiss him if he could walk the two feet to meet me."

"Oh no!" I started laughing hysterically. "Did he even try?"

"Yes," she grumbled. "The dirty old bastard walked all the way up to me, then kissed me on the cheek and took his walker back."

I laughed harder.

She threw a piece of pepperoni at my face.

"Anyway, the residents are pretty cool." She shrugged.

This was my chance. To ask about Gabe or at least find out more details about Princess. I cleared my throat and began. "That girl, you know… the one in the wheelchair?"

"Which one?" She suddenly found great interest in picking the toppings off her piece.

"The one they call Princess."

Her hand hovered over the pizza. "Yeah."

"Her and Gabe… they seem really close."

She sighed and gave me a helpless shrug. "Gabe's like that with everyone."

I felt my face fall. Was that what he was doing with me? Was I just like Princess? Was he just helping me because he wanted me to feel good about myself? About my music? Maybe that's why he hadn't called. I was… just like Princess… a charity case?

"No!" Lisa put down her pizza and held out her hands. "Not like that, I mean… No, no, no, you're different."

Yeah, the last thing I needed was to look desperate enough to try to pry details out of his cousin. "It's fine. Let's not talk about him."

"Who?" The door opened and Wes's head poked around. "Who are we not talking about?"

"Gabe," Lisa answered honestly while I smacked her on the arm.

"He's a crap cook. Don't know what anyone would see in

him anyway." He winked at both of us and then stepped fully into the room. "Hey, Lisa, Kiersten needs help with... cooking."

Lisa's eyebrows knit together. "Cooking? What does she need help with?"

Wes looked between the two of us helplessly. "The pan?"

"Are you asking?"

"Can you just help?" He put his hands together in a begging motion. "Please?"

"Men." Lisa shot up off the floor and left the room.

Wes sat down in her spot and took a piece of pizza.

"Yeah, you're the worst liar I've ever seen."

"Tell me about it." He winked. "Anyway, we're having a surprise birthday party for Lisa tomorrow night. I want you to come." He held up his hand. "Correction. We want you to come. We all do."

"But—"

"Nope, the only way you're getting out of is if you have a high fever, get hit by a car, or you're puking into a toilet. And even then I'll need to see the thermometer, the doctor's bill, and-or the puke."

I hesitated a breath, taking in his piercing blue eyes and chiseled features. "You're weird."

He set the pizza down and leaned forward. Holy crap. How was Kiersten able to actually look at him in the face without falling over and swooning? It wasn't that I was attracted to him or anything, but man, he was pretty.

"Yeah, well..." He shrugged. "Let's just say I don't want you to miss it, okay?"

"What time?"

"Five."

"Do I need to dress up or anything? I'll be volunteering tomorrow at the Pacific Northwest Group Home again."

"Nah." He waved me off. "Just wear clothes."

"Good advice."

He laughed. "I'm the king of advice, what can I say?"

"Aw, you two kids bonding?" Lisa said entering the room again. "Oh and Wes, Kiersten needed help with finding the cooking spray for the pan."

He snapped his fingers. "That was it."

Lisa's eyes narrowed. "Sometimes I wonder about you."

I took a sip of soda.

"It's the drugs," he said in a serious voice, causing me to choke on the leftover Diet Pepsi in my mouth.

"He means the good ones," Lisa added.

I looked between them.

"Legal drugs," Wes explained. "To keep me healthy. Just in case cancer tries to come back and make me its bitch."

"R-right." My voice was hoarse from choking.

Wes smiled that same blinding smile that belonged on every freaking billboard in America and pushed to his feet. "Alright ,ladies, have fun with your pizza party. I'm going to go help my *fiancée* in the kitchen."

"Kissing her and trying to make her wear the sexy apron isn't helping!" Lisa shouted after him.

"A guy can try!" he yelled back.

The minute the door shut behind him Lisa's gaze narrowed in on me. "What did Wes want?"

"Uh, to give me advice."

"He should have majored in Psychology." She shook her head.

"Yeah, that or modeling."

Snorting, Lisa tossed a piece of sausage in her mouth, "Ain't that the truth. Alright, let's finish writing up our stupid reports from the past four weeks so we can watch crap reality TV."

"Deal." I pulled out my computer and started typing.

Three hours later and we were halfway through the first season of New Girl. Every time the door opened my heart sped up a bit – hoping to catch a glimpse of Gabe. Lisa said they hung out twenty-four seven.

Just as we were starting the second season, the door flew open and Gabe strolled in, his eyes focused on a box in his hands. "Lisa, it's time for you to dye my hair again. It's already lightning up and I'm getting strange looks from—"

Lisa cleared her throat.

Gabe looked up.

"Hi." I waved from the couch. Lame. I should have at least smiled brighter, but I was too busy being completely affected by his proximity and a bit confused as to why he needed to dye his hair — as if he was keeping it dark for a reason.

A muscle clenched in his jaw. "Hey."

"He gets gray hair," Lisa explained.

"What?" he roared.

"And old ladies hit on him." She examined her nails. "Pisses him off, so he makes me dye it. Isn't that right, Gabe?" She smiled brightly while he glowered at her like she'd just kicked him in the balls and said you're welcome.

"Right. I'm a cougar magnet."

"Cool." I fought a smile. "So why do you dye it darker? Why not go blond or something?"

The smile froze on Lisa's face.

Gabe smirked. "Black, just like my soul."

"Wow. Should have seen that one coming," I replied, falling into an easy laughter with both him and Lisa.

"Why don't you do it?" She pressed pause on the TV.

"Do what?" Both Gabe and I asked in unison.

Lisa huffed and got up from the couch. "Dye Gabe's hair. Besides, I just got my nails done." She snatched the box from his hands and threw it at me.

I caught it midair and watched as Gabe's eyes narrowed in on his cousin, that same jaw flexing even tighter this time like he'd just bit down on something hard. "But Lisa, you actually have experience dying hair."

"Hey!" I acted offended. I had no idea what I was doing.

Lisa smacked him. "She's a girl. Dying hair is as natural as breathing."

"Doubt that." They engaged in a silent stare down while I looked on.

Gabe tore his gaze away from her and swore. "Fine, but if I wake up with bald spots and earn the nickname patch for the rest of the semester I'm blaming you."

"As much as I'd enjoy that…" I got up from the couch and made my way toward the bathroom. "I'll do my best to make sure all hair stays on your head and not in my clutches. Deal?"

"On second thought…" Gabe came around the couch with a wolfish grin. "If you're pulling my hair — damn, I may like that."

"Dip your balls in some cold water before you go in that bathroom and shut the door, will ya?" Lisa asked. "I don't want my friend getting taken advantage of on school property."

"Chill." Gabe winked at Lisa and licked his lips. "If I wanted to take advantage of her I sure as hell wouldn't start on your bathroom floor."

"And the visual images just keep coming," Lisa sang. "Remember, Gabe. She walks in with her virtue. I expect her to leave with the same."

"Yes, ma'am." Gabe called, then followed me into the bathroom, slamming the door behind him. The bathroom suddenly felt fifty times too small as he maneuvered around me, put the toilet seat down, and sat.

Hands shaking, I pulled out the instructions and started reading.

All the while noticing that Gabe hadn't said a word once we were alone.

"Your hands are shaking." He finally pointed out.

"Well. you're making me nervous because you keep

tapping your foot." I snapped.

"Oh." He stopped tapping. "Sorry."

I blew out the breath I'd been holding in and concentrated harder on the instructions. "It's fine."

A few seconds went by.

"If you stare any harder at that paper you're going to burn holes through it."

"Do you mind?" I asked. "Or are you a fan of going bald at twenty-one?"

"Twenty-two," he corrected. "And sorry."

I read the last bit of instructions and went to work, all the while hoping that I really didn't end up burning all of his dark hair off. Though I had to admit, I wouldn't mind… because for some reason, dark hair really didn't suit him.

Chapter Twenty-Nine

The most erotic touch a man can experience is that of a woman digging her nails into his scalp and giving a little tug. —Gabe H., Wes M., and all men… everywhere.

Gabe

So the whole ignore Saylor for a few days and try to get her out of my head thing? Didn't go as planned.

I dreamt of her.

I dreamt of her music.

Her kiss.

Her stupid laugh.

It was aggravating to say the least — especially when I was supposed to be focused on making sure my dad didn't pop up at the Home again.

Things had been quiet. Too quiet. Even Wes was a bit concerned. He helped me hire the best private investigator money could buy. And still nothing.

We had no leads. It was like — he just disappeared. Which made me almost as nervous as if he was snooping around.

When I called my mom, she said he simply left and said he had something to do. Granted, she was used to his escapades. He was pretty unstable most the time but she still loved him — would do anything for him. I wasn't sure what made me feel sicker — the fact that my dad's number one desire in life was to bring me to my knees — or that my mom was still capable of loving someone who wanted to destroy her flesh and blood.

Saylor started combing out my hair, and I literally had to hold onto the countertop so I didn't slam her against the nearest wall, plunge my tongue down her throat, and beg her to kiss me back.

And I would beg.

I would plead.

Damn, it had been forever since I'd felt so attracted to a girl — the all-consuming feeling was starting to grate on my nerves.

"I've been practicing every day," Saylor said quietly, her fingers parting my hair as cold liquid made its' way onto my roots.

"Oh yeah?"

"Mmm." She started rubbing the dye in, then moved to another spot on the back of my head. "I think you'd be proud of me."

"I'm sure."

"I want you to watch."

Holy shit, I almost choked before answering. "Yeah, I would love to." No seriously… I would love nothing more.

Maybe I could.

Maybe my dad really was gone.

Maybe being with Saylor was possible.

Yeah. I was starting to throw myself tiny crumbs from the table in hopes that one day I could have the full meal. Yet I knew as much as anyone that by the time I made it to the buffet, the food would be gone — as if it was a mirage in the first place.

Saylor moved from my side and stood in front of me, her legs almost straddling mine as she leaned over and started dying the hair in the front.

I stared straight ahead, at her hips.

And groaned.

"Did I hurt you?" Her hands briefly left my head.

"No." I coughed. "Sorry."

Her hands returned. I fought the urge to close my eyes.

Her hands paused.

"Something wrong?"

"No." She sounded like she was thinking. "It's just… your hair's really light right here."

Damn it. I played dumb. "Oh yeah? Weird."

"Gabe…"

"What?"

"Your hair's almost blond."

"Maybe it just looks that way because the dye's so dark."

"But—"

"Saylor."

"What?

"I missed you."

I felt like an ass for distracting her like that, but at least what I was saying was true. It wasn't like I was lying.

She started rubbing the dye in again and sighed. "I missed you too."

A smile spread across my features before I could stop it.

"And you're a jackass for using something like that to distract me from the fact that you're a natural blond and for some reason don't want to talk about it."

"Sandy blond," I grumbled. "And it's the truth. I did miss you."

"Enough to help me more with my music?"

A cold spot of dye dripped down the side of my head

and onto the towel across my shoulders. "After all, you said five tears."

My shoulders relaxed. "I've only made up for one."

"I know."

"Tomorrow." I licked my lips and tried to keep the next smile in but it was impossible. "Tear number two."

"I have class all day, then I'm at the Home tomorrow."

"Weird, me too."

She laughed and grabbed my head. "Stop leaning forward or we're going to end up dying your eyebrows too."

"Fine, fine."

She worked in silence and I was happy watching her legs…

"Okay." She set everything down on the counter then sat on the floor facing me. "Tell me one true thing."

My eyebrows shot up in surprise. I swallowed and answered. "I hate dying my hair."

It was her turn to look surprised.

"Then why go to all the trouble? And don't spout crap about gray hair. I saw no gray hair, and you're not the type of guy to turn down any female, cougar or otherwise…"

"Ouch." I laughed.

Her eyes narrowed. Oh, I loved those eyes. They changed colors when she was angry. Hot. So damn hot.

"It's a necessary evil."

"Because."

"You said one true thing."

"This is part of the true thing."

"Nope. I told you one true thing. I hate dying my hair."

She sighed, crossing her arms over her chest.

I looked away, focusing on the bar of soap in the corner of the bathtub and the slow drip of water coming out of the leaky faucet. "Light hair was the old me — too recognizable. And that's as close to the truth as I've told anyone."

Saylor's lips pressed together, causing her cheeks to

tighten just a bit, which also caused her neck muscles to strain. Man, every inch of her was perfect. I wanted to touch every part of her. I've never seen a girl look so sexy without trying.

She was in skinny jeans and a black t-shirt for shit's sake, and it was a tie between wanting to strip her first and lick her later or lick her first then strip her later.

"Thank you," she finally said, getting up off the floor and checking my hair with her fingers.

"Not so fast," I murmured, grabbing a hold of her waist. "Now it's your turn. Tell me one true thing."

My fingers dug into her skin, her breath caught.

"I think you'd be hotter as a blond."

I released her and burst out laughing. The sound of it echoed around the bathroom walls like a damn ping-pong ball. "Honey, you have no idea how true that is. No. Freaking. Clue."

She swatted me with a towel, and just like that—

I was back to being obsessed.

Back to trying to figure out possible scenarios where the endgame wasn't me packing up and leaving.

But keeping her all for myself.

Except — I had a nagging suspicion that if she ever found out who I really was, the normalcy of our relationship would take a nosedive and head straight for the pit of hell.

Chapter Thirty

The hardest thing I've ever done is watch my family suffer through my illness, knowing there was nothing I could do to comfort them… until I saw the look on Gabe's face when she came into the room. And then, like watching the saddest part of a movie, I saw their story unfold. And the ending? I closed my eyes. I couldn't watch. Because I hated those types of stories — ones that gave you no hope but left you empty — and searching. —Wes M.

Saylor

I pulled into the parking lot and hurried out of my car. An accident on the freeway had made traffic complete insanity. Clenching my keys in my hand and some sheet music in the other, I ran toward the doors. Two men, big enough to cause serious damage to any action star, blocked my way. My eyes fell to two huge guns. Had there been a break-in or something?

One of them held up his hand, stopping me in my tracks.

"Do you have an appointment?"

"Um." I looked around them. "I'm one of the volunteers

from UW."

The one picked up a clipboard. "Name."

"S-saylor."

"Last name?"

I froze, literally forgetting my last name, then one of them pointed at something on the clipboard and nodded.

"Go on in." They moved to the side and let me pass. I pulled my cell phone from my back pocket for them to hold at the front desk, and completed my usual sign in.

Once everything was said and done I was fifteen minutes late.

I ran through the doors and nearly collided with Gabe.

He gripped my shoulders and steadied me. "You're late."

"I know," I huffed. "Traffic was horrible, and then two huge guys stopped me outside the building. Did something happen? Why is there more security than normal?" I vaguely remembered the conversation Gabe had on the phone when our kiss happened. I mean, I'd noticed that more security had been added over the past four weeks but two goons in front? Really? Had he said something about more security in front of the building? To be honest, I'd been so shocked about the kiss that his entire conversation fell on deaf ears. Now I wished I could remember it.

Gabe removed his hands and shrugged. "Who knows? Maybe some of the residents are trying to escape."

"It's not like we don't try," Old Man Peterson grumbled, shuffling up next to us.

Gabe gave the old man a high five and pointed at his retreating form as he used his walker to make his way across the floor. "My point exactly."

I rolled my eyes and walked by Gabe to the front of the room.

"Sorry I'm late, everyone!"

They quieted down and took their seats.

"Today I thought it would be fun to break out into

groups and write our own scales. When you're done, you can either hum the song to me or you can use your instrument to play the notes. We're just going to work with the major scale today, so use any four notes you want, but only four. We don't want to make it too difficult. I have examples on the worksheets — oh, and please make your notes colorful. If you use an F or a G make sure it's always the same color as the previous F and G. Any questions?"

They never had questions.

Probably because they never actually followed directions, but hey that was fine, at least they were enjoying themselves.

For the next hour, I made my way around the group tables and offered my assistance, but I stayed away from Princess.

Gabe was with her, hovered over the piece of paper while she instructed him on what to do.

Ha, and he thought I was bossy.

I had nothing on that girl. She knew exactly what she wanted and why.

"No, Park! I want you to use the same note again! It needs to be pink!"

I watched them interact, watched how he patted her hand every once in a while, or how he adjusted her chair so he was closer, or even wiped some of the spit from her mouth.

I'd already suspected there was something more.

I wanted to ask him, because I was beginning to wonder if she was his sister or some other family member. It was the only logical explanation as to why he would not only volunteer but be the only person who was with Princess the most. Then, on the other hand, Lisa somehow had to fit into the picture. I just didn't know how. Ugh, I was giving myself a headache.

"Sorry." He laughed and tapped her nose with the pink crayon. "So what notes do you want?"

"I want—" She started coughing wildly.

Gabe shot to his feet. "Get it out, Princess, that's right, just cough it up."

He put a napkin over her mouth and then wiped it.

"That's my girl."

"Parker..." She coughed again, and he repeated the process, rubbing at her nasal tubes. "I hate coughing."

"I know. It's because you got the sniffles, but you're getting better, right? It's easier to breathe because of them putting air inside?" He winked and tapped against the little machine attached to her wheel chair.

"A bit." Her face looked paler than before. "I'm so tired though."

"Maybe—"

"Parker!" she yelled, her voice almost piercing my ears. "I said I'm tired! I'm tired! So tired! And I keep dreaming of the Christmas tree. But it doesn't have lights. Why doesn't it have lights, Parker?"

Gabe froze. I'd never seen him look so pale before.

"The tree!" she yelled again, and then seemed to almost seize in her chair as her mouth dropped open.

I ran over just as she started coughing and snatched the napkin from his hand and held it up to her mouth.

She hacked a few times. I wiped her mouth and offered her a small smile.

"All better?" I asked.

"N-no." Giant tears started falling down her face.

"Hmm, why don't we sing then? Would you like that?" I was grasping at straws. It always seemed to calm her down when Gabe sang.

She didn't answer, and I knew I was playing with something fragile. Without thinking I shoved the napkin back into Gabe's hands and went over to the piano and started playing one of the songs that I'd learned from the Little Mermaid when I was little.

"Part of Your World!" Princess shrieked.

Gabe still stood motionless.

Princess tried singing, and even though the words didn't come out right, her smile returned. Best of all, no more coughing.

When the song was done, it was time for class to be over. Martha came in and wheeled Princess to the corner, while I approached Gabe and played with the idea of clapping in front of his face.

"What's wrong?" I tugged his hand.

He blinked and looked down at the napkin in his hands. It was stained red. Covered in blood.

Princess was coughing up blood.

Chapter Thirty-One

Red— amazing how one color can transport me back to that moment. There had been so much blood and it was all on my hands — it's still on my hands. —Gabe H.

Gabe

The dream was back.

The dream usually came when she was feverish... Princess couldn't remember much about her accident, only that there were trees. In her mind, they looked like Christmas trees, which meant we had a hell of a time during the holidays, considering she was petrified of them.

I had to agree with her.

Trees reminded me of it too.

Just like her damn Oregon Ducks sweatshirt and the scarf tied around her wheelchair.

"Gabe..." Saylor repeated my name a few times. I looked down at my hand and tried to find words, but nothing would come.

"Gabe..." She grabbed my arm and walked me out the

back doors to the outside "Is she sick?"

"Pneumonia." My voice cracked.

Saylor's hand didn't leave my arm. "I'm sorry, Gabe. That's... horrible, I know—"

"You don't know anything." I sneered, lashing out because I needed to hurt her like I was hurting, because I was losing my mind, because I was losing the girl I used to love and it was my fault all over again.

"Don't yell at me." Saylor squeezed my arm and pushed me away, releasing my arm in the process. "I'm only trying to help. I know she's important to you. She's family? Like your sister?"

I let out a harsh laugh and threw my hands in the air. "My sister? Is that what you think?"

Eyes wide, Saylor nodded quickly.

"Wrong." I scoffed and stalked toward her until I towered over her body. "She was my *fiancée.*"

Swearing, I walked back into the building and slammed the door behind me. I was going to puke.

I barely made it to the bathroom in time before all the contents of my stomach made their way into the toilet.

I puked until I was doing nothing but dry heaving, then washed my mouth out with water and made my way to Martha's office.

She was sitting demurely at her desk, sipping coffee, and looking over paperwork.

"She's coughing up blood, Martha."

The coffee cup paused mid-air to her lips. "Yes, we didn't want to worry you."

"Worry me?" My voice raised. "Worry me?"

"Gabe, sit down."

"No." I swore and slammed the door shut so nobody would hear us. "If she's sick we need to get a better doctor."

Martha's smile was kind. "Thanks to you we have the best money can buy. It's not that the doctor isn't skilled."

Dread filled my body as the clock ticked on the wall, as if waiting for the perfect time to go off. "I'm afraid the infection is worse than before. She's stopped responding to antibiotics."

"But you said—"

"Gabe." Martha sighed. "You look exhausted. Go home, get some rest. I'll keep you updated when I know more. As of right now, the doctor is still extremely optimistic that she'll pull through."

"But if she's stopped—"

"Gabe." Martha's voice was more stern this time. "She's a strong girl. Go home."

With a nod, I opened the door and stepped through then slammed it behind me, noticing the crazed looks I was receiving from staff members as my feet pounded against the tile floor.

When I reached the parking lot, Saylor was waiting by her car.

Hell, that's just what I needed. More tears to make up for.

When I approached her, she opened the passenger side door. "Get in."

"I brought my bike and—"

"Get in the damn car, Gabe."

So no tears — just a really pissed off freshman. Great. Wonderful. What a terrific freaking trade-off. Made my whole day, dammit!

Grumbling, I got into the car and buckled my seatbelt. We drove in silence, and then it started to rain.

Yes, it was slowly becoming the worst day ever.

Saylor didn't say a word to me the entire ride. And it wasn't a short ride to campus — with traffic it took at least twenty minutes. By the time we pulled onto campus I was ready to scratch my way out of the car so I could be free from the anxiety.

Saylor passed her dorm... She passed mine... and parked in front of the music building.

She turned off the car. "Come on."

Sighing, I followed her into the building and up the stairs, down the hall, to our private room. I walked into the room and waited for her to sit on the bench, but instead of sitting, she went behind me, pushed me toward the piano, then pulled down on my arms, forcing me to sit in front of it.

"Today we're going to trade," she whispered in my ear.

"Oh yeah?" I stared at the keys. "How so?"

"You said you'd make up for the second tear today, but instead, I'm going to make up for yours."

"But I haven't cried."

"Just because we aren't crying on the outside doesn't mean we aren't completely wrecked on the inside." Saylor's hands rested on my shoulders. "I figure you have more than one tear I can make up for, and even though I'm not the cause of them, I know exactly what you need to feel better."

"What?" My voice was a hollow whisper as I swallowed the lump in my throat.

"Play." She lifted my hands on the piano. "Let it go, Gabe."

And just like that. I played.

For two hours straight.

While Saylor sat silently in the corner and waited.

And she was right, damn but she was right, because I did have tears. I had gashes and scars that were so horrendous I sometimes felt like the monster I'm sure Princess's parents saw me as.

When I hit the last note, a weight lifted. "How'd you know?"

"Musicians." Saylor got up off the floor and approached me, laying her hand on my shoulder. "We share the same soul."

Slowly, I raised my head to look at her. "When I look… I see *you*. Beyond the music, beyond your smile, your touch, your laugh." My voice caught. "I see you."

"I see you too."

Chapter Thirty-Two

Baring your soul to someone is like purposefully stabbing yourself in the heart and waiting for the person you love to stop the bleeding — Wes M.

Saylor

My hands shook as I held on to him. As if he was leaving me — because that's exactly the look he had on his face. Like he wanted to run, like he was *going* to run.

I didn't know how to help. All I knew is that deep in his soul, music was his therapy — his everything.

So I brought him home.

To his real home — at the piano.

"We were super young." Gabe licked his lips and stared at the piano, his voice low and gravelly. "I proposed when I was seventeen — I was a kid, but I was in love, you know? Not the type of love most people at that age feel. It was huge — epic — like I'd finally found the person I was supposed to partner up with. And then she was just gone."

"The accident..." I asked, sitting next to him on the piano

bench. "What happened?"

"A tree." He swore and started tapping the middle C key. "We'd been out partying — nothing crazy, but we'd had a few drinks…"

Drinking at seventeen? I mean, I wasn't perfect. I'd done my fair share of wild high school parties. But it just didn't fit him, not when he seemed so controlled.

His rhythm faltered for a couple of beats before he continued, "I wanted to go for one more run down the mountain. We were both skiing. I thought it would be fun before we met up with our friends. She said no." His fingers moved to the piano, he played softly as he spoke. "I finally convinced her to go with me — only she was complaining about forgetting her helmet, and me being slightly buzzed and not thinking about the ramifications of a human hitting a tree at breakneck speed, blew her off — said not to worry. I discounted her fears when she had an actual reason to be afraid."

Gabe's voice shook. "We went down the hill. I heard her scream." His voice cracked again as his left hand joined his right, playing across the piano. "And then silence." He closed his eyes. "Sometimes I wonder what's worse… the scream or the silence afterwards."

He sighed, his shoulders hunching over as if someone had physically put weights on his body.

His left hand stopped moving.

And when I went to grab it, to offer some comfort, I noticed the tattoo on his ring finger.

It was the letter K, wrapped around like bow, with a tiny music note on top.

And I realized whatever Gabe and I had? It stopped at music — because I would never be able to replace what he'd lost — not while he still held on for dear life.

"I'm sorry," I whispered.

"Me too." Gabe paused. "Do you hate me now?"

"No."

"You should." He sagged heavier against the piano. "I do."

My phone buzzing interrupted the silence. I wasn't going to answer it but the buzzing was persistent.

"Hello?"

"Hurry up!" Kiersten shrieked in my ear. "Lisa's going to be here any minute, and we have to surprise her!"

"Oh, crap. Okay, we're on our way."

"We? Is Gabe with you?"

"Oh, yeah."

"Thank God!" She sighed. "Okay, just hurry. Do you need directions or are you good?"

I eyed Gabe's hunched form and wondered how he was going to be ready to party when he looked suicidal. "Yeah, we're good."

If good was finding out he was engaged to a paraplegic who was coughing up blood and was hiding his identity for no reason other than it seemed he hated the guy he used to be and wanted to be different.

Just. Peachy.

Gabe's eyes searched mine once I ended the call. "Party?"

"Yeah, I totally forgot."

"I never forget." He rose from the bench, his eyes darkened as he stared right through me. "Maybe that's my damn problem." He turned off the light to the practice room and offered a small smile. "Let's go."

And just like that, I watched him pull on the mask again and pretend like the sun was still shining, like he wasn't taking care of his paralyzed *fiancée* and blaming himself for the reason she was in a wheelchair.

Huh. And I was complaining to him about having performance anxiety. Yeah. He should have probably told me to go to hell.

My problems? Nothing compared to the load he was

carrying.

I followed him out of the building and unlocked the doors to my car. It was weird, seeing the other side of him and knowing he was choosing to still wear his mask.

I imagined it was like finding out who Superman really was one day only to see him try to pull the wool over your eyes the next day.

But my memory? It was perfect. And I wasn't sure I'd ever get over the look on Gabe's face when he was playing — pouring his soul out onto the piano. He may as well have slit open his wrists and let the blood trickle out of his body as he pounded each note.

Watching Gabe perform such a normal task as buckling his seatbelt was almost unnerving. I wasn't really sure how he was able to function with all that guilt on his shoulders.

"What?" His eyes flashed.

Caught. I'd been caught staring.

I shoved the key in the ignition. "Nothing, sorry. Just tired I think."

"You don't have to go to the party."

You. Not us. But you. As in he didn't want me to go or would be totally fine with me staying at home and napping like a senior citizen.

"No." I pulled out of the parking spot. "I think I should. After all, Wes didn't really give me a choice."

Gabe fumbled with the heat. "Yeah, he's intense like that."

"How did you and Wes meet?"

Gabe's hand froze midair before he pulled it back and crossed his arms. "Kiersten was Lisa's roommate. I'm Lisa's… cousin. Remember?" He rolled his eyes. "So I met him through Kiersten and the rest is kind of history."

"Through Kiersten," I repeated, the wheels in my head turning.

"Stop." Gabe growled. "It wasn't like that with her — it

hasn't been like that with anyone."

My heart dropped to my knees as my lower lip threatened to quiver out of control.

"Until you," he said it so softly I almost didn't hear it.

I chose not to speak the rest of the way to the restaurant, because I didn't trust myself, and — thankfully — Gabe didn't ask any questions.

Maybe it was one of those understandings... Too many questions had been asked; too many answers given. A person can only handle so much, and I was officially past my limit.

Chapter Thirty-Three

Sometimes I wonder if we ever truly let anyone completely in. The desire for another human being to know you, all of you, all the pieces, even the ones you're ashamed of — is huge. But too often, we sit down and sort through the pieces only picking out the pretty ones, leaving the ugly ones behind, not realizing that choosing not to share with someone else is like committing a crime against our very soul — for how can we ever be free? When we purposefully place what we struggle with the most — in the dark? —Wes M.

Gabe

She knew.
She knew.
She knew.

Wasn't I supposed to feel lighthearted now that Saylor saw just a glimpse of my reality? Instead, the urge to tell her everything, to cut open my own beating heart and slam it down on the table for her to fix — to mend — was so intense, it was staggering.

Finding it hard to breathe, I'd barely managed to make it

to the restaurant without breaking down in the car. How was she able to carry on as though nothing had changed? How was she able to act like what I'd just shared with her was nothing out of the ordinary? A normal person would be freaking the hell out.

So either she wasn't normal—

Or she was a saint.

Was it wrong to wish for the second choice? I was abnormal enough for the two of us.

"You made it!" Kiersten launched herself into my arms. I twirled her around, as per usual, and set her on her feet, kissing her forehead as she leaned forward and gripped my shoulders. "I was worried."

"Have I ever let you down?" I winked. Though on the inside I knew… I let her down a lot. And I wasn't the only one carrying that particular gem.

"Not yet." Her bright red hair was snaked around her head like a crown. She looked like a fairy princess in her short white dress and brown sandals. It immediately made my chest hurt. Princess would have loved to dress up like that — to walk.

"Gabe." Wes came up behind me.

I turned.

He was wearing jeans and a t-shirt with some indie band on it. His eyes were focused intently on me, as if he was a freaking vampire trying to read my mind.

"So…" Saylor said from behind me. "When does Lisa get here?"

"Fifteen minutes. We were able to stall a bit." Kiersten gripped Saylor's hand. "And thanks for coming, I know things have been really busy lately with practice and trying to fit everything in at the Home."

"No problem." Saylor's voice cracked. Damn. I was the reason she was going to have the most stressful night of her life. No way was she able to process everything that just went down and still function like a normal human being.

I had four years.

And I still wanted to slam my face against a brick wall.

The restaurant, Marlin, was a small bar and grill on Puget Sound. I knew Kiersten had rented out the back room which led to the dock. I'd told her I'd pay for everything. When she'd argued Wes had told her it wasn't a big deal and that she should let me do something.

But Wes knew.

He knew he wasn't the only one who could buy not just the damn restaurant but half the property on Puget Sound and still not feel the squeeze.

"Music!" Kiersten shouted, scaring the shit out of me. "I almost forgot!"

She ran to the back of the room and plugged in her iPod then turned up the volume.

I chuckled. The room was way too big for us. I mean, it was huge and there were going to be five of us, but still it was nice. To not have to worry about anyone recognizing the walking miracle and famous duo that were Wes and Kiersten — or worse, recognizing me.

Not that it had happened in the last four years.

But I could never be too careful.

I self-consciously rubbed my hair, my dark-as-sin hair, and hated myself all over again as Saylor's words replayed in my mind.

She'd said I'd be hotter as a blond.

Well, damn, if that didn't make me want to chop off the Captain Jack Sparrow thing I had going on and go all natural.

Kiersten and Saylor were busy talking about something while Wes watched me.

"Creepy, dude." I shook my head.

He shrugged.

And then the music changed.

My entire body seized up. As if someone had just told me

to stop breathing at once and turn into a zombie.

"Oh my gosh! I used to love this song!" Kiersten all but shouted as she and Saylor started singing along.

"When you take my heart, I give you my soul, but baby, you screwed up and let me go! Whoa, Whoa, Whoa." Kiersten belted it louder. "You let me go, go, go, baby, no no, whoa. I should have known things would get sticky when I wanted you to be with me and only me, but no, no, no."

Wes's eyebrows shot up as he sent me a knowing look.

Yeah, yeah, bastard. Thanks, caught that.

Saylor fell against Kiersten laughing when Kiersten started doing the exact choreography from the music video. I was almost tempted to join. But pretty sure that would give me away.

No man should know that choreography.

Well, that, and Wes would shit his pants. That was so not the way to tell people the truth. Just bust a move like a white guy who actually knew how to dance and break out into song.

Dark hair or light. It wouldn't matter. They'd see right through my disguise. It always amazed me how much people only saw what they wanted. They saw tattoos and thought bad ass. They saw muscles and dark long hair and thought I was a total loser.

They had no flipping clue that I'd had straight A's my entire life.

That until a starlet seduced me — I'd promised myself for marriage.

That at night I used to cry when my parents wouldn't let me stay up late and write music.

Beer. Hell, I needed beer or something stronger than bottled water. But the joke was on me — because this was not the type of place to flash my ID.

Dark gritty bars with bartenders who didn't even know their own names? Couldn't care less.

Nice restaurants with a peppy college student as your

waitress? Yeah. Not smart.

"She's coming!" Kiersten hushed everyone and turned down the lights.

The door clicked open. High heels clamored against the floor as a figure was silhouetted in the doorway.

In perfect timing, we all jumped up and screamed in unison. "Surprise!"

The lights flared to life.

And I knew, in that moment, my life was officially over.

"Hi, son." My dad had his arm wrapped around Lisa. Her cheeks were stained with a mixture of tears and black mascara. "I don't know why I never thought to locate your ex-girlfriend first and track you that way. Oh…" He turned to Lisa and kissed her on her cheek. She tried to jerk away from his touch but he held her firm. "Happy Birthday, Mel."

Chapter Thirty-Four

You can tell a lot just by reading the expression in a person's eyes — and Gabe's… it was the same expression a trapped animal gets before it's shot in the head. His dad was the hunter — and Gabe was the deer. His time was up. And I wasn't sure if I was supposed to feel sorry for him or horrified at the revelation. He was a stranger to me. A complete and total stranger. —Saylor

Gabe

"Let her go." My nostrils flared as I stalked toward my dad, a man that, if I had it my way, was about to get thrown into Puget Sound and held under the dark murky water until he stopped fighting back. "Now."

"What?" Dad's face was indifferent. It always was. It was part of the reason I hated him. Because I got my talent to act — directly from him. One minute he was the happiest man in the world, the next, you'd think he was working for the mafia or high on drugs. "No hug?"

"Hell, no." I spat. "Let her go."

With a cruel smile, he pushed Lisa away into Kiersten's

waiting arms. Wes strode over and stood in front of the girls. At least I knew if there was a fight we'd win. My dad didn't stand a chance.

Then again, he'd just sue the shit out of us if he survived and I wasn't about to let my best friend go to prison for murder, so yeah. We were screwed.

"New tattoo?" Dad motioned to my neck.

Damn, but I felt every muscle strain in my body. Begging for a fight.

"Your mom misses you."

I laughed and crossed my arms. "I'm sure she's fine. After all, she has all the money she needs to be happy, right?"

His cold blue eyes narrowed in on me. He looked dirty, like he hadn't slept in days. He smelled like he hadn't seen a shower in weeks.

"Been camping in your car?" I mocked him. "Or did you have to sell that in order to pay your debts?"

"You think—" He smiled and shoved his hands in his pockets. "—that you're in any position to toss insults around, son?"

"Don't call me son," I all but yelled.

"Oh but, why deny it? Especially since we're going to be spending so much time together. I have everything worked out — long lost son finally comes home to family after four years of solitude!" His eyes pooled with tears.

Son of a bitch!

"Oh, yes, Miss Walters, it was such a happy reunion, having our little Ashton back."

I reared back and punched him in the face.

He fell to the ground, cursing.

Wes came up behind me and grabbed my arms. I pulled against him trying to lunge for my dad.

Dad looked up at me through watery eyes, as blood dripped from his nose. "You're stronger than you used to be."

"I'll kill you."

"Do it." He smirked. "I'll still be smiling from the pit of hell."

I lunged again, but Wes held me firm.

"After all..." Dad stood. "All I've ever wanted is the truth Isn't that what they say? It sets you free?" He sniffed. "Isn't that what you want, to be free? Finally free?"

"You're insane," I ground out, injecting as much hatred as I could into those two words.

"Tomorrow." Dad handed me a piece of paper with his phone number on it. "We'll talk about your return."

"I'd rather die."

Dad made his way toward the door then paused and turned. "Oh, I know that. You would never do it for me, son. But for Mel?" His eyes fell on Lisa. "Or how about Kimmy?"

With everything in me, I fought the arms banded around me like a vise. "I'll kill you for this!" I screamed.

"Tomorrow," Dad repeated and left.

I thrashed against Wes — until Lisa walked up and stood in front of me. "Just you and me, okay? It will be okay. I promise." Her eyes pooled with tears. "Screw him, let them find out about me, I don't care, just—" Wes released me into her arms as she hugged me. "I'm so sorry."

"Me too, Mel." I sighed. "Me too."

We hugged for a few brief minutes before Wes cleared his throat behind us.

"Gabe?" Saylor spoke so softly I wanted to cry. "What's going on?"

Without looking at her I answered, "My names not Gabe. It's Ashton Parker Hyde."

And I finally understood the expression of hearing a pin drop in a room. I might have just said I was Spiderman.

Chapter Thirty-Five

The truth really does set you free — but what they don't tell you is the process hurts like hell. —Wes M.

Saylor

I felt my mouth drop open as the mask fell completely away from Gabe — or rather, Ashton's — face. His eyes, those blue eyes, and his dark hair. Mortified, I wanted to cover my face with my hands. I'd told him he'd look better blond — because his natural color? A honey blond, that for years, people swore couldn't even be copied… He was my generation's version of the perfect Ken Doll. Everything about him was worshipped, revered as though he was some sort of god. It had been devastating when he abandoned the industry and fell off the face of the planet.

Girls full on wept for months.

There were reports that he'd died of a drug overdose, or worse yet, committed suicide after his famous girlfriend was killed in a tragic skiing accident.

All lies.

Every last one.

Princess.

My knees buckled beneath me as the lies swarmed around the room, stealing the oxygen my body so desperately needed.

"Hey." Kiersten knelt down by my side and pulled me into her arms. I'd met her what? Three times? And I clung to her like she was my mom. Like she would protect me.

"Y-you aren't cousins?" I pointed between him and Lisa, my stomach getting sicker. Funny, how I'd thought he and Kiersten had a thing. So was it Lisa all along?

Not only was he engaged to a *fiancée* who — surprise! — wasn't dead. But the girl he'd been introducing as his cousin was—

"Holy crap!" Kiersten yelled in my left ear. "Lisa, you could have told me. I would have… understood."

"I know." Lisa shrugged. "I did it for Ashton, not me."

Who was she?

I struggled to remember my fourteen-year-old self, to visualize my old room littered with teen magazines.

"Melanie Faye." I choked on the name.

Lisa's face went from pasty white to deathly gray in less than three seconds. She gave a firm nod as fresh tears streamed down her face. "I didn't want anyone to get hurt. And I — I just wanted to help Ashton. I loved him. I was so jealous at first, and then when everything happened. I couldn't abandon him."

"She found me…" Gabe said in a low voice. "After I tried to overdose."

"It was my idea." Lisa looked down at the ground. "To run away. To leave our lives behind and start fresh, especially when we found out Kimmy was going to make it. The world that used to be so fun and shiny had become our own personal hell."

Melanie Faye had been mentioned in magazines only

because she'd been Ashton's best friend. People always said they were dating but no one had ever actually confirmed it as truth. They had grown up next door to one another. She was a model; he was a triple threat Hollywood heart-throb. A match made in heaven.

I used to want to be her.

Because at fourteen I'd been obsessed with all things Ashton Hyde.

Fantastic.

"I, um…" I pushed away from the floor. "I need to go."

Without looking back, I ran out of the restaurant, my chest heaving with exertion as my feet pounded against the pavement.

"Wait!" Gabe yelled from behind me.

I lifted my left hand mid-air, waving him off, pushing him away as I reached for the car door with my right, my breathing ragged. I couldn't look at him. I just… couldn't. I felt betrayed. Lied to. All I'd asked for was truth, and he'd given me lies.

A part of me understood the need to protect himself.

But I wasn't one of those friends. The ones that you gave a sliver to while you sucked them dry.

That wasn't friendship.

"What?" My voice cracked. "What more could you possibly say?"

"You promised."

"Excuse me?" I turned in a flash, ready to slap the crap out of him when he stalked toward me.

I backed up out of total self-preservation. I didn't trust my emotions around him, not when it was like staring at three different people. Was he Ashton, the famous actor and pop star? Was he Gabe, the wounded bird that just needed someone to talk to? Or was he Parker, the broken *fiancé*?

Gabe's eyes were wild. "I can't lose you. I can't."

"Funny." I swallowed the lump in my throat. "Because

I've already lost you. I lost Gabe. I never knew Parker. And now I'm losing Ashton all over again. I wonder how much more I can lose — before I'm empty."

"Saylor—"

"I asked for truth. You gave me lies."

"When?" He pulled me against his chest. "When did I lie to you?"

My mind searched for situations where he'd out right lied… and I came up with nothing. Absolutely nothing, except for one thing. "Your name."

"I told you," he muttered, his lips nearly touching mine, "I told you there were things I kept hidden — is this it then? You're rejecting me?"

"Me?" I tried to jerk free. "Reject you? No, Gabe. That's like saying I'm setting a caged bird free without ever being given the bird in the first place. What we had wasn't real. You can't base what we had on truth when nothing was actually real. God…" I started shaking. "I was falling for you. Falling for you, Gabe! How do you think that makes me feel? Do you even know who you are?"

"No." He sighed. "I guess that's the problem when you spend four years trying to forget."

We stood in silence. So many words rushed through my head, things I could say that wouldn't actually make anything better because at the end of the day, our worlds should have never collided in the first place.

"Saylor," he pleaded. "Let me make it up to you. Let me tell you the truth — can I have one chance, one chance to come clean?"

"Why would I give you this chance?" I slowly pried myself free. "When you haven't even made up for the tears you caused the first time? Why in the hell would I give you the opportunity to cause more?"

Gabe stared at me for a few minutes, his shoulders slumped. He nodded slowly.

And then he walked away.

He walked away.

And a part of me hated him for it. Because for once in my life I understood what it meant to be at a crossroads where someone either chooses you or them.

He didn't choose me.

I was alone.

Just how I started.

Only now, I realized how lonely I actually was.

I wiped away a few more stray tears and got into my car. Rain started pounding against the windshield as I drove toward campus.

My life wasn't over.

So why did it feel like it?

Chapter Thirty-Six

Sometimes by holding onto what you love the most — you end up choking the very life from the thing you want to keep on living. It's possible to try too hard, to love something so deeply that you lose yourself. The danger is never in loving someone — but losing your identity in the process. Because what happens when tragedy strikes? You're left an empty shell. You're left with nothing. It's why I tried to end things. Why I didn't want to go on living — because I'd been living through her, not with her, and I had forgotten how to be myself. How to be normal. The only problem was — I was okay with it. —Gabe H.

Saylor

I took I5 and kept driving.

When I pulled up to the small subdivision in Mill Creek. I turned off my car and stared at my mom's apartment.

Once we'd lived in a nice neighborhood, but because rent always went up over the years we moved around a lot.

Luckily, she was a nurse, so she had a good job, but still… We'd never had a ton of money, so we didn't have a large home, just a different apartment every few years.

I grabbed my purse and slowly took the stairs to the third floor, two at a time, then let myself in the apartment. Everything was pristine. Clean. Beautiful. I hadn't been back since Christmas, and even then I'd only slept there. I spent most my time on campus practicing.

"Say?" Eric walked down the hall, his smile wide. "Is that you?"

"Yeah." My lower lip quivered. "It's me."

He was fifteen now, tall enough to be almost at eye level. His wide-set blue eyes looked me up and down. They were slanted just slightly, making his smile even warmer as he grinned.

And then he opened his arms. Just like that, I ran to them and started bawling.

"Shhh, Say, it will be okay. I promise. I promise, Say." He rubbed my back and rocked me back and forth. "I'm sorry you're sad."

I didn't trust my words, so I only nodded and clung to my brother like he was my lifeline. He was wearing a Seahawks sweatshirt and smelled like he'd just taken a shower.

"Mom's home soon." He released me and gave me one of those silly grins. "I've been cooking more."

"Really?" I wiped my eyes.

He nodded. "Food makes things better."

With a laugh I croaked, "Yeah, it does, doesn't it?"

"Sit," he commanded, in his soft voice. "I'll make you eat, Saylor."

"Eric?"

He turned around, his eyes smiling just as much as his actual mouth. "What?"

"I'm glad I'm here."

He shrugged and started pulling food out of the fridge.

Chapter Thirty-Seven

If only alcohol actually made you forget. Instead, I figured it would do nothing more than remind me of everything I wanted to bury far, far, away —Gabe H.

Gabe

"I'm sorry," I mumbled as we all piled into Wes's Porsche and made our way back to campus. "For ruining everything."

Kiersten cleared her throat. "Well, at least it's a birthday Lisa won't forget."

Wes chuckled. "How's that for optimism?"

"She hates me." I banged my head against the window, "How the hell am I supposed to deal with both my dad and making sure Saylor knows that—"

I stopped talking.

Wes cleared his throat. "That…"

Lisa squeezed my hand encouragingly.

"That—" My throat constricted. "Holy shit, I can't even say it out loud! No wonder she hates me."

"You..." Lisa said slowly.

"Love." Wes added.

"Her!" Kiersten smirked at me through the rearview mirror.

"I'm not two." I pressed my fingers against my temples. "Does anyone have any ideas? Wes? You know how I usually tell you to stop being such a wise ass?"

"Yup."

"I need you to forget I said that."

"Nope."

I groaned again.

Wes pulled into his usual spot in front of the dorm complex. "Look, Gabe, I can't fix this for you. None of us can. And trying to figure it all out tonight is going to do nothing but stress you out more. The only thing I will say is... your time's up."

"No shit," I spat, wanting to hit something with my fist.

"Gabe." Wes unbuckled his seatbelt and turned around. "It's time. You're done being Gabe. You were never him to begin with. You've always been Ashton — a name doesn't change someone no matter how hard you want it to. Your identity is found in your heart. Not your job, not your status, your name, what your major is, how much money you have. Your heart has been the same the entire time. So, be who you've always been."

"So pick one?" I shook my head confused.

"No." Wes offered a sad smile. "Fuse them."

Chapter Thirty-Eight

Sometimes you have to simplify in order to process. Eating an omelet while listening to my brother talk about football? Free therapy. — Saylor

Saylor

Eric fixed me the best omelet of my life then patted my hand and started jabbering on and on about football and all the different plays. From there, conversation quickly fell to the Seahawks.

"Russell Wilson." Eric sighed dreamily then pointed a fork in my direction. "He's better than Tom Brady."

My mom chose that moment to open the door. She was in her pink nurse scrubs and looked like she'd had a bit of a rough day.

"Eric, how dare you say something against my Patriots!" She grinned and put her hands on her hips. "And what are you doing up so late, young man?"

Eric pointed at me.

"Hi, Mom."

"Saylor!" She wrapped me in a giant hug and kissed my forehead. And just like that I was a little kid again, wanting my mom to fix things. Wanting a hug and a chocolate chip cookie with milk. "Is everything okay?"

Eric shouted. "She was crying, Mom, but I made her eat."

"Thank you, Eric." Mom beamed with approval. "Now, why don't you go get ready for bed, alright? Can you do that for me?"

Eric started to pout, his lower lip stuck out as his forehead creased.

"Brush your teeth first. Remember to put in your retainer, then crawl into bed." We'd learned early on that by just giving him an order of direction, he was able to accomplish basically anything, but if I was to tell him to go clean his room he'd throw a fit — the task was too big, too overwhelming. So I had to say things like, pick up your books first, then put them in your backpack, and then find your colored pencils.

"Fine, Mom." Eric gave me one last hug and marched down the hall to the bathroom.

Mom took one look at me, offered her hand and led me to the couch. "What's going on, sweetie? I hardly see you and suddenly you show up with tear-stained cheeks."

"It's a long story," I croaked.

"Well…" She checked her watch. "We have all night."

It took me three hours to explain. Part of me felt like I was betraying Gabe's secret, while the other part needed someone to talk to so bad I didn't really care all that much. Besides, my mom was a vault.

By the time I was finished, I was severely dehydrated, but I felt better. Mom didn't say much, just nodded and listened.

Finally, when my voice was hoarse from talking, I waited for her to offer me advice.

"So?" I asked. "What do I do now?"

Mom's smile erased some of my angst, but her words

brought it right back to full force again. "I think that's pretty clear, don't you?"

"If it was clear, I wouldn't be feeling like my life was over, sobbing on the couch and dealing with my heart getting ripped out of my chest."

"Love." Mom sighed and scooted closer. "It does that to you."

"Mom, I've only known him for a few weeks—"

"Love has no time table, no rules. It is what it is, Saylor." She gripped my hand in hers. "I'm not saying what this Gabe did was alright, Saylor. I'm not condoning any of it. What I am saying is that everyone deserves a second chance. That's what life's about."

"But—"

"The thing about second chances," Mom interrupted, laying a hand on my arm, "is we always walk into them assuming we'll feel better, when nine times out of ten things get worse before they ever get better. If you give him another chance, it's not going to feel good. It's going to be painful. It's going to be hard, but in the end, if things work out..." She shrugged. Her eyes seemed to shine with her smile. "...totally worth it. Wouldn't you rather suffer for a few days — in order to gain the love of a lifetime? Given the chance, people say they'd suffer for two days if only the rest of their lives they could be happy. The reality? Most people quit after one hour because things prove too difficult." Tears pooled in her eyes, "Don't quit Saylor. It seems Gabe's entire life has been summed up into that one word. People quitting on him, him quitting on himself. Don't do what he expects."

"But it hurts," I argued, my voice shaking. "So bad."

Mom cupped my face with her hands. "So use the pain."

It was the same exact thing Gabe had said to me when we'd gotten into our second argument. What did that even mean? Use the pain?

"I don't understand," I mumbled.

"Don't let pain keep you from moving forward. It shouldn't stop your progress — it should drive it."

I sighed and started picking at the blanket in front of me. "When did you get so wise?"

She smiled fondly. "I had a patient once." Her eyes glazed over a bit. "The odds were against him in every way possible. I was in the room after his MRI. It broke my heart to see such a promising young man have his future stolen from him. And then the strangest thing happened. When I went to the door to leave — it was locked. I turned the knob and heard footsteps, and after the footsteps I heard him talking to someone. It was a lady. She had a beautiful voice, but it wasn't her voice that struck me, it was the words.

"She said, 'Sometimes when we think God has written the end, what he really means is the beginning.'" Mom wiped a stray tear from her eyes. "It's haunted me, that phrase. Sometimes I wake up in the middle of the night and still hear that woman's voice."

Mom licked her lips and gripped my hands. "How often do you think we write our own ending before the story is even finished? How often do we give up on ourselves when our lives are just starting? Things get hard and we immediately back away and assume that means we're going in the wrong direction, doing the wrong thing. If anything, when the waters get thick, that's our sign to keep going."

"So you're saying it's not the end," I whispered.

"It rarely is," Mom replied.

We sat I in silence for a bit until the clock chimed. It was one a.m.

"Mom?"

"Hmm?"

"How long were you trapped in that room, anyways?"

I couldn't read her face. She shifted in her seat and answered, "I wasn't. Once I overheard that conversation, I tried the door and it wasn't locked anymore. When I told the janitor, he said I must have been confused. That door doesn't have a lock. It never did."

Chapter Thirty-Nine

I looked at the three masks I wore and realized something — they were all monsters of my own making. I did this. Nobody else. It was my choice. And I had chosen wrong. —Gabe H.

Gabe

"You ready?" Wes asked for the tenth time.

"Just do it already," I grumbled leaning my head into the shower as he started rinsing the black out.

"So this is a fun bonding experience." Wes laughed and started whistling.

"Please don't whistle," I grumbled. "Do anything but whistle."

Wes started to hum one of the songs from my first albums.

"Freaking hilarious."

"I thought so." He continued humming.

"Just—" I tensed my hands against my knees as I leaned farther in. The black swirled into the drain as if my sins were getting washed out right along with my hair. "Just don't do anything."

"Gabe..." Wes dunked my head farther under the warm water. "You're doing the right thing."

"Yeah, that's what you keep saying."

"It's true."

"How do we know this doesn't backfire and shoot me in the ass?"

"We don't."

"Imagine, there was once a time I thought you should be a therapist. Do you want me to kill myself?"

Wes laughed, pissing me off more. "Sorry, man, but think of it this way. The worst has happened and you're still alive."

"I—"

Holy hell he was right. The worst had happened. My dad knew where Lisa and I were. He was going to expose us. He knew about Kimmy, and Saylor hated me. My life was over, but I was alive.

"I can literally hear your brain frying right now."

"Shut up."

Wes turned off the water and threw a towel over my head, using a little bit too much aggression as he did so. The ass.

When I turned around he brandished a pair of scissors in his hand and a smile I can only describe as way too eager.

"No." I shook my head. "Hell, no."

"Oh, come on." He held the scissors up in the air and snipped. "Go big or go home."

"No."

"Afraid?" He tilted his head.

"Shit." I wiped my face with my hands. "Maybe a little."

"Try having cancer." His eyes narrowed. "Now stop being a bitch and sit down."

I shook my head. "Being healthy's changed you."

"No." Wes gave me a sad smile. "Almost losing my best friend — that changed me."

"Wes—"

"I know you're sorry." He cleared his throat. "But if you ever go to that dark place again, I'm following you and I can be annoying as hell. I think we both know that. So, sit down while I cut your hair. We're doing this together."

Giving in, I nodded. "Thanks, Wes. For... everything." Because he'd stayed up for twelve hours — missing sleep, missing food, missing everything — to help me come up with a plan.

He'd said he owed me.

But in the end, I think I'd always owe him for everything he did, for everything he'd done, for everything he was still doing by just being Wes. Freaking. Michels.

Shit. I would not cry.

As pieces of hair fell in front of me, and the sound of snipping clamored in my ears, I felt the weight lifted. I stopped slumping. Instead of leaning forward, I sat up. Instead of feeling emptier and more horrified...

I felt... invigorated.

I was able to smile — because the pieces of hair on the floor weren't black. They were golden blond.

When Wes was finished he handed me a mirror and slapped me on the back. "Welcome back to the land of the living, Ashton Hyde, nice to meet you."

Chapter Forty

He was just a man. Just a very, very, very attractive and popular man. And I had kissed him. A lot. Funny, when I was sixteen I imagined what it would be like to kiss Ashton Hyde. Never in my lifetime did I think it would actually happen — or feel so right. — Saylor

Saylor

The sweet smell of my mom's pancakes woke me from my fitful sleep. When I opened my eyes, the clock on the bedside table confirmed that I'd totally slept in. Grumbling, I rolled over and threw on a pair of ripped jeans and a white t-shirt. After eating my body weight in pancakes, I left her apartment and drove, as slow as humanly possible to the Home.

It was one of my Friday afternoons and as much as I didn't want to face Gabe, I knew my mom was right. Besides, no way could I abandon everyone.

As luck would have it — no traffic.

Of course.

I don't know what I expected when I pulled up to the Home, but everything seemed normal. As if a movie/pop star hadn't just come out of hiding last night, as if Gabe and I were still friends.

As I got out of my car, I shivered. The air was thick with mist. The two security guards nodded at me and let me through.

Martha was at the front desk, a smile on her face. "Ah Saylor, how are you today?"

"Good." I'd be lying if I said my eyes weren't darting all over the place, looking for traces of Gabe.

"He's already inside," Martha answered, pulling my cell phone from my clenched hand. "And he's waiting for you."

I cleared my throat and suddenly found great interest in staring at the countertop. "Who?"

She laughed.

Was I that transparent?

Sighing, I walked, again, as slow as my legs would allow me while still moving, and opened the doors to the game room.

Greedily, I searched for Gabe.

But Gabe wasn't who I found.

Because Gabe didn't exist anymore.

My breath caught in my chest as Ashton freaking Hyde rose from his chair and moved toward me.

The only thing that was the same? The tattoos. No piercings. No dark hair.

He was wearing blue skinny jeans, brown boots, and a tight tan Henley that opened up revealing a few chest tattoos.

His hair was golden blond. The type you see on TV and swear isn't real. The type that looks like dark spun gold.

"You came." He sounded relieved.

"Yeah." I couldn't look at him in the eyes. Not now. Not knowing what he did to me, how he affected me. My heart might as well have been exposed for all to see — no doubt he heard it.

Gabe or Ashton, or whoever he was — I guess in my mind he was still Gabe — reached into his pocket and pulled out a tiny bottle. It was the size of a keychain and made of glass.

"What's this?"

Gabe smiled. That paired with his dark skin and bright eyes, I had to blink to keep my mouth from falling open. "Five tears. You're right. How dare I cause more — when I don't even fix the first ones that fell?"

Speechless I stared.

"A tear for a tear," he whispered then shook the tiny bottle.

"You—"

"It was only fair." His eyes fell to my mouth. "By my count that means I have three more to make up for. So you better prepare yourself."

"Prepare myself?" I repeated, still in shock.

"Yeah." He smiled again and started to walk away toward Princess. Then as if forgetting something, he turned and said simply, "I'm falling."

"Huh?"

"I'm falling for you too. I haven't fallen. Falling. As in still falling, still in the air, still trying to get used to the idea that I've just nosedived off a cliff with every intention of making sure the landing doesn't break my fall."

"And if it does?"

"Then at least I still jumped."

My breath caught in my throat, my body responded to his words as if he'd physically picked me up and twirled me around the room and kissed me senseless.

"Alright, everyone, take your seats." I clapped my hands four times.

They followed. Princess shouted. Normal. Everything felt normal.

"We've been at this over four weeks." I looked around the room. "Last time we met, we worked on our own songs. Does anyone want to share?"

A few people volunteered. Each of them trying hard to sing the notes they'd colored on their papers. Even Princess shouted the notes Gabe had colored for her.

"Anyone else?" I looked around the room, most everyone was distracted by his or her own worksheet, looking at each other's, whispering.

"I want to go," Gabe's voice pierced the air.

"Oh yes, Park!" Princess shouted. "Play a song! Play your song!"

Gabe's smile was for her and only her as he bent over and kissed her forehead. I would have never recognized her. But it was Kimmy. Kimmy Paige. Eighteen-year-old starlet. I really honestly thought she'd died. She'd been in a coma for so long, the media had lost interest.

"Parker!" Princess shouted, excitement evident in her twinkling eyes as her gaze followed him to the piano bench.

The songs he sang. They were hers. Ashton had been famous for it. He would write love songs for her then upload them to YouTube. One time, he'd even filmed himself singing her to sleep.

Was it any wonder women everywhere about killed themselves when he disappeared?

Gabe sat at the piano looking like he'd been born there. His hands hovered over the keys. "A new song. For new beginnings." He lifted his eyes just slightly and met my gaze. And then he began to play.

Transfixed, I watched him while he played — his eyes never left mine.

"How could I let a love go — one I'd been holding onto for so long — one that felt like home? It's not easy to let go of the pieces, even though they're the reason for my pain. I gripped them so hard that my blood fell like rain. But nothing,

nothing could have prepared me for a new life with you — one I didn't deserve, one I want to pursue." He leaned over the piano, closing his eyes, as the music dipped. The song was both beautiful and haunting, his body was one with the piano, and in turn I felt like I was the piano. Like he was playing me, every stroke of the keys was him kissing my skin.

"If beauty is pain — let me get lost in it. If you're my salvation — I want to earn it. If love is all I have to give — then let me give it. You. It's all for you."

Gabe's eyes opened and locked in on mine.

"How can I prove that what I feel is real? You ask for truth I give you lies. You ask for joy I make you cry. But I don't want to lose you. Not like this. Not when I've left your heart in such a mess. Give me one chance — I'm letting go of the past — but I need you here to know."

"If beauty is pain — let me get lost in it. If you're my salvation — I want to earn it. If love is all I have to give — then let me give it. You, it's all for you." He paused, hitting the last few notes, and the song ended.

Gabe's smile lit up the room.

But I was frozen in place.

Me. He'd sung that to me.

I wiped a stray tear from my eye as Gabe approached me yet again. Was the man trying to kill me? I mean, there was only so much a girl could take.

His eyebrows drew together as he reached out and touched my wet cheek.

"It's okay." I whispered. "You earned it."

"I want more songs!" Princess shouted breaking our moment.

I'd forgotten there were people all around us. Feeling my face heat, I sighed and walked back to the front of the room. "Alright, today we're going to work on adding to the songs we created last time. Use four different notes and I want you to add a chorus."

I walked from table to table helping.

When I reached Princess and Gabe, she was sleeping, which was weird to say the least. She never slept. I was beginning to think tired wasn't even a word in her vocabulary. Then again, recently, she'd been mentioning it more and more.

"Is she okay?" I asked, my eyebrows drawing together in concern.

Gabe looked up from his chair and sighed, shoulders hunched he said quietly, "The infection is getting worse."

I pulled a chair next to him and sat, without realizing I'd done it. I grabbed his hand and squeezed. "She's strong. It will be okay."

"Yeah." He squeezed back and smiled. "It really will."

Chapter Forty-One

Watching your best friend smile when he looks in the mirror? No words. Just. None. —Wes M.

Gabe

"Wear the dark jeans."

"Do you mind?" I snapped.

Wes held up his hands. "All I'm saying is they hug your ass and if you're still tiptoeing around Saylor, it couldn't hurt."

"Remind me again why you're here?"

"Best friend." Wes pointed at himself and smirked. "Besides, it was either me or Lisa, and we both know how she is when people go on dates."

"Good point," I grumbled.

Lisa and Kiersten were spending the evening together. Kiersten wanted answers, and Lisa owed her some. Besides, it wasn't my truth to tell, not by a long shot and I had my own demons to face — no chance in hell was I going to try to tackle all things Lisa as well.

I sighed. It seemed like we all needed our own night of truth. Yay. Hold me back while I pump my fist into the air and dance a little jig.

I'd met with my father earlier that morning before I went to the Home. His demand was simple.

Go with him to the media.

Or he'd expose me, as well as Lisa and Princess.

I told him to go to hell.

His way meant I had no control — my way meant that at least in the end I could control how everyone found out. The only issue was that Princess had no idea and was going to have to blindly trust me. And Lisa? Well, her family had always known where she was.

Because unlike me, she wasn't hiding from her family or from the media, not really.

She was hiding from *Him*.

With Wes's support I called every freaking news station in the area offering them the story. Let them fight over the exclusive — in the end it would be my choice.

The only catch? I didn't want to be interviewed, not yet, and I didn't want to bring Princess into it. I hoped it was a bit like calling my dad's bluff — I'd show him I'm not afraid to go to the media myself, and he'd walk away.

He still hadn't returned my phone call.

So now it was a game of chicken.

Either way. The truth was going to come out — Wes was right about that. But at least this time, when I thought about that ticking time bomb, I was clipping at the wires. I wasn't just staring at it waiting for it to scare the shit out of me. Funny, how all it takes is a different perspective for you to snap out of a fearful situation and empower yourself.

Awesome.

Now I sounded like Wes.

The walking Hallmark card.

And shoot me now.

"Dude, the jeans don't look that bad," Wes scoffed. "Stop being so dramatic. Damn actors."

I pulled the trigger and mouthed *poof* right in Wes's face and smirked. His response was to tilt his head to the right, feel my forehead, and then smack me on the cheek *Godfather* style.

"I think you're more fun to irritate when you have light hair."

"Hilarious." I threw on a black t-shirt and grabbed my keys.

"Gabe—"

"What?" We'd decided it would be weird for him to call me anything else. I was so damn relieved he didn't want to call me Ashton because I knew it was only a matter of time before the whole freaking universe was going to be shouting that name. And I didn't mean that because people loved me — no, I meant that just because once reporters had a bone it was chewed on until only tiny shreds remained, once the bone disappeared, they'd just cough it up and start the process all over again.

"Thanks for trusting me with her."

I couldn't look at him.

So I looked at the floor. "Just, don't freak her out. She likes to play board games, but you have to move the pieces for her. And the only reason I trust you with her is because…well, you're you. Besides, she has a thing for guys with light hair and dimples."

Wes threw his head back and laughed. "She has good taste, that's what you mean."

I joined in. "Yeah man, the best."

"So I'll see you later at the home then?"

"Yeah." I scratched the back of my head. Why the hell was I so nervous? I felt like a parent leaving my child for the first time. Is that what Princess had become to me? Wes was the first person other than Saylor who was going to meet her and I wasn't even going to be there to see it happen. But, the only way I could actually go out tonight and be with Saylor — be the man she needed me to be — was if I had someone I trusted keeping their eye on Princess.

And Wes did kind of come along with two of his best security.

Add them to the security we already had at the Home, and we had six guys who wouldn't let a soul through the doors if they as much as sneezed in the wrong direction.

"Go." Wes pointed to the door. "Just make sure your pants are still on by the end of the night."

"As opposed to what? Down by my ankles?"

"As opposed to what, he asks." Wes rolled his eyes. "Need I remind you how many compromising positions I've walked in on in this room?"

"Oh that." I waved my hand into the air. "Water under the bridge. I buried that mask."

"Huh?"

"You said to fuse them together." I flashed him a triumphant grin and waved goodbye. "So I only put together the good parts. Princess's favorites, Saylor's favorites, yours, Lisa's… the rest of that shit? It was better left behind. Baggage, you would say."

"Well, well, well." Wes clapped. "The student becomes the teacher."

"Bye, Sensei." The door clicked behind me to Wes's laughter. I had trouble fighting my own smile as I put on my baseball hat and walked down the hall.

So far, nobody had said much to me. Besides, who actually suspects that they've been living next door to a long lost celebrity for four years?

As unbelievable as it sounds, when you live in the real world, outside of Cali or New York, people don't give a shit. In LA people are constantly looking for famous people, hoping to catch one as if we're animals you have to trap or something.

But put me in Boise, Idaho? Seattle, Washington? They

don't expect it, so they just see a guy tatted up.

That being said, though, it had only been four years, so I kept the hat low, I didn't want anything ruining this night with Saylor.

I'd never pursued a girl before.

With Princess it had just happened.

And as for the rest of the girls I slept with – it was the only way to promise myself that Ashton Hyde was gone. He would have never done that. After all, Princess was the second girl I'd ever slept with, and I'd believed I was going to marry her. I'd thought she was it.

Recreating yourself via turning into a monster? Not the smartest idea I'd ever had – especially considering putting my whole body at risk.

Shit. I'd even messed up my own suicide.

I was too naïve to even know what the hell I was doing.

I'd cut my wrists the wrong way and hadn't bled out.

My first tattoos covered my scars – as best they could.

Self-consciously I rubbed the scar on my right wrist as the elevator doors closed in front of me.

Five minutes.

Around seventy-two steps later... I was in front of Saylor's door.

It was just a door.

But beyond that door?

Was not *just a girl.*

Inhaling, so I didn't forget to breathe and pass out, I knocked twice and waited.

The door swung open.

Saylor was wearing a short black dress with gold high heels. Her hair was pulled back in a low messy bun and her lipstick was red.

Red.

Red.

Red.

For some reason, repeating it in my head just made me all the more aroused over the fact that those perfect lips, her perfect mouth, was red, and it was going to be pressed right against mine.

That is if she didn't impale me with something first — we did have a tendency to fight a bit.

"You look…" I licked my lips and let my eyes roam over her body for a second time. "Stunning."

Her mouth widened into a smile.

Holy shit.

I coughed and looked away. Freaking gorgeous was more like it.

"Thank you." She stepped toward me, making me naturally step backward and nearly collide with someone else walking down the hall.

The girl almost face-planted on the wall then flipped me off.

"Sorry," I croaked.

Saylor smirked and locked the door to her room. "So, where are we going?"

"Ah." I grabbed her hand. "So the lady's curious."

"The lady's intrigued."

"Intrigued?" I stopped walking. "Not excited?"

Her poker face told me nothing.

I traced my finger along her smooth jaw line and then reached for the back of her head, pulling her into my space as I blew a kiss across her lips. "And now? Now are you excited?"

"You're getting warmer," she whispered.

I sucked on her bottom lip then let my mouth hover over hers as I answered, "I want you to be on fire. Not just warm, but blazing. Not intrigued, but impressed. Not just excited. I want you enthralled. And at the end of the night, what I really want…" I closed my eyes so I wouldn't kiss her again. "…is for those tears to be washed away from your memory for good."

"Why's that?" Her body arched toward me.

"I want old memories gone… bad ones. So I can create new ones. Ones so powerful that the old ones don't even stand a chance."

"So what are we waiting for?"

Smiling, I stepped back and reached for her hand. "Good point."

Chapter Forty-Two

He seemed normal but I had so many open-ended questions with absolutely no clue how to get the answers. I was torn between wanting to just have a normal date — and a desire to shake him until all the answers fell from his lips. Even if it hurt to hear, I had to know. —Saylor

Saylor

I let him kiss me.

Oh, who was I kidding? Not kissing him would have been a crime against my own body. I liked him. I more than liked him, and not kissing him just because I was still a bit hurt, upset? That was a total girl move. And I hated girls like that. The whiny types that withheld all things physical until they got their way. Yeah, it also meant that at the end of the day I might need a pint of chocolate ice cream from all the emotional damage done to me, but hey, at least I had one kiss.

I wasn't sure when I'd started looking at it like that.

Maybe it was when he sang his song yesterday afternoon.

Or maybe it was when my mom started talking about

endings and beginnings.

I was in charge of mine — my end or my beginning. I could end things with him now and hate myself for the rest of my life. Or I could choose to do the scary thing and jump off that cliff right along with him.

I chose the cliff.

And the minute I leapt — I knew it was right.

That's how risk works. You don't know it's the right choice until you're freefalling, and even then you still have butterflies — but at least you were the one to take that step over the ledge.

I wasn't pushed. I was proud of myself, for being able to come to that conclusion — pretty sure I had my mom to thank for that.

That was me. Going on a date with him.

In my head, I was sitting at the piano, authoring my own story, the story Gabe encouraged me to play. And the music — damn, but it was good.

"You seem deep in thought," Gabe said once we were a few minutes into our drive. I tried desperately not to look at him. I knew he was still the same guy, but he made me nervous. This guy was different than before, there was a sense of raw vulnerability about him. No layers remained. They'd been peeled back and destroyed.

"Dangerous. I know."

"I'm glad you said yes." Gabe cleared his throat, steering the car onto the freeway. "And I'm going to start right now."

"Start? What do you mean start?"

"When I was five, I had a pet rat. His name was Thomas. I wanted a train set. My parents got me a rat, go figure. Since the train set I wanted was Thomas, I just decided to name the rat that." He shrugged, "He got a tumor when I was six. We took him to the vet. He died in my arms."

"Gabe, I'm—"

"Thomas number two was a Chihuahua, who I can only

imagine was actually birthed in the pits of hell and then sent to earth to set about destroying every single piece of furniture and every shoe in my bedroom."

I covered my face with my hands to keep from laughing. "Did he die?"

"Of course not." Gabe's voice was irritated. "He's like a cat, has nine lives, maybe more. He's broken almost every bone in his tiny possessed little body, and is totally blind in one eye. He walks with a limp and sleeps in my old bedroom. Refuses to go anywhere else."

Why did I suddenly feel like buying him a nice big dog like a golden retriever or a collie?

"I got my start doing hair product commercials. My dad always wanted to be an actor but could never make it, so he pushed me into it at an early age. When I was thirteen and doing my first movie, he locked me in my trailer after one of the older actresses approached me and offered her services for oral sex."

"Uhhh."

"I was twelve freaking years old," he ground out. "And she was twice my age — literally. I hated my dad a bit after that. He said in the entertainment business I'd never survive if I was innocent."

"Gabe—"

"He introduced me to drugs. At sixteen I'd already done seven movies. I was on my way to burnout when I met Princess. I was dropping my second album and seriously starting to hate my life. It helped that I had Mel — Lisa. She'd had a crush on me when we were little. We were neighbors and all that, but I never even kissed her. I knew who I wanted. And she wanted me too."

He cleared his throat.

Rain pelted against the window.

"I believed in true love — I still do. Sunsets still take my breath away, pizza makes me a bit sick, but I'll eat it. I love dancing almost as much as I love playing instruments. I can play almost all instruments just in case you were wondering. It was how I passed my time when my dad would lock me in the room for going against his wishes."

"And your mom?" I asked, looking out the window. Where the heck was he taking me? We were officially outside of Seattle.

"She loves green." He shrugged. "Anything green. So she let him do what he wanted because she got a happy husband and lots of houses out of the deal."

He drove over the floating bridge into Bellevue.

"I had a twin sister," he whispered. "She died from SIDS. My mom says I was in the crib with her when it happened. Apparently she'd been dead for about three hours before my mom came in to check on us."

My breath hitched.

"She'd been drinking." Gabe swore and hit the steering wheel. "I hate the Oregon Ducks."

"Okay…"

"No. Seriously. Hate. Them." His muscle clenched. "It's the only damn sweatshirt Princess will wear."

I reached across the consul and grabbed Gabe's free hand, clenching it within my own. "Why is it the only sweatshirt she'll wear?

"Because…" His eyes were like glass, he blinked a few times. "It used to be mine. I was wearing it the night she hit the tree."

"Oh."

"It's the same way with her pink scarf. For some reason the only thing she remembers is that she forgot her pink scarf – not her helmet. I don't know why she fixates on certain things. But she has to have her pink scarf tied to her wheelchair at all times or she has a meltdown."

"And the singing?" I cleared my throat. "Is it the same with the singing?"

Gabe took the second Bellevue exit that led to the west side. Curious, I looked out the window and tried to keep my heart in check. He was cutting himself open, bleeding himself dry, and waiting for me to either accept or reject him.

He was brave.

Braver than me.

"The minute she hears my voice, she's taken to someplace safe, different. Stupid, right?"

I turned and looked at him, focused on his full lips, gorgeous mouth, strong jaw.

"No." I squeezed his hand. "Not stupid. If positions were switched, I can imagine, hearing your voice would be the most soothing thing in the world. Like the quiet after a storm, the peace you crave in a lifetime full of noise. You're her peace."

Gabe nodded. "I guess that's something, right? I both destroy and bring peace?"

"You didn't cause the destruction, Gabe. You were just an unfortunate victim — and sometimes that's worse than being the cause."

He nodded, but didn't say anything as he drove the car around a curvy road and then pulled up to an immaculate house.

"Where are we?"

Gabe turned off the car and stared straight ahead. "Seattle was far enough away that it made sense to disappear here, but..." His nostrils flared. "She'd seen this thing on HGTV about homes in Bellevue and fell in love."

I looked back at the house. My heart pounded. "Gabe..."

"I bought it." He clenched the keys in his hand. "For her. I bought it for her."

I didn't want to know, yet I had to. "Was she able to see it, before?"

"No." Gabe's voice was filled with pain. "She never saw it. I was going to fly her up here as a surprise."

We sat in silence. He stared at the house. I stared at him.

"So." Gabe nodded. "This is it. You know how people always come with baggage? I don't have baggage. I have a freaking house. I don't have a closet full of skeletons. I have seven bedrooms full of them. And I can literally walk up those stairs and open the door and let you see all of them, but I'll have nothing left. This is the last possible thing I have protecting myself. I have no more masks, no more façades, no jokes, no personalities, nothing. Absolutely nothing. This house? This is it."

I released his hand and reached for the door. "Well, what are you waiting for?"

His head snapped to the side, his eyes narrowing in disbelief. "Pardon?"

"We didn't drive all the way out here to stare at a house." I stepped out onto the gravel. "We're going in."

"Are you sure you want to do that?" Gabe asked, doubt lacing his every word. "This is heavy stuff, Saylor. I wouldn't blame you for running, for getting back into that car and deciding it wasn't worth it."

"I'm falling." I shrugged. "Not fallen, as in I've already landed, but falling, in the process. I'm falling with you, not jumping after you. Don't you think it's about time you let someone share the load?" I offered a small smile. "Besides, who actually likes jumping out of a plane by themselves? Tandem, all the way."

"One day…" Gabe whispered. "When my heart is mine again. When I'm not sharing it with a dying girl… I'll give you everything."

"Gabe," I said, sighing. "Right now? I'm perfectly happy with the pieces. No matter how broken they may be."

"Damn, you really mean that, don't you?"

"Yeah. I do." I reached for him.

He took my hand without hesitation. We walked up the stairs together, slowly approaching a house that was getting bigger and bigger by the second.

From the outside, it was a two story masterpiece. He put the key in the lock and the door creaked open.

He turned the lights on.

And I gasped.

It wasn't just beautiful, it was out of this world. Like something I'd only ever seen on TV or in the movies.

Exposed wood beams lined the ceiling, creating a trail from the living room into an open floor plan kitchen. The colors were a combination of white and wood. A stone and copper fireplace dominated the center of the room with a plush white couch wrapped halfway around the front. Splashes of red — throw pillows and blankets — decorated the living room area. I stepped further into the hall and saw another open room, this one with vaulted ceilings.

And a baby grand piano waited in the middle.

"Afraid?" Gabe's voice whispered in my ear as he wrapped his arms around me from behind.

"Ha." I exhaled and stared, a bit jealous that he had his own practice room — a happy room I could imagine myself sitting in for hours on end while the roaring fireplace crackled in the background.

It wasn't until I took my eyes off the piano that I noticed what was on the walls. It was like watching a movie without sound. Black and white pictures went from left to right, all the way across the room.

Slowly, I walked up to the first one. Gabe and Kimmy were wrapped around each other kissing.

I touched her face — the same face he wiped the drool from every single day — and completely lost it.

The tears wouldn't stop coming. I cried, and I cried, and then I cried some more. I cried until my body shook. I cried until I had nothing left.

And Gabe held me.

The thing about people revealing their pain to you?

More often than not. It becomes your own.

And I was wrecked.

Chapter Forty-Three

Music without passion is merely noise. A life without passion? You may as well be dead. —Gabe H.

Gabe

"Shh." I pulled her into my arms and dragged her to the couch, then I turned on the fireplace in front of us. I was thanking my lucky stars that I'd had a cleaning crew go through the house and air everything out so we weren't sitting on dust. "You know, you're going to give me a complex. I'm supposed to be making it so you don't cry."

Saylor sniffled against my chest, not raising her head. "I'm so sorry. I just—"

"What?"

"You found the one. At the right time. The girl you loved. The girl you wanted everything with. You were so brave, so... raw. You gave her everything and..." Saylor's breath hitched. "Looking at pictures of you guys together... it destroys me, Gabe. It's not fair."

I closed my eyes and held her tighter. "I know."

"It's not fair," she repeated. "It's not fair that I'm here and she isn't. It's not fair that you have to show me your house and that she can't be the one to make cookies for you every Christmas. She's never going to come through those doors and walk into your embrace. That is never going to happen."

I fought the tears clogging in my throat. "I know."

"I feel unworthy," Saylor whispered. "To see this. To be with you. It should be her."

"You're not unworthy." I stroked her arm. "I'm sharing this with you. You, Saylor." I pried her away from my chest so I could look into her clear blue eyes. "The thing about life? It never goes as planned. But, right now, in this moment, with you in my arms. I wouldn't want it any other way. Please believe me when I say that. This moment — it's a gift. Just by being here, you're making that pain a little less sharp."

A tear slid down her cheek.

"Number four," Saylor whispered.

"What?" I watched her lips as she spoke.

"Tear number four. You just made up for it."

"By making you cry more?" I touched my forehead to hers.

"No." Saylor cupped the back of my head. "By understanding the tears in the first place."

With a shaky voice I answered, "They weren't because of me."

"No."

"They're for me."

"Yeah. A tear for a tear," she said softly. "Isn't that what you said?"

I didn't trust myself to speak. I could only nod as I watched the flames lick wildly in the fireplace.

After a few minutes of silence, I looked down at Saylor. Her hot little dress and high heels were still on.

We were alone in an amazing house that I hadn't visited in four years.

And we were sitting on a couch.

Depressed.

"Am I the worst date ever?" I blurted.

Saylor's head jerked up, a watery smile appeared, "Well..."

"No more tears." I got up and marched toward the kitchen. "You've seen the house. You know the story. Now we're going to be awesome."

"Oh?" Her eyebrows shot up as her gaze followed me into the kitchen.

I didn't really know my way around anywhere, but I did know that the staff had stocked food in the pantry and that a few menus for takeout were lying around just in case we got hungry.

"Next person who cries has to run around outside naked," I declared, lifting the menus into the air.

Saylor tilted her head. "You do realize that just makes me want you to cry right?"

I smirked. "There are easier ways to get me naked, honey."

She blushed and looked down at her hands.

"Aw, the pink pony's making a comeback," I teased.

Saylor crossed her arms, and lifted her head, eyes sparkling with indignation. "It was purple."

"A pony's a pony — you still ride it."

Saylor's face flamed red.

"Gotcha." I winked.

"You're too confident for your own good." She scowled.

"Does the fact that I slept with my rat next to my bed until he died make me any less confident sounding?"

"No."

"I hate spiders?" I offered. "And I'm slightly terrified of them?"

Saylor took a few steps toward my spot in the kitchen. "How afraid? Like if a small spider skittered across the floor, what would happen?"

"I'd scream and squash its hairy ass."

"Hmm." She tapped her chin and took a few more steps, "And if I put a spider in your bed?"

"I'd weep," I answered honestly. "Honest to God tears. And then I'd scream and squash its hairy ass."

She flashed a grin and leaned against the counter, which meant her entire body was outlined by the back glow of the fireplace. I swallowed the dryness in my throat. "And if I was dressed as a spider?"

My eyes didn't leave hers when I answered, "I'd pin you against the floor, strip the costume off and then attempt not to squash your very pretty, gorgeous, infuriating ass."

I wasn't sure who reached for whom first.

But all of a sudden our bodies collided, our mouths met in a frenzy. I lifted her onto the countertop as she wrapped her legs around my waist. With a moan, her body trembled beneath my touch. I cupped her face with one hand while I steadied her body with the other. I wanted to kiss her until my lips were sore, until my mouth was swollen, until my body was spent, so basically I wanted to kiss her until forever.

This kiss was different.

A lifetime of kisses — and nothing compared to her mouth, her touch, her taste.

It was shattering to realize how incredible of a pull another human being could have on someone — just by touching them.

But Saylor wasn't just touching me, she was enveloping me with her body, she wasn't just kissing me, she was sharing her soul with me. Saylor was showing me what words couldn't express.

Her tongue drove me wild as it swirled around mine — I dug my hand into her hair grabbing a fistful of it as I tried to pull her tighter against my body.

Saylor's arms tightened around my neck as the sensation

of our bodies colliding, rubbing against each other, nearly had me passing out.

Every touch was like getting permanently branded.

She pulled back, her eyes glazed.

I stared at her.

She stared at me.

Weird how people can communicate without saying one damn word. Saylor, slowly, pried herself from my body and hopped off the counter, then grabbed my hand and dragged me to the couch.

I followed. There wasn't any other option.

When we reached the couch. I didn't hesitate to pull her into my arms and fall backward onto it so that she was on top of me.

We started kissing again.

This time slower. I took my time tasting her, exploring every inch of her mouth until I thought I was going to go insane. She responded to my every touch, with little sighs.

It was killing me.

"Say…" I nipped her upper lip.

"Don't stop," she whispered. "New memories, Gabe. In this house, just you and me."

I pushed the ghosts of Kimmy away from my mind and focused on the present. Focused on Saylor, and only Saylor, as we kept kissing. I pushed my hand against her stomach, brushing my knuckles against her ribs. Saylor gasped. I tore my mouth away from hers, making eye contact with her briefly before she tangled her hands in my hair and pulled me hard against her mouth again. Another kiss, this one stronger, hungrier, deeper. Her mouth moved from my mouth to my ear, her hot breath giving me chills all the way down my spine. I was consumed by her, each touch and kiss made it harder for me to keep clothing between us — when all I wanted was to make her mine.

My hands pushed against her bare skin, inching higher

and higher, a soft moan escaped. My body cried out, and I slowly pulled back the pressure of my kiss, because as hard as it was, each kiss also reminded me that I wouldn't be giving Saylor everything I had — because I wasn't in possession of everything right now.

Because how could I truly take from Saylor? How could I truly give myself to her? When part of my heart was still missing?

And that was the problem.

My heart had never been engaged with other girls and one night stands. But with Saylor? I was pretty sure had I had my heart in the palm of my hand I would have handed it to her then lain prostrate on the floor. Just hoping, begging, for her to accept it even though it didn't look like other hearts. Even though it was damaged.

Saylor's hands dug into the sides of my body as she moved on top of me. H-o-o-ly shit. This wasn't going to end well.

"Say—" I was cut off by another kiss. "Saylor, we can't. I can't sleep with you."

She pulled back, a smile forming at her swollen mouth, "Who said anything about sleep?"

"No." Why the hell was my face heating up? "I mean we can't have sex."

Her smile returned. "Did I tell you I was going to have sex with you?"

"Well… no." Damn it.

"So?" She leaned down until her breasts were brushing against my chest. Hell. Turn on the AC already. Great plan, Gabe. A fireplace? What was I thinking?

"So." I licked my lips. "I'm confused."

"You ever make out?" She kissed me softly. "Do you ever just kiss to kiss?"

"No."

"You should." She brushed another kiss on my neck. I

groaned, grabbing her body and pulling her hard against me. "Sometimes, the appetizers are better than the main course."

At that, I laughed. "Oh yeah? Prove it." I put my hands behind my head and winked.

"Rule number one." She traced the outline of my jaw with her finger. "Never let your guard down."

"Why's that?"

"Because I may just take you up on your offer." With a smirk she pushed up my shirt and started licking.

Licking.

She was licking me.

And I was liking it.

Way. Too. Much.

"Say—"

And then she bit me, right where she'd licked me. There was sucking, something that I could only describe as swirling even though I knew it sounded insane. And more kissing.

I fought to keep my hips from driving toward her — from making this more than just kissing.

Her teeth nipped at my lower stomach where my jeans met skin, and then that damn tongue of hers went to work again.

I couldn't focus on anything because my vision kept going blurry, so I closed my eyes.

Her hands dipped behind me, gripping my ass and then gripping harder as her fingers dug into flesh and then started to slowly massage.

Erotic, yes. Relaxing, even more so.

And before I knew it. I was getting sleepy. Not because I wasn't as turned on as hell, but because she was just — everywhere. I felt her everywhere. I was like a fat happy cow before getting sacrificed. No doubt about it, I was going to most likely explode from want.

But in that moment… I savored every damn touch.

And allowed myself to succumb — to her.

Chapter Forty-Four

Funny — I'd never realized how stressed out Gabe was until I finally saw him resting. His face was slack, his jaw unclenched. He was male beauty personified — and all mine. For now, at least. For now, he was mine. —Saylor

Saylor

The bastard fell asleep.

I laughed softly and tucked my body next to his on the couch. My stomach was grumbling, but I decided to nap for a bit with him before ordering food. The minute my head fell against his chest, he wrapped his arms around me.

Gabe's mouth found mine again.

We kissed, lazily kissed, neither one of us reached for each other, we merely lay there and let our lips graze and nip at one another.

It felt beautiful.

If our first kiss was a chaotic symphony exploding with all the wrong notes in the wrong places — our third kiss? Our fourth? Were a song. A very pretty, perfectly played, song.

"I miss her," he whispered against my hair. "I miss her so much. How can I be so happy to be with you, to be in your arms? How can I want you so badly? Yet still miss her?" Gabe's eyes didn't open, if anything he squeezed them shut tighter and pulled me against him.

"Because…" I played with his golden hair, in the firelight it looked like a halo. "She was your first love, and every day you see her face you're reminded that although she's still here — she isn't."

Gabe sighed. "I feel like my heart's getting ripped in two. I feel like one day you're going to wake up and realize that this drama isn't worth it. That I'm not worth it. Saylor, tell me tomorrow things won't be different."

"But they will be." I sighed and tucked the hair behind his ear. "Because the skeletons are finally gone, the scales from people's eyes are going to eventually be lifted, and you're going to have to make a choice."

He shuddered. "I would never choose her over you."

"But Gabe…" I felt the tears well in my eyes. "You already have. Even if it wasn't on purpose — you already have."

His eyes flashed open. I could tell he wanted to argue with me just by the way his eyes bored into mine as if pleading for me to take it back. But that's the thing with truth — once you speak it out loud…

It's out there.

He kissed my forehead. "I could love you."

"So you keep saying." I offered a sad smile. "But for what it's worth. I could love you too."

We didn't eat.

We spent the rest of the night kissing, falling asleep, only to wake up kissing again. I had no idea what time it even was. The house felt like a fairy tale. I imagined if we stayed there forever we'd be happy — we'd still be kissing — and we'd be happy, but that wasn't life.

The universe must have heard my thoughts because Gabe's cell started buzzing in his pocket.

With a curse he pulled it out. "Hey, Wes, sorry… fell asleep."

Gabe closed his eyes and let out a long sigh.

"What channel?"

Dread exploded all over my body as Gabe slowly rose from the couch, walked over to the large flatscreen, and grabbed the remote.

Color invaded the living room.

The picture on the screen took my breath away. It was one of Kimmy before the accident, so full of life, so gorgeous it hurt to look at her. And then a photo of Ashton Hyde.

And finally a photo of Gabe's family with the caption. "Devastated Father finally reaches out to long lost son."

"He's finally come home!" Gabe's dad said on the TV screen. "The prodigal has returned after our insistence that he allow us to be a part of his life again. We're so saddened that he felt the need to go to such extremes to push us and the rest of his beloved friends and fans from his life. But know this, Ashton Hyde." His dad stared through the TV screen. "Nothing will ever be the same. Now that you've returned — we won't ever let you go."

Gabe sank to the floor on his knees.

I ran to him, wrapping my arms around him as I rocked him back and forth. "It's going to be fine," I whispered. Even though I knew it was a lie. The thing about lies? They only work if the other person doesn't know the truth. And we both knew.

Nothing. Would ever. Be the same.

Chapter Forty-Five

Life was passing me by. I was alive, but not awake. I hadn't been awake in a really long time. Funny, I thought the prince was supposed to wake Sleeping Beauty. Never in my wildest dreams could I have imagined that I wasn't the dragon or the prince. But the one in need of a rescue so epic — that my world shattered. The scary thing about waking up? You're reminded how much of your life was a nightmare — and again remember why you went to sleep in the first place. —Gabe H.

Gabe

The lights had never bothered me. They flashed in my face, made me feel like I was going to have a seizure, but it was a necessary evil. People had a fascination with pictures — because then they could fantasize about what it would be like to be with me, to see me in the flesh.

I swore to destroy every last picture of myself. But when that didn't work. I destroyed the perfect image they had of me. It was the only way.

And now I was regretting it.

Because the Ashton Hyde they wanted to take pictures of? He didn't exist anymore.

But for the first time in four years, I was okay with that. I was okay with myself… who I was.

I gripped Saylor's hand in mine as we drove toward the group home. After watching the morning news show. I knew things would get crazy with the media. I needed to make sure that everything would be set up to protect Princess from reporters.

Wes, being Wes, said he was already on top of things, which I could only assume meant he'd called his dad and brought in the US Army or something equally huge. He didn't do anything half-assed. Hell, I wouldn't be surprised if the SWAT team was standing outside the group home with Tasers set.

Saylor didn't say much, but I kept squeezing her hand. I wasn't sure if it was because I needed comfort or because I was trying to comfort her. Her lips were drawn into a smile, but I could tell she was putting on a face for me.

Which sucked, because how many times had I been on the offering end of that same smile? Giving a fake smile in order to make people feel good? Felt like hell.

"We're here." I pulled the BMW into the parking spot. Both of us were still wearing our clothes from the night before. When Wes had called it was five in the morning and I'd wanted to get to the home right away.

"We are." Saylor looked around.

The sun was just beginning to rise over the Sound. There were only two or three reporters in front of the Home. No doubt, hundreds would be staked out later.

"I want to stay in the car," I admitted. "I want to turn around and go back to the house and lock myself in there with you."

Saylor turned and looked at me, her fake smile turning real, revealing her perfect pink mouth. "Let's pretend."

"Alright." I wasn't sure what she was getting at.

"We met at college," Saylor began, licking her lips. "We collided in the hallway and immediately hated each other."

"Because you were snarky." I smirked.

She giggled. "Only because you were cocky and made fun of me."

"True." The sun peeked over the mountains. "And I couldn't get you out of my mind."

"So days later, when we met again, it was chaotic because we both despised and intrigued one another," she continued.

"I pursued."

"Oh?" Her eyebrows arched.

"Yeah." I nodded. "I pursued… wanting you, needing you. I went about it all wrong, as most guys do, thinking that if I could just make you hate me you'd leave me alone to wallow."

"Silly boys, that never works," Saylor whispered, her eyes welling with tears.

"Never." I shook my head and clenched her hand. "Because we forget that hate and love are sometimes impossible to tell apart." My voice went hoarse. "And then I fell."

"Me too."

"I took you out on… ten dates?"

"Wow!" Saylor laughed. God, I could listen to her laugh forever. It was deep and sounded real, not fake or high pitched. "Someone's optimistic."

"And we hung out every second of every day."

"Made music together." Saylor grinned. "For hours on end."

"Kissed." I sighed. "For hours on end."

"And what started out as hate…" I shrugged. "…blossomed into full out love. And neither of us wanted to be without the another."

"So we stayed." Saylor's eyes watered as she looked at

the sun rising, lighting up the inside of the car. "We stayed that way forever."

"In our house." I focused my attention on the Sound and squeezed her hand as tight as I possibly could.

"And lived…" Saylor whispered. "…happily ever after."

"Yeah." I nodded. "Happily ever after."

"It would have been a great story." Saylor sniffled, tears streaming down her face.

"With a killer ending." I cupped her face in my hands.

"Too bad it's just a story." She bit her lower lip and shrugged as more tears dripped over her lips.

"Yeah." Something pierced my heart, made it hurt so damn bad I thought I was going to die right on the spot.

"Gabe…" Saylor kissed my mouth. "For what it's worth, I still want to be in the story, even if it means… I walk away empty-handed. Even if it means I walk away without my heart. You've made your choice. And I've made mine."

"Even if it means you're left with nothing?" I asked.

"Just because the girl doesn't end up with the boy in the end — doesn't mean she ends up with nothing. Life's a gift. I just want to share yours, no matter how small the pieces that are shared may be."

"God…" I was going to swear, but her mouth covered mine.

"God…" Saylor tapped my chin. "Wrote the ending before the beginning was ever even realized." She shrugged. "Let's write our story the same way."

I nodded and reached for the door. Because really what else could I say to make everything better?

She knew as well as I did that the minute we both got out of the car, Gabe would officially be nothing but a memory. The normal college life, walking around the home and helping out.

Life would change.

And the biggest change would be that people finally knew about Kimmy. They finally knew she was alive, and would soon know we were engaged.

Which left Saylor out of the picture.

I was torn. Because although my heart belonged to another — I really wished that it belonged to her.

Because what I had with Saylor it was a living breathing thing, and what I had with Kimmy? It was like trying to revive something that had been dead a long time.

I loved her — but I wasn't in love with her. Yet my heart wouldn't allow me to completely let go. It hurt too much to think about. No matter which direction I walked in — it hurt.

"Ashton!" A reporter charged toward me. Saylor gripped my hand the whole time I walked slowly toward the building. "Ashton, tell us. Is it true? Have you been secretly hiding out in Seattle? Going to school and passing off as a student all these years? And your *fiancée*? Rumors were she passed away in an accident. What really happened all those years ago?"

I sighed as the weight of the world nestled onto my shoulders. "I'll answer all your questions." I offered a polite nod. "But right now, I really need to check on my *fiancée* — she's been sick, and that trumps giving you guys a story. Please, respect my privacy a little while longer."

The reporter's eyes narrowed. "Who's this?" She pointed to Saylor, who was still at my side.

I opened my mouth to say… I don't know what the hell I was going to say. My girlfriend? Because that would sound all kinds of horrible, considering my *fiancée* was lying inside the home not a hundred feet away from us.

"His best friend." Saylor smiled warmly.

"Rumor has it your best friend is Wes Michels." The lady smirked.

"What is this, first grade?" another reporter lashed out. "He can have two best friends."

"Mike." I breathed a sigh of relief. I'd known him since I'd gotten my start. He was a reporter for HollyWood Today and then went into retirement. "I thought—"

"I've lived up here for years Ashton. Thought I'd come out of retirement and see how my favorite kid was doing."

The other reporters were silent as Mike and I talked.

I slapped him on the shoulder. "You." I nodded as relief started tampering down the adrenaline that was surging through me. "You I'll talk to."

"Good." His eyes crinkled. "Kimmy would have liked that."

"Yeah." I bit my lip to keep from crumbling. "She would have."

"Go on in, son." Mike nodded. "I'll take care of the swarms out here." He put a card in my hand and smiled. "When you're ready, we'll do it however you want. Your terms, Ashton. Don't let them make you into something you're not."

I clenched the card like a lifeline as I stared at Mike's name and contact info stamped on front. Then I shoved it into my jeans pocket.

Saylor was silent as security let us by. The Home looked the same, but the expressions on everyone else's face? Different.

Martha walked up and sighed. "I'm sorry. Short of smashing in all the TVs and stealing everyone's computers for the day, I couldn't keep them from finding out."

"Well…" I sighed. "Everything has an expiration date, right?"

"Right." Martha's eyes moved to Saylor standing next to me and then warmed. "Glad to see you back, young lady."

"Gabe…" Wes was walking down the hall like he was marching to war. "She's been asking about you – I don't know if Martha said anything but, the infection it's… it's getting worse, man."

Wordlessly, Saylor and I walked down the hall with Martha and Gabe. Princess was lying in her bed with an oxygen mask over her nose and mouth.

Saylor's breath hitched.

"Helps her breathe," Wes explained. "But the coughing makes it difficult. I swear I didn't sleep at all last night. Every time she coughed sounded like..." His voice trailed off as he spread his hands helplessly.

"The last." I sighed.

"Yeah." Wes rubbed his face with his hands. "Her body isn't responding. It's like she's..."

"Princess?" I let go of Saylor's hand and walked toward the bed. Her eyes flickered open.

She smiled and said my name fogging up the oxygen mask.

"You look like you've seen better days." I smiled and sat on the bed.

She nodded.

"You feeling better?"

Nothing. No nod. Nothing. The light in her eyes died a bit, and then she started coughing out of control. I held the mask in place and helped her as best I could. By the time she was done coughing, a wheezing took the place of her breathing, making it sound like she was choking.

I turned around to see Saylor and Wes were gone.

Martha's eyes were sad. "I think..." She placed her hand on her chest. "Gabe, I think it's time to call hospice."

"What?" I stood. "Do you think it's that bad?"

"The infection is worse." Martha sighed heavily. "I've seen healthy individuals die from this type of infection, not to mention she's already in a weakened state. I just think it would be wise to call them. In the end, it's your call. And hospice doesn't necessarily mean the end. People come off hospice all the time."

Then why did it feel like I was sentencing her to death?

"I need to think about it," I answered honestly.

"I figured." Martha smiled. "Just let me know once you decide."

She left me alone with Princess.

Her form was so frail. Funny, I never really said Kimmy in my head anymore. To me she was simply Princess. Kimmy — the girl I had known — was gone. But she had left me with a gift in the form of a princess.

A princess sent from heaven.

I took her hand in mine, then kissed it. "You're beautiful, you know that?"

Her eyes welled with tears.

"To me," I whispered, my lips grazing her hand, "you will always be the most beautiful thing I have ever had the pleasure of laying my eyes on."

A single tear spilled over and rolled down Princess's face.

"You really are a princess, you know that? Like the ones from the stories I read you. So, I have one question, my little Princess. Will you let the prince rescue you? Can I take you on my horse to my castle? Can I fight for you, even when you won't fight for yourself? Will you let me love you, even when you're sick and broken? Will you let me keep the vow I made to you all those years ago?"

Her eyes fluttered shut.

"Gabe?" Wes's voice sounded from the hallway. "More reporters just came. I know this is a lot to take in one day, but the sooner you break your silence, the better it will be. Trust me."

"Right." I swallowed the tears thickening around my throat and reached into my pocket. "Do me a favor?"

"Anything." Wes walked into the room.

I handed him the card. "Call him and set up the interview. We can do it here at the Home. I just… I need to get it over with."

Wes took the card. "Done."

"Where's Saylor?"

Wes's eyes were sad as he answered. "She wanted to give you guys some privacy. Martha said coffee was the best way to start a morning, so yeah, she left. She'll be back though."

My eyes never left his. "That's what I'm afraid of."

"Let her," Wes commanded, his voice firm. "Let her be that person for you. She knows what she's getting into, and she's still here. That's saying something."

"I have nothing to give her." Clenching my hands into fists, I tried not to cringe as I recognized the unmistakable sound of desperation in my voice.

"Who said you had to give her anything?" Wes answered and walked out of the room.

Chapter Forty-Six

You know you're in love with someone when the idea of them being in love with someone else doesn't just wreck you, it invades every part of your being. Yet, how could I be upset that Gabe loved her? When his love for her was one of the very reasons I loved him? — Saylor

Saylor

The coffee was bitter.

It didn't help.

I took a seat on the cold metal chair and tapped my nails against the coffee mug. An hour went by, and finally someone walked into the tiny hospitality room.

"Found you." Lisa winked then plopped down next to me. "So are we wallowing or are we just… thinking?"

I smiled. "A little bit of both."

"He loves you." Lisa's eyes didn't meet mine. "For what it's worth, I've known Ashton all my life, and he loves you, loves you something fierce." She covered my hand with hers, "You may be sharing him for now, but considering the circumstances, I can't imagine a better person to be sharing him with. And that's the truth. Kimmy… she would have loved you."

For some reason that made me want to cry. "What was she like?"

"Talented." Lisa removed her hand. "Loud." Laughing, she rose and grabbed her own cup of coffee. "I looked up to her so much. It's funny, even though she and Ashton had something special, they never left me out, even though I was two years younger and ridiculously naïve."

"Freshman?" Everything sort of clicked. "You just started school though."

Lisa's face darkened. "Yeah, well, I didn't go to school right away. I mean, it was my idea to help Ashton escape everything, but I didn't follow him right away. I um, I stayed in LA for a bit."

"And stopped modeling?" I asked. "What happened?"

"I think," she said, taking a seat, "that we've had enough sad stories for one day." Her smile returned. "I just wanted to let you know — just in case you were having doubts — he needs you."

"Thank you." The room fell silent.

"I overheard them talking about hospice," Lisa mumbled. "I hope that doesn't mean what I think it does."

"It does." Another voice chimed in. Kiersten walked into the room, looking about as crappy as I felt, and sat at the table. "I just talked with Wes. The infection's getting worse, not better. I just… I don't know. I wish there was something we could do." Her eyes met mine. "When Wes went through his surgery and everything, at least he knew we were present, you know? He was able to talk with us, cry with us." Her voice wavered. "But Kimmy? Or Princess? She's hurt and doesn't know why. All she knows is Gabe's sad and she can't figure out why. You know? I just wish we could give her happiness."

I listened intently, my mind reeling. What could we do?

How could we make it easier? Not that it would ever be easy.

"I think—" I croaked out. Then I cleared my throat and tried again. "I think I have an idea."

Kiersten's and Lisa's heads both snapped up.

"But, I need your help, and Kiersten, we're going to need Wes."

Kiersten grinned. "We always need Wes. He's like a superhero."

I had to agree with her. The man was probably Batman in another life or something.

"Okay." I leaned forward. "This is what we're going to do."

****

After the girls and I talked, we decided to go grab lunch at the cafeteria and then find Gabe.

He was in the game room with that man he'd seen earlier, Mike. Wes was there too. All three of them looked tense.

A camera crew was setting up, and one of the assistants was putting a microphone on Gabe.

"Fifteen minutes." Gabe spoke slowly. "I can do fifteen minutes before I crack. My strength… it's going to get zapped fast."

"Alright." Mike cleared his throat. "Just talk, Ashton, and I'll make sure the story gets told the way you want it told."

"Has he heard from his dad?" Lisa whispered in my ear.

"No." I sighed. "At least not that I know of. After this morning I'm pretty sure the last person he wants to see is his dad."

Lisa snorted. "Ain't that the truth. I'd probably run him over with my car, so it's probably good he's hiding out."

"Ready?" Mike asked.

Gabe's eyes flickered to mine, his mouth relaxed.

I licked my lips and mouthed, "I see you."

His shoulders instantly relaxed as he mouthed back, "I see you."

"So, Ashton Hyde," Mike started. "It's been a while. Why don't you start off by telling us where you went?"

"I think the important part," Gabe said, nodding and leaning forward, "is not where I went but why I went." He looked down at the ground and then directly at the camera. "Boy gets famous, boy meets girl. Boy's world is flipped upside down, boy makes a bad choice, girl gets hurt. Boy's heart shatters inside his chest, but doesn't stop beating. It just continues to beat through the brokenness, even though each pump hurts like hell." Gabe sighed. "I disappeared because suddenly my life didn't matter anymore. It was all about hers. Getting her the best care, getting her away from the watchful eyes of the media."

"And her parents?"

Gabe sighed, his face darkened. "The minute she became what she is now, her parents bailed. They couldn't handle it. It was too hard, and they signed over guardianship to me. I have power of attorney, everything. We belong together. As if we'd actually gotten married."

Mike nodded. "Yet you never wed?"

"No." Gabe licked his lips. "We never did, but I took care of her — *take* care of her — as if I made those vows, even though I tried really hard to be something I wasn't."

"Meaning?"

"My escape was creating a new identity. I thought it would be easier. When I came to the Home I was just Ashton. When I went to college, I was Gabe, a completely different version of myself. I thought… I thought separating the two would make it less painful."

"Did it?" Mike leaned forward. "Did it make it less painful?"

"No." Gabe exhaled. "If anything, it made it worse, because Gabe fell in love with a girl too." His eyes met mine.

"But he shares a heart with Ashton, and Ashton's heart will always be in limbo — waiting for his princess to either wake up or go to sleep."

You could hear a pin drop in that room.

Lisa gripped my hand while Kiersten wrapped her arm around me. Gabe was already starting to sink lower into his chair. Emotionally, he was done.

"Let's talk about your father." Mike began, "What's this business about your parents wanting you home? What's the truth?"

"My father wants what used to be his cash cow…" Gabe shrugged. "Had he offered me love, acceptance, understanding, I would never have been put in the position I am now. I begged him to leave me in peace. Instead, he threatened the well-being of those I love the most. So that's why I'm here, giving this interview. He can say whatever he wants, but I want my fans, my family, my friends, to know the truth. I never left them because I hated them, I didn't lie because I wanted to. I did it because at the time, I didn't see any other choice. And every single one of my choices was made because of her."

"True love." Mike nodded his approval and smiled warmly. "It sounds like true love."

"Yeah."

"Ashton, anything else you want to say to your fans?"

"Thank you." Gabe's voice dropped. "For understanding."

"Alright, that's it." Mike waved at the camera crew while someone stood up and grabbed the microphone from Gabe.

Everyone started packing up while Wes approached Gabe and pulled him in for a tight hug then handed him a phone.

Gabe dialed a number, then held the phone to his ear, face tight. He looked ready to unleash on someone.

"Yeah, you wanted me parading in front of the media?

You got it. I suggest you watch Mike's show tonight. Should be on around six," he ground out. "And when you do, just know I did it all for you, you sick son of a bitch." He sliced the air with his hand and started pacing back and forth. "Shut up and listen, old man, because I'm saying this once. You and me are *done*. You can't hurt any of us anymore, and you and your sorry ass are going to fade into the pit of hell where you belong or I will hunt you down… and kill you."

He listened, but I couldn't tell what his dad was saying because Gabe's expression never changed. And then he cracked a smile. "You finished?" He waited a brief moment then nodded. "Good. Because those are the last words you will ever say to me, you money-hungry, piece-of-shit bastard." He stabbed the *end* button on the phone and looked like he was about to throw it when Wes intervened and grabbed it out of his hands.

The silence was broken by Wes chuckling. "If ever there was a time when a person needed a drink – now's that time."

"Here, here." Gabe's smile didn't reach his eyes, but when he looked at me, I could tell some of that weight was beginning to fall off.

I just hoped that by the time my surprise happened, he would be receptive and not angry that I'd overstepped my boundaries.

"Whiskey." Wes pointed us toward the door. "It's time for whiskey."

Chapter Forty-Seven

If God meant for us to carry baggage around, he would have made our skin have little pouches like kangaroos. Or maybe he would have just made it so that each and every one of us were born with huge-ass shoulders to carry the load. Clearly, we weren't made to carry the weight of the world, kinda makes you wonder why we do it anyway, huh? —Wes M.

Gabe

For the first time since Wes punched me, I drank. I didn't drink a ton, because I wasn't optimistic that my *body* would actually forget the trauma of that day, let alone my *mind*.

When Wes drove the car toward the dorms I asked him to turn around and drive me to the house instead.

Saylor offered to stay with me.

I turned her down.

Not because I didn't want company, but because I knew I was in bad shape. I was a bit buzzed, emotionally distraught, and she just looked so damn pretty that I knew I'd make a giant ass out of myself and either try to seduce her in order to feel better, or end up weeping on her shoulder. Maybe both.

At this point, it was a toss-up.

I still felt pissed. I still felt angry, but that's the thing about feelings. They don't have to force you to make choices you know may sound good at night but ruin you come morning.

So I went to bed — by myself.

I punched my pillow a few times, letting the alcohol soothe my nerves as I closed my eyes. Sleep. Sleep would cure everything. With a sigh, I let myself fall off the ledge into a deep slumber.

I would have followed her anywhere.

It's funny isn't it? People claim to know what love is — yet the minute they're given the opportunity to prove it — they bail.

I wish I could have bailed. I wish I could have walked away four years ago, then maybe I'd have the strength to walk away now. To look her in the eyes and say, "Sorry, but I can't do this again."

People rarely mean what they say. To me, sorry was just another word in the English language that people misused, just like love.

I love ice cream, I love pancakes, I love the color blue — bullshit, because when I said love — I meant I bled for you. When the word love actually leaves my lips — I'm speaking it into existence. I'm empowering my soul — I'm joining with yours.

I'd always heard about crossroads, how people are given choices in their lives, choices that either make or break them. I never realized that I'd be given that second chance. I never realized I'd fail to take it.

Her eyes pleaded with mine. My heart shattered in my chest, my lips moved to speak — to say anything to get her to understand the depth of what I was feeling, but I knew the minute I told her how I felt — it would be all over with.

My heart, my soul, it couldn't survive anything happening to her. If she wasn't in my world, my heart would stop. I knew it was killing her — because it was destroying me.

But going back to that life.

Even for her.

Was out of the question.

Falling in love, jumping out, even knowing full well that she'd catch me. It wasn't an option. Because everyone knows, when it comes to love, it's not the fall that hurts… it's the landing. And I knew it was only matter of time before she gave up on me too and allowed me to break.

Because in the end… that's all I was — broken. A shell of a human.

"I don't understand!" She beat against my chest with her fists, "You promised me! You promised you'd never leave!" Tears streamed down her face, the face I used to love. I closed my eyes then looked behind me as Saylor clenched the keys in her hand, waiting for my decision.

I was at a crossroads all right. One path led to my future — the other to my past and utter self destruction.

I couldn't look at her. I ignored every thread of feeling — and relished the pain of my heart breaking into a million pieces as I held out my hand in front of me, "You're right, I promised."

"Gabe!" Saylor yelled from behind me. "It doesn't have to be like this."

"Don't you see?" I said quietly without turning around. "It's always been like this. It will always be like this. I warned you."

"But—"

"Enough." I yelled, tears threatening to stream down my face. "I said enough. You should go."

I heard the door slam behind me.

"It's okay!" she said, cupping my face. "It will finally be okay!"

"Alright, Princess." I choked on the word. "Alright." I tightened the pink scarf around her neck and put my arm around her.

"Thanks." She sighed happily. "You always promised you'd take care of me. You can't leave. You can't—"

"I won't," I vowed, because it was my fault. Just like everything else.

"Can we go play now, Gabe?"

"Yeah, sweetheart, we can." I folded the blanket around her legs and pushed her wheelchair out of the room, knowing full well that I was choosing the wrong path — with every step I took.

I jerked awake in a cold wet sweat. It wasn't real. It was just a dream, but why did it *feel* so real? I really did believe all those things.

Sick to my stomach, I barely made it to the bathroom before I lost my dinner and those four shots Wes had fed me.

As the water flushed down the toilet, taking the remnants of Wes's good idea with it, I grabbed a towel and wiped my face, then sank down onto the cold tile.

I missed Saylor.

I also missed Princess.

I didn't want my choosing Princess to make it so that Saylor left me. How selfish could I be? I wanted both? Did I even deserve both? I knew I didn't, but that didn't make me want her any less. It didn't make the cravings for her kiss, for her touch, go away.

"Damn." I wiped my face again, stripped off my soaked clothes, and jumped into the shower. I'd only gotten six hours of sleep, but at least I'd slept.

Today was the day I had to decide whether or not to call hospice, and I still wasn't sure what I was going to do.

After my shower, I walked numbly across the cold slate floors that led into the kitchen.

The sun was just starting to peek over the city.

It was beautiful — I wished Saylor could be there to watch the sunrise with me. I wished so badly that I was whole for her.

Just as I was getting ready to turn on the coffee pot, the doorbell rang. Curious, I walked over and prepared myself for some low-life reporter who'd somehow discovered my secret house.

I opened the door.

It wasn't a reporter.

Saylor stood smiling at me. And Princess was with her, all cuddled up in her chair with blankets spread over her, an oxygen mask on her face.

A pretty woman in scrubs stood behind Princess, beaming.

"What are you doing here?" I asked, after finally discovering my voice again.

"I came here to bring Princess home." Saylor smiled.

"Home!" Princess shouted then started coughing. "Ashton, it's my home. From the picture!" She coughed some more as her chest rattled.

I knelt down on to meet her face to face. "Do you like it?"

She nodded. "Because you know why?"

"Why?" I asked.

"It's a castle," she whispered.

"Fit for a princess." Saylor finished.

I couldn't talk even if I wanted to. Without saying anything else, I opened the door wider and helped them pull the chair into the living room.

"The doctor's okay with this?" I asked.

"Well…" Saylor chewed her lower lip. "Let's just say Wes had to do his fair share of throwing his weight around and even then the only way they'd release her was if your signature was on the paperwork."

"So?" I crossed my arms. "How'd you do that?"

"Martha signed." Saylor cracked a smile. "She's pretty good at doing your signature too by the way. Oh, and she said if you fire her she'll hunt you down."

"Ha." I wiped my face with my hands. "She's the best head nurse we have. I'd never fire her."

"Good." Saylor's smile was wide and happy.

"I still can't believe you're here."

A throat cleared. I glanced to the right. The nurse was folding her arms over her chest, looking between the two of us with interest.

"Oh, and I almost forgot! This is the nurse who's going to be taking care of Princess, and even if you call hospice she won't leave."

The nurse tilted her head and held out her hand. "I'm Tara."

Saylor went and stood next to the lady then wrapped her arm around her shoulder. "Gabe, meet my mom."

Stunned, I could only stare and then hold out my hand. "Pleased to meet you, ma'am."

She nodded and politely took my hand. "Where would you like me to put Princess?"

"Ahh..." I sighed and looked around the house, momentarily confused as to which direction to take them. "Guest rooms are down here, let's go."

It wasn't until I was halfway down the hall that I realized Princess hadn't called me Parker — Ashton. She called me Ashton.

How was it possible for a heart to be so full of dread and excitement at the same time?

I paused in the hallway.

"Gabe?" Saylor turned. "Are you coming?"

"Yeah," I croaked. "Sorry."

Chapter Forty-Eight

Watching someone you love... die? There are no words for how broken that makes a person. It's like waking up from a bad dream only to find out that it's you reality, it's like watching sunlight fade from the sky, like watching death suck the one you love dry, and being powerless to stop it. You may as well try to stop the waves from rolling in, or the sun from rising. In the end, the waves will roll, the sun will set, and death will come. The only thing you have a choice in? How you deal with it...when it does. —Wes M.

Saylor

Two days later, I was sitting next to Gabe while he read to Princess. She was still failing so he'd called hospice in. One of the nurses from the main hospice team came a few times a day to check on things, but since my mom was constantly around they didn't stay. It wasn't normal for hospice to approve of something like this, but in the end, it was about the patient. And Gabe was high profile so they didn't mind. Besides, my mom wasn't just any nurse. She was amazing, the best at what she did.

Eric called at least thirty times a day — he was staying with his best friend and thought it was the coolest thing in the world that he could spend the night on school nights for the entire week.

And I was stressed.

Not because of the situation.

But because I couldn't focus on anything, not even my music. It was like, the passion that had once been there, the passion that Gabe had introduced me to, had been sucked dry. I literally had nothing to offer, nothing to give.

That evening, I walked into the piano room — the one littered with pictures of Gabe and Kimmy — and sat at the piano.

My fingertips grazed a few of the notes, but nothing. I felt nothing.

"Sometimes," Gabe's voice said from behind me. "It's not passion that brings forth the music, but desperation."

"I feel desperate," I whimpered. "I also feel a bit lost."

"Hmm." His hands moved to my shoulders. "Play it out."

"I can't even find the beginning, let alone the ending, Gabe."

"So?" He pushed down on my shoulders. "There's gotta be a middle in there somewhere. Find that."

I slammed my hands down onto the piano.

"Good," he encouraged.

I slammed them again.

"Better."

I lifted my hands to slam them a third time, then cracked as my hands fell gracefully across the keys, playing a song I didn't even remember practicing.

My hands flew across the piano as I played.

Body overheated, sweat started to pool at my temples, threatening to drip down my face.

By the time I was finished, my chest was heaving, like I'd

just run for hours without stopping.

"Beautiful." Gabe took a seat on the bench and faced me. "Thank you, for what you did, for what you're still doing."

I looked away. "I feel helpless."

"Don't we all?" He sighed. "Sometimes, there's really nothing to do but sit and stare at a wall... and wait for the inevitable."

"Stupid wall," I grumbled.

Gabe cracked a smile. "I miss you."

"I'm right here."

"You know what I mean."

I did. I wasn't avoiding him, but I was giving him space. Allowing him time to grieve, allowing him moments with her.

"I need you," he whispered. "Even when I'm with her, my thoughts are with you, my heart was never fully given back to me, but the pieces I still had, were stolen the minute I kissed you. The minute our lips met. So don't for a second think I don't need you. Don't think I don't want you. Because I do. I. Need. You." His mouth met mine, gently at first, and then with more urgency as his hands dug into my hair and tugged. "So beautiful."

"I think I love you," I blurted. "I'm so sorry." I collapsed against his chest. "I'm so sorry I love you. I'm sorry." I trembled. "I can't help it."

"That's romantic." He chuckled against my hair.

I smacked him, as tears threatened to pour. "I'm trying to apologize."

"For loving me?" Gabe asked, just before his mouth met my cheek. His eyes roamed over my body then my face. "Why the hell would you apologize for giving me one of the most treasured gifts in your possession?"

"Because..." My lips trembled. "It makes it harder on you."

"Isn't that for me to decide?" He tilted his head. "And just so you know, Saylor, you're mine. That love you feel for me? It gives me strength. Your face is all I see when I close my eyes, Saylor. So please don't apologize for your love — don't say you're sorry… when I'm not…"

I sighed and hugged him.

Gently, he pushed me away, and his hands fell onto the piano.

"Split in two," he sang, *"Loved by one, and then another. Pulled in a direction and then the other. If I could breathe you in, all of you, every day of my life, it wouldn't be enough. My heart was captive long ago — then you stole it away, you helped me grow. Now I'm staring at my crossroads with a choice to make, wondering how in the world I even thought there was one way to take."*

His hands flew over the piano, muscles tightened in his forearms as he leaned forward and continued singing.

"My biggest fear, is not the ending of this life, but going through it without you by my side." He repeated the chorus and closed his eyes, humming the haunting melody in such a way that I felt hypnotized.

"Letting her go will be the hardest thing I've ever had to do — but I'm doing it so I can say goodbye to her — and good morning to you. Tell me it's not too late to ask for a second." He smirked but continued singing. *"Third, fourth, tenth date."* His hands slowed. *"Loving you will always be easy because when I look into your eyes I know you see the real me, so be my love, be my rain, be my clouds, be my pain."*

"My biggest fear, is not the ending of this life, but going through it without you by my side." He stopped playing.

The room fell silent.

"That was beautiful."

Gabe turned. "It's your song."

"My song?" I repeated.

"Saylor's song." His smile returned. "I know it's not very creative, but, it's yours."

"No." I put my hand over his. "It's ours."

Gabe's smile lit up my world as he leaned in and kissed

me across the mouth.

"One more left," I whispered against his lips.

"One more?" He pulled back.

"Tear." I released a deep sigh "You only have one more to make up for."

"I thought that's what all this kissing was for." He teased.

Laughing, I kissed him harder as his arms wrapped around me. He lifted me into the air and pushed me against the wall, assaulting my lips with such force that I let out a pitiful moan. And then another as his tongue twisted around mine, retreated and then pushed forward again. The guy could kiss. Seriously. Could. Kiss.

My knees weakened as he pressed his hands to my stomach steadying me on my feet.

"Gabe? Saylor?" My mom's voice echoed down the hall.

I sighed in frustration as Gabe pulled back and bestowed one more kiss on my mouth.

"In here," he called.

Mom walked into the room, took one look at me, and stumbled a bit. Once she regained her posture, she cleared her throat. "The oxygen mask is helping her breathe during the day, the ventilator at night, but… Gabe, I don't have a good feeling. Her coloring is very pale, and her face…" Mom sighed. "What I'm trying to say is, she's transitioning. I can see it. I can feel it. She's starting to go."

"Go?" Gabe croaked.

"Gabe." Mom reached out and grabbed his hand firmly in hers. "Kimmy's dying, but you need to let her go. Do you understand? People… even in Kimmy's case, they try to hold on. They hold on and it's so very painful when they do. The best thing you can do for her is allow her to rest in peace. Give her permission not to be strong."

Gabe swayed on his feet. "I've been saying goodbye for years."

"Maybe this time…" Mom said wisely. "You should

mean it."

Chapter Forty-Nine

It was like the accident all over again. I felt powerless — until Saylor grabbed my hand and didn't let go. I used her strength — I used all of it. And for once I didn't feel guilty for needing someone else. She was my savior. —Gabe H.

Gabe

Saylor held my hand as we walked into the room. It was nearing midnight, so the room was blanketed in black.

The only sound was that of the machine breathing for Princess, and the noises from her chest that would follow.

The ventilator was attached via a tracheotomy so that she could still talk, but Princess had stopped talking two days ago.

Now, she just stared at the ceiling, as if waiting for someone to call her home.

"Princess?" I kept my voice quiet, kneeling in front of her bed. Grabbing her hand, I whispered, "Kimmy, sweetheart?"

Her head turned, just enough so I could see the whites of her eyes. With a smile she nodded. "Tired, Ashton."

"I know, sweetie," I croaked. "I know you are."

"Coughing." She sighed, her chest rattling. "Hate this."

"I know." Was that the only phrase I could speak? I squeezed her hand tighter even though I knew she couldn't feel it.

Her body was so broken that she couldn't even feel my reassurance as I held on for dear life. And now her spirit was following that same body into heaven.

"I love you," my voice cracked as tears trickled down my face. "But sweetheart, sometimes, it's okay to stop fighting."

"So tired," she repeated.

"A nap sounds good, doesn't it?" I said hoarsely. "Wouldn't that feel good, sweetheart? To take a nice, long nap?" My voice cracked as Saylor came up behind me, placing her hands on my shoulders.

"Yes…" Princess said slowly. "Ashton, will you sing me to sleep…" Her eyes welled with tears. "One more time?"

"Yeah," I whispered through my tight throat "I can do that."

"And Ashton?" she pleaded, her voice so weak I was sick to my stomach.

"What sweetheart?"

"Thanks for being my best friend." Her voice was so weak, it was hard to discern what she was saying.

I nodded. I couldn't talk. Whatever words were forming in my mind wouldn't make sense. They'd come out as a pitiful sob.

Without letting go of her hand, I leaned in and started to sing, while Tara went and slowly started pulling the equipment from Kimmy's throat and body.

"I love my Princess, my favorite girl. Every time I hear her laugh, I want to save the world — cause she's my, my, my girl." My voice cracked and wavered as my mind replayed images of our times together.

Our first movie, her laugh, her smile, the way she kissed me, the love she gave me. The gift of her life was more than I'd ever deserve.

I kept singing. *"My girl, my girl, she'll always be my girl, and when the tears fall from her eyes, I'll swear to never let her cry… never alone, never without me, never without us together. My girl, her and I will rule forever. My girl. She'll forever be my girl."*

Princess smiled and closed her eyes.

Her chest stopped moving.

I knew she was gone — and I knew in that moment that God had received another princess into his arms. It happened so swiftly so beautifully that had I not been watching her face, I would have never known that she'd slipped away.

A vision of Kimmy running through Heaven brought a sad smile to my face — she was gone. And she was finally whole.

Chapter Fifty

If I could take away his pain… If there was a way to transfer it from his soul onto mine. I would take it. Without hesitation I would take it all. Maybe that's how you know you love someone. When you actually feel each tear they cry as if they were your own. When you feel each cut, each bruise, each hit as if you're the one suffering. I bled for him. And in turn, he bled for her. Funny, how life comes full circle. —Saylor

Saylor

"She's gone." My mom said it softly, but it may as well have been a scream for as much as the announcement penetrated the room. "I'll make the call to hospice."

Slowly, Gabe released Kimmy's hand and stood. "I need to call her family, make an announcement, get the funeral arrangements—" He staggered, nearly collapsing on the floor.

Without thought, I grabbed his hand and led him down the hall until we were in the music room.

I closed the doors.

I locked them.

And led Gabe to the piano seat.

"We'll stay here…" I squeezed his hand. "…for as long as it takes."

"What?" His eyes were glassy with tears.

"For as long as it takes for the sorrow and pain to transfer into acceptance. I'll stay here. With you. By your side. I won't leave."

"Promise?"

"Vow." I placed his hands gently on the piano. "I vow."

"I can't." Gabe's hand were lifeless against the keys.

With strength I didn't even know I had within me, I put my hands over his and started playing. "Then let me play through you. Let me help you push through that pain until there's nothing left."

Gabe hung his head and let me help him.

Soon, his hands were gliding over the piano with such perfection, I was able to remove my own.

Tears collided with his hands. The drops caused his fingers to sometimes slip as he moved from one song to another.

Three hours we were in that room.

The only noise was the music Gabe played. Some sad songs, some happy ones, but in the end, sometimes words can't express what's in your soul. And talking to Gabe about what he just went through? Seemed silly compared to letting him bare it all to me with his music.

When the last note ended, Gabe stood.

I was sitting on the floor against the wall.

He walked over to me and dropped to his knees staring into my eyes for what felt like an eternity. Then he took my hands in his and pulled me to his chest. "I love you. If you remember nothing else for the rest of your life, if you fall and hit your head and can't remember my name, if you get so sick you're unrecognizable, if you hate me, if you're on your deathbed and can't manage to even lift a finger — remember this. I. Love. You. Always. Forever. Eternally. Is that kind of love something you can handle, Saylor?"

"I already am." I choked back the tears. "I love you too."

The room fell silent, only our ragged breathing kept me aware that time was passing. That it wasn't a dream.

"Come on." Gabe got up and held out his hand. "It's a new day."

I smiled and gripped his hand with mine. "It's a new beginning."

"That…" Gabe smiled and kissed my head. "It is."

Chapter Fifty-One

Death and love are the only two things that exist in this world that are strong enough to alter the course of your life, of your destiny. They either propel you or paralyze you. In the end, the choice is always yours. —Wes M.

Gabe

The funeral was over with before I even realized it started. I got up to say a few words and almost cracked. Then Saylor smiled.

And I was able to finish the eulogy.

I sang her song.

It was bittersweet. When I'd written her that song it had been during a time in my life when things were still so innocent. When she was still Kimmy to me, when I thought I would spend the rest of my existence in her arms.

If there was anything I learned in this situation it was that we weren't promised anything. All we had was moments strung together. Each one is over in a blink of an eye. I'd understood this to an extent when Wes went through his surgery. I'd been so bitter about that. So angry because it hit so close to home. Because I'd known I was doing a crappy job of pushing away my demons.

But now? Now I just wanted to do right.

And doing right started with Saylor.

"Hey," Saylor walked up and gave me a hug. We walked hand in hand out of the church. Oddly enough reporters had respected my wishes and laid off a bit. There were still cameras but the buzz felt different, as if they were mourning right along with me.

"You wanna go somewhere with me?" I asked.

Saylor shrugged. "Are you sure you're up for it?"

"Yeah." I nodded, feeling the corners of my mouth turn up in a smile. "I really am."

"'Kay." She squeezed my hand.

We said our goodbyes to Lisa, Wes, and Kiersten, and drove in silence down I5.

"Where are we going?" she asked.

"It's a surprise." I laughed. I actually laughed. Damn, it felt good. My hands were sweaty as I gripped the steering wheel and drove into downtown.

It was crowded for a Wednesday afternoon.

Saylor was silent as I parked as close to Pike Place Market as I could.

"Come on." I laughed again and slammed the door. A smile formed at her lips as she grabbed my hand and giggled a bit.

My heart hammered in my chest as we ran down the streets. What started as brisk walking turned into a full out run. I had no idea why. It just felt — necessary.

Once we reached the bottom of the hill right in front of Pike's Market. I held up my hand and went over to the spot.

"Fish." I pointed to the sign. "Our first date was fish."

Saylor burst out laughing. "So are you saying every date from here on out is going to involve fish?"

"Only the important ones." I winked and went up to the guys working the seafood for the morning. "I need salmon, a big-assed salmon."

The guy nodded. "Alright, you ready for it?"

"Oh…" I held up my hands. "I'm not catching it. She is." I pointed to Saylor.

She gaped. "What if I drop dinner?" She held up her hands.

"Chill, Nemo's not alive." I winked. "Better get ready, Saylor, becauase they throw hard."

The guys started counting. "One—"

"Ahhh!" Saylor clapped her hands and gave me a panicked look.

"Two!" I joined in.

"Oh, my gosh!"

"Three!" The man threw the fish.

Screaming, Saylor closed her eyes but still managed to catch the giant fish.

Cheers erupted from the crowd as Saylor lifted the fish in triumph. "I did it!"

"I knew you could." I kissed her temple.

"Are we really eating all this fish?"

"Maybe not all of it." I shrugged and offered a wink. "Unless you've suddenly developed the appetite of an NFL lineman."

"Hey!" Saylor nudged me with her body. "You said you'd love me regardless…"

"Truth." I nodded and pointed at her. "That's the truth."

"So the fish?" She lifted it in the air.

"Oh no, you can keep it." I patted her head in teasing. "We're going to cook it tonight, and I'm going to make good on my promise to strike out the very last tear."

"How do you expect to do that?" Saylor's shoulders lifted. "By feeding me?"

"You'll see." I rubbed my hands together. "Now, let me

go pay for Nemo before we go back home."

"Your car's going to smell!" she called after me.

"So will your hands!" I fired back.

Her eyes narrowed.

By the time I paid for the fish and helped her carry it up the hill and place it in the car, my stomach was already growling for food.

"Hey, you do know how to cook salmon, right?" Saylor asked once we walked into the house that I was hoping, praying, she'd still want me after I said what I was going to say.

"What?" I dropped my keys onto the counter. "You mean, you can't cook?" I threw my hands up in the air. "How can you even call yourself a woman? What have I gotten myself into! I'm going to starve!"

Saylor crossed her arms over her chest. "You done yet?"

"Make me food, woman."

"So here's the line." Saylor made a motion with her hands. "You just jumped over it then burnt the village on the other side."

"Aw..." I winked. "I can cook, but I am bit sad I won't get to see you in some apron, sweating over the stove looking all hot and bothered."

"Because cooking does that to women." Saylor nodded. "We also have pillow fights in our thongs and look forward to doing laundry."

Laughter bubbled out of me before I could stop it.

She hit me again.

"Stop hitting me." I stepped away. "And be useful."

"Useful?" she repeated, her eyes narrowing again.

"I'm cooking in my boxers." I shrugged. "So I need you to get me an apron, just in case Nemo decides to come back to life and tries to nibble off Gabe Jr."

Saylor closed her eyes, then opened them. "So many, many, things..." She opened five drawers before she found the apron. "…wrong with you."

Keeping my eyes locked with hers and feeling no shame whatsoever, I peeled off my button up and stepped out of my pants.

Saylor's mouth dropped open a bit.

"You were saying?"

"Stop flexing."

"I'm not."

"Damn it!" She stomped her foot.

"Apron?" I held out my hand, palm up and waited.

Saylor's eyes ate me alive as she examined me from head to toe. "No." She hid the apron behind her back. "I think you should take your chances with Nemo. Prove you're a man and all that."

"Wow." I teased. "I didn't know it was up for questioning."

"What?" her head jerked up.

"My manhood." I grinned. Saylor's cheeks went bright red. "You know I could always cook naked."

She swallowed… slowly. "Oh?"

"Keep your pants on." I winked. "I kind of want to savor the moment when I'm with you for the first time, and I really don't want you to be covered in fish."

She exhaled a long breath as her eyes once again greedily took me in from head to toe.

"Now, honey… I could go for some honey dripped all over your body." I stalked toward her. "Or maybe even some chocolate." Leaning in, almost touching her, I nipped at her lower lip. "Right here." I traced the line of her face and then moved my finger down her neck to her chest. "Or some whipped cream, right here." I licked the hollow valley between her breasts and sighed happily.

"I forgot." Her chest heaved.

"What?"

"How dangerous you are," she breathed.

"And now?" My mouth sucked the skin just below her left ear. I moved up until my lips tugged at her ear. "Now what?"

"What?" She arched toward me. "I forgot the question."

"Fish," I whispered in her ear. "We have to cook the fish, and then — maybe — I'll show you what I mean." I stepped away from her body, feeling cold, wishing I could just press against her and stay there forever. But fish. I had fish to cook.

"Gabe—" She groaned. "Come back."

"Nope. Gotta feed." I stepped away farther and started getting busy with the food.

"Does it bother you?" She handed me the apron. I pulled it over my head and paused.

"Being shirtless? No."

Saylor sighed and leaned against the counter top. "Not that. I still call you Gabe."

I thought about it for a minute and answered. "Say, you met me as Gabe. All you know is Gabe. To you, I'm Gabe… so what if to the rest of the world I'm still Ashton? We're the same person, and both Gabe and Ashton are in love with you."

"That sounds like you have multiple personalities." She teased, tugging the un-tied apron strings back so that I was plastered against her.

"I gotta admit, I kind like the idea that you'll have a variety of names to choose from when I make you scream."

Saylor's face flamed red.

"Don't worry." I kissed her mouth. "We eat first."

"And then?" Her voice wavered.

"And then…" I shrugged. "Forever. We have until forever."

Chapter Fifty-Two

Healing doesn't come right away — and even though I was still in pain, this time I embraced it, because the pain was a reminder that she had existed. The pain reminded me — she'd lived. Funny, how I used to think numbing my pain would make it go away. But the only way to fully rid yourself of the pain is to go against nature and embrace it. —Gabe H.

Gabe

My eyes roamed greedily over her lips. I couldn't manage to pull my gaze away from her mouth as she took a sip of water and leaned back in her chair.

"Finished?" I stood and walked over to her side of the table.

"Yeah." Saylor sighed. "No more fish."

"So…" I held out my hand and pulled her to her feet then wrapped my arms around her. "About that last tear."

Her eyebrows knit together in confusion. "I thought that the whole fish throwing thing and naked cooking got rid of that last tear. Besides, enough tears have been shed on both ends, Gabe."

"True." I pressed a kiss to her mouth and smiled against her lips. "But I want to be really sure."

"Really sure?"

"Yup." I laughed. "I don't want to leave any room for doubt."

"Doubt about what?"

"The way I feel about you. The way I feel about us. The way I feel about everything." I sighed and released my hold on her hands, taking a step back so I could gather my thoughts better. "Today was Princess's funeral. But Kimmy? She's been gone for four years." I shrugged. "Honestly, I thought I'd feel broken forever."

Saylor didn't move a muscle.

"But…" I paced in front of her. "I don't. For some reason, in her death, I finally feel whole. Like everything's come full circle. But there's still something missing."

"More fish?" Saylor offered.

"You're getting warm." I smirked and purposefully strode toward her.

"Water?"

"Even warmer." I grinned, tilting her chin toward my face.

"More… boats?"

"With sails…" I sighed. "And people who man them…"

"You lost me."

"Saylor." I kissed her mouth. "I'm missing *you*. You're the final piece to the puzzle, the star on the top of the Christmas tree."

"I have always wanted to be a star." She grinned.

"Be serious."

"Call me a star again."

"Say…" I groaned her name. "I love you."

"I love you too." Saylor's arms snaked around my neck as she pressed her lips against mine, once, twice, three times.

And then pulled back.

"I know you're young..." Damn, my throat was dry. Stupid nerves. "But, I want to start a life with you — I want to be with you. Forever."

Saylor's face lit up. "What exactly are you asking?"

"You're going to make me say it, aren't you?"

She nodded.

I fell down on one knee.

And that's when she started sobbing.

"I swear the harder I try to fix your tears, the more you cry. I'm going to be a nervous wreck around you for the rest of my life."

She nodded again, wiping the tears from her eyes.

"Saylor." I cleared my throat "I know you're young. I know you need to finish school. I'm great with that, because I'm not going anywhere. I want to build my life here, with you. I want to have a beginning, a middle, and an end to our story. I want to create music with you. I want to take care of you. The last thing in this world that I deserve, is the gift of your love, the gift of your commitment to me. I realize that..." I shrugged, using the shrug as a way to actually process this huge moment.

Funny, my whole life had been based around Princess, but now that I had the freedom to have a future. All I saw was Saylor. Living wasn't living without sharing that life with her.

"But I want you anyways, by my side. I want you to marry me." My hands shook as I grabbed hers and squeezed. "Damn, I think I'm doing this wrong." Nervous, I briefly broke eye contact and then looked up at her perfect face. "I love you. I love you more than life itself. I never want to say goodbye. And I don't want to pretend ever again. Please, be my wife?" *Please say yes, please say yes. Please don't kick my ass...*

Saylor nodded and then jerked me to my feet. Our mouths met when I was about halfway off the ground.

"I'm excited," Saylor sobbed, "to start our story."

"Sweetheart..." I kissed her soft mouth. "Our story started the first time I laid eyes on you and you fell on your ass."

"Thanks for the reminder."

"Stalker."

"Turtle."

"Maybe we'll come up with better nicknames." I kissed her harder across the mouth and pulled back.

"Later." Saylor's tongue pushed past my lips.

Groaning I lifted her into the air and assaulted her mouth, "Right. later."

Epilogue

Gabe

6 months later

"Wife!" My yell echoed around the house. A smile formed on my lips when Saylor walked around the corner with her hands on her hips and glared.

"When I said new nicknames I meant something sexy."

"Sorry." I shrugged helplessly. "Wife..." I said it in a deep sultry voice and then started peeling off my clothes. First my shirt, second my jeans, third my boxers.

Saylor's breath hissed out of her mouth as I stood in front of her naked. "You were saying? Wife?"

Saylor focused in on my abs, legs, arms — really every part of my body but my face.

I snapped my fingers. "Hey, up here. We're about to have a serious talk."

"Like that?" She pointed at me and squeaked.

"Yup." I crossed my arms.

"Fine." She pulled off her shirt.

"Wait." I held up my hands. "What are you doing?"

"Two can play this game." Her hands moved to her jeans.

We'd been married two days. Two actual days.

Rather than waiting, Saylor and I decided that, doing the whole long engagement thing? Not working so well, especially considering it felt like we were practically living together anyway.

Besides, if there was one thing we learned it was that we weren't promised tomorrow, only today, so we got married.

"Say…" I groaned once her jeans fell to the floor.

She stepped out of them, clad in only her bra and underwear and then moved her hands.

"Wait!" I shouted my eyes fighting to figure out where to look first. "Our very serious discussion can't happen if we're both naked."

"Oh?"

"Yeah." I moved toward her, slowly, "It's against the rules."

"And who put you in charge of the rules?"

"Sweetheart, I'm Ashton freaking Hyde."

"Ah," Saylor nodded, a knowing gleam flaring in her eyes. "Pulling the celebrity jackass card… classy."

I tilted my head to the side and lifted my hands helplessly into the air. "If the shoe fits."

"The shoe's about to find its way to Gabe Jr. and we all know how fond you are of every part being in working order."

Snorting, I rolled my eyes, "Please, I didn't hear you complaining last night, or this morning."

"Whore."

"I'm your whore." I pointed out. "So it's totally legal."

"What's this discussion about?" She crossed her arms making her breasts pop up in her bra, distracting me considerably from my goal of winning the battle I'd started.

"Up here." Saylor snapped her fingers in front of me. "You have three seconds."

"Dishwasher." I pulled her against me. Damn, her skin

felt good. "You forgot to load it."

"False." She breathed, arching her body into mine. "That was your chore for the week, check the chart."

"I made the chart."

"Aw, Ashton freaking Hyde, are you pouting?"

"No." *Yes.*

"The chart," Saylor pointed out, "was only established for what reason?"

I glared.

"Sorry, I didn't catch that." Saylor cupped her ear.

Grumbling, I looked down and answered, "Because I have a bad habit of baking too many cookies, feeding them to you, and then not cleaning up my mess."

"Right." Saylor nodded. "So technically this discussion is a moot point."

"Not really." I smirked, reaching behind her back and snapping her bra off. "Pretty sure I just made it a real discussion again."

"Oh yeah?" She put her hands on her hips, letting me openly gape. "How do you figure?"

"Now we can discuss how beautiful you are." I kissed her hard on the mouth and retreated. "How damn sexy I find you." I sucked her lower lip. "And how excited I am that one day I'll have little princesses running around that look exactly like you."

"Charmer." Saylor breathed as my hands reached for the last shred of clothing that was separating our bodies from one another.

Laughing, I picked her up into my arms and carried her to the couch, careful to kiss her lips, plunder the depths of her mouth, and tease until she was ready to either scream at me or hit me.

I tossed her onto the couch.

"Gabe…!"

"Love you." I hovered over her, kissing every inch of

skin, savoring the feel of her warmth against my mouth.

"I need you," she moaned.

My body was already on fire — being with her did that to me, made me want to seriously spend my days having sex and never doing anything else with my life. Ever. But when I brought up that topic to Saylor, she said the only people who made careers out of sex were prostitutes.

I, of course, pointed out that since we were married it didn't matter.

She said if money changed hands, it did.

With a grin I kissed her neck and finally entered her with excruciating slowness. I would never tire of that feeling — of being one with the person I loved.

Saylor whimpered as I brought her body to the brink of release, only to slow down again.

Teasing her, even in intimate moments was my favorite thing in the world.

"Gabe!" Saylor yelled.

I chuckled. "Louder?"

"I—"

My mouth crushed hers as her body tensed and then went limp against mine.

Careful not to squash her, I managed to lie next to her.

"Tell me…" she whispered. "One true thing."

"I love you." I kissed her cheek. "And a lifetime of days like this? Won't ever be enough."

"I like that truth."

"Yeah." I wrapped my arm around her. "I do too. What about you? What's your truth for the day?"

Saylor shifted toward me. "Someday, when we do have kids… and we bring a little princess into the world, I think we should name her Kimmy."

I couldn't find my voice. I could only nod as I felt my eyes well with tears. "I think— I think she would have liked that."

"Yeah." Saylor sighed. "Me too."

The doorbell rang.

Panicked, I jolted up and nearly knocked Saylor off the couch.

"Who is it?" Saylor called in a totally calm voice while I was busy trying to locate articles of clothing. Why was I only finding my socks? How were socks going to cover this up?

I mean, seriously.

"Hurry up, guys, it's freezing!" Lisa shouted.

"Shit!" I found my pants, only to fall on my ass, because my feet slid on my shirt. I looked at Saylor as the light bulb clicked on in her brain too.

"Taco Tuesday!" We shouted at the same time.

"Guys! Come on!" Lisa pounded the door again.

"Keep your pants on!" I yelled back.

Saylor sighed and quickly buttoned her jeans.

I wasn't as fast.

I was like a turtle. Ha, that damn nickname wasn't ever going away.

Finally, we opened the doors to see Wes, Kiersten, and Lisa waiting.

Wes took one look at me and burst out laughing. "Shirts on backwards, man. Welcome to matrimony."

"Gross." Lisa side-stepped me.

As everyone talked at once and piled into the house, I was left staring at the sunset, the same sunset that I'd seen at the end of every day. Last year it had reminded me of loss — and now? It reminded me of life.

"Hey, you coming?" Kiersten called.

"Yeah." Smiling, I closed the door. "I am."

Haven't read enough Wes and Kiersten? You're in luck! Their novella *Fearless* releases March 9th! Turn the page to see an excerpt from the book, and be sure to check my website for the release date for *Shame,* the third book in the Ruin series and Lisa's story!

Acknowledgements

First two weeks proceeds going towards non-profit in Uncle Jobobs Honor

I really, really, need to thank God for all of his many blessings and allowing me to live my dream day in and day out.

When I first started the Ruin series, I had every intention of just writing Wes's story. Many of you know that I was inspired by my Uncle's battle with cancer, and in order to deal with all the emotions I was going through decided to not only write a book about it—with him as one of the characters—but donate some of the proceeds toward his medical bills.

Uncle Jobob is now pain free… he passed away this last November and though it was horrible to see him suffer—I'm so relieved that he is now cancer-free. Some of our stories don't end like Wes's, but that doesn't mean we lost the fight with cancer. Regardless of the ending, you still win, because you fought.

With Gabe's story… I wanted to keep the topic close to home. My Uncle has two daughters, one of them, Kimmy, is mentally handicapped and the sweetest girl you will ever meet! I based Kimmy's character on her and used part of her story as inspiration to write the rest of the book. I thank my family for allowing me to use real characters to bring the story I had in my head to life.

When I first started writing *Toxic,* I wasn't sure which direction I was going to go. I mean, I knew who Gabe was, but I wasn't sure how I was going to be able to tell his story and actually do it justice. I had this vision in my head, and for some reason, it just wasn't transferring to the pages. I ended up taking a few weeks off and just praying. I really did. I sat at my computer, cried a bit, and was like WHY ISN'T THIS WORKING!

Eventually, I gave up. I shook my head and said, "Okay, fine. This isn't working." I ended up calling my mom in tears—I was so worried about people comparing it to *Ruin* that I was over-thinking it. But finally it occurred to me. This isn't about Wes. This is about Gabe. To even make it about Wes would be unfair to all the characters, which is why I wrote the novella, *Fearless*. I knew some of you wanted to see more details of Wes's and Kiersten's life, so I wrote *Fearless* for you guys. ;) Well, and for myself, because I'm selfish like that and I want to know what happens with their story too!

Thank you so much for reading and for reviewing. Know that I do truly read every review you guys post as well as every Facebook comment, Tweet, email—just know it's so so appreciated, and I love the feedback guys!

If you hated the book, write a review. If you loved it, write a review. This is how authors get better and it's also how I know what you guys like or don't like.

As always, bloggers, readers, you guys rock my world. I can't say enough about the tireless hours that go into blogging. Thank you so much for hosting me and for reviewing my book, as well as pimping it out. I so appreciate you!

Readers, gosh, you guys are amazing!!! I love connecting with you and honestly just love talking books! Thank you so much for your continuous support and love!

If you want to connect, find me on Facebook www.facebook.com/rachelvandyken, or Twitter @RachVD.

Other Books by Rachel Van Dyken

Forever Romance

The Bet

The Wager

Elite

Elect

Seaside Series

Tear

Pull

Shatter

Forever

Fall

Wallflower Trilogy

Waltzing with the Wallflower

Beguiling Bridget

Taming Wilde

London Fairy Tales

Upon a Midnight Dream

Whispered Music

The Wolf's Pursuit

Renwick House

The Ugly Duckling Debutante

The Seduction of Sebastian St. James

The Redemption of Lord Rawlings

An Unlikely Alliance

The Devil Duke Takes a Bride

Other Titles

Every Girl Does It

The Parting Gift

Compromising Kessen
Savage Winter
Divine Uprising
Ruin
Fearless

About the Author

Rachel Van Dyken is the *New York Times, Wall Street Journal,* and *USA Today* bestselling author of regency and contemporary romances. When she's not writing you can find her drinking coffee at Starbucks and plotting her next book while watching *The Bachelor.*

She keeps her home in Idaho with her husband and their snoring boxer, Sir Winston Churchill. She loves to hear from readers! You can follow her writing journey at www.rachelvandykenauthor.com.

www.rachelvandykenauthor.com
Twitter: @RachVD
Facebook: RachelVanDyken

Made in the USA
Lexington, KY
03 September 2014